Untangling her fingers from the mahogany silk of Cole's hair, Tori flattened her palms against his massive chest and forced herself to breathe.

Though he still had her perched on the desk, Cole, too, was making a visible effort to slow his breathing and ease his grip on her. He peppered her face with tiny kisses, drawing out the last sparks of her combustible reaction to him.

He wanted something from her. But why?

Tori sorted her thoughts and calculated possibilities, trying to regain the upper hand, which she feared she'd lost for good. She raised an eyebrow and challenged his high-handed behavior. "I don't know what kind of game—"

"Believe me, sweetheart, this is no game." His deep voice dropped back to a whisper for her ears alone. He smoothed his palms up and down the bare expanse of her upper arms, raising goose bumps and placating her for the benefit of the witnesses behind her. He brushed the warning against her ear under the guise of yet another kiss. "Follow my lead and we'll both walk out of here."

Tori's entire body went rigid with protest. "You want me to pretend—?"

"And I expect you to be a very good actress."

Dear Harlequin Intrigue Reader,

As you make travel plans for the summer, don't forget to pack along this month's exciting new Harlequin Intrigue books!

The notion of being able to rewrite history has always been fascinating, so be sure to check out *Secret Passage* by Amanda Stevens. In this wildly innovative third installment in QUANTUM MEN, supersoldier Zac Riley must complete a vital mission, but his long-lost love is on a crucial mission of her own! Opposites combust in *Wanted Woman* by B.J. Daniels, which pits a beautiful daredevil on the run against a fiercely protective deputy sheriff—the next book in CASCADES CONCEALED.

Julie Miller revisits THE TAYLOR CLAN when one of Kansas City's finest infiltrates a crime boss's compound and finds himself under the dangerous spell of an aristocratic beauty. Will he be the *Last Man Standing*? And in *Legally Binding* by Ann Voss Peterson—the second sizzling story in our female-driven in-line continuity SHOTGUN SALLYS—a reformed bad boy rancher needs the help of the best female legal eagle in Texas to clear him of murder!

Who can resist those COWBOY COPS? In our latest offering in our Western-themed promotion, Adrianne Lee tantalizes with *Denim Detective*. This gripping family-in-jeopardy tale has a small-town sheriff riding to the rescue, but he's about to learn one doozy of a secret.... And finally this month you are cordially invited to partake in *Her Royal Bodyguard* by Joyce Sullivan, an enchanting mystery about a commoner who discovers she's a betrothed princess and teams up with an enigmatic bodyguard who vows to protect her from evildoers.

Enjoy our fabulous lineup this month!

Sincerely,

Denise O'Sullivan
Senior Editor, Harlequin Intrigue

LAST MAN STANDING

JULIE MILLER

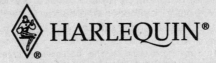

TORONTO • NEW YORK • LONDON
AMSTERDAM • PARIS • SYDNEY • HAMBURG
STOCKHOLM • ATHENS • TOKYO • MILAN • MADRID
PRAGUE • WARSAW • BUDAPEST • AUCKLAND

ISBN 0-373-22779-5

LAST MAN STANDING

Copyright © 2004 by Julie Miller

ABOUT THE AUTHOR

Julie Miller attributes her passion for writing romance to all those fairy tales she read growing up, and to shyness. Encouragement from her family to write down all those feelings she couldn't express became a love for the written word. She gets continued support from her fellow members of the Prairieland Romance Writers, where she serves as the resident "grammar goddess." This award-winning author and teacher has published several paranormal romances. Inspired by the likes of Agatha Christie and Encyclopedia Brown, Julie believes the only thing better than a good mystery is a good romance.

Born and raised in Missouri, she now lives in Nebraska with her husband, son and smiling guard dog, Maxie. Write to Julie at P.O. Box 5162, Grand Island, NE 68802-5162.

Books by Julie Miller

THE TAYLOR CLAN FAMILY TREE

Mary Cantrell (d) m.
(stay-at-home mom)

Mitchell Taylor Sr. (d) ~ Sid Taylor
(police officer)   (butcher)

m. Martha MacKinley
(stay-at-home mom)

1. Mitch Taylor
(precinct captain)

~~~~~~~~~~~~

m. Casey Maynard 2. Brett Taylor
(medical journal editor) (contractor)

m. Ginny Rafferty
(homicide detective)

Mitch Taylor III

3. MacKinley Taylor
(forensic pathologist)

m. Julia Dalton
(trauma nurse)

5. Gideon Taylor
(arson investigator)

m. Meghan Wright
(firefighter)

Alex (a) Matthew (a)

Edison (a)   Mark (a)

m. - married
e. - engaged
a - adopted child
~ - brothers
~~ - raised by
      aunt & uncle
d - deceased

7. Cole Taylor
(former detective)

6. Jessica Taylor
(antiques dealer)

e. Sam O'Rourke
(FBI agent)

4. Joshua Taylor
(detective)

m. Dr. Rachel Livesay
(psychology professor)

Anne Marie Livesay Taylor

1. *One Good Man*
2. *Sudden Engagement*
3. *In the Blink of an Eye*
4. *The Rookie*
5. *Kansas City's Bravest*
6. *Unsanctioned Memories*
7. *Last Man Standing*

CAST OF CHARACTERS

Cole Taylor—He was once the finest that the KCPD had to offer. But two years under deep cover is enough to break any man. He's lost his soul to death and lies.

Victoria "Torie" Westin—She's been assigned an impossible mission—one where she'll have to choose between her life or her heart…and might very well lose both.

Jericho Meade—An aging, ailing crime lord. A lot of people are vying to take over his position in Kansas City. And someone doesn't want to wait until he dies of natural causes.

Chad Meade—Jericho's nephew and the #1 candidate for his uncle's position in the family business.

Daniel Meade—A haunting memory? Or a very real threat?

Paulie Meredith—Meade's right hand since their early days on the streets.

Lana Shepherd—She's the mastermind behind Meade's criminal campaigns. But she has a bad track record with men.

Aaron Polakis—Not your typical butler.

Backer and Brady—Who are those guys, anyway?

Lancelot—A mystery man with a grudge against the Meades.

A. J. Rodriguez—Cole's former partner on the police force.

The Taylor Clan—Someone's out to get them. They've banded together time and again to protect each other in times of crisis. But this time they may not be able to save one of their own.

In memory of Margaret Miller.

With special thanks to the gang
on the CODE NAME: INTRIGUE discussion loop
at <www.eHarlequin.com>.
I appreciate your enthusiasm for Intrigue,
your support for the authors and each other,
your insightful ideas and all the fun we have
hanging out together.

Prologue

"One should be all dead when one is half dead..."
Edgar Lee Masters—SPOON RIVER ANTHOLOGY

Amazing what kind of dull, dreary errands a sixteen-year-old boy with a new license would run with his grandmother, so long as the opportunity to drive was involved.

Martha Taylor grinned, taking good care to keep her amusement out of sight behind the muscular shoulders of her newly adopted grandson. Already they'd been to the cleaner's, the post office, and now the grocery store without a single complaint about boredom or getting up early on a summer vacation morning. She'd gone through this same spate of volunteerism with all six of her boys, starting more than two decades ago. Some things never changed.

A young man's appetite didn't change, either, she noted, following Alexis Pitsaeli Taylor as he pushed the shopping cart across the parking lot to her teal van. He'd already dug into the sacks and opened a box of cream-filled cupcakes. The first one had disappeared in two bites and now he was working on his second.

"Let's put the sacks in the back, Alex." Martha opened her new straw purse and fished out her key ring to unlock

the doors for him. But he already had his shiny new keys—
a spare set copied and given to him by his grandfather—in
hand and had pushed the unlock button. She halted a step
as he lifted the hatchback and started unloading the cart. He
paused just long enough to pop the last of the cupcake into
his mouth. Martha grinned. "I think we'd better go home
and get some lunch before all these groceries disappear into
that bottomless pit you call a stomach."

Alex made a choking sound and spun around, apparently
downing that last bite without chewing first. A stricken look
dulled those soulful onyx-colored eyes that were going to
make women weak in the knees as he matured. "Sorry,
Grandma. I was hungry."

Grandma. Was there any sweeter word?

Martha curled her fingers around the handle of her purse,
resisting the urge to reach out and hug the teenager in public. "Oh, honey, I'm teasing you. I do that with all my boys.
I just don't want you to ruin your appetite."

"Not possible." His rare smile gleamed against the olive
tint of his skin. "If you're cooking, I'm eating."

Martha laughed at the compliment. She was used to shopping for a big family—she'd raised six boys and a girl, after
all. But a whole week watching her four newest grandsons
while their parents, Gideon and Meghan, finally took a well-
deserved honeymoon worried her that she might be a little
out of practice. "I hope I bought enough food."

He eyed the seven sacks. "This should get me through
the day. And I'd be happy to run to the store again tomorrow."

Ah, yes, another chance to drive. Sharp kid. Thank good-
ness he could joke with her. Alex seemed like such a serious
boy. No wonder. He'd already outlived his abusive birth
father, and his birth mother had lost her battle with drugs
long before he'd joined a gang and eventually reformed
himself. Martha's smile became forced as she watched him

diligently unload the groceries and push the shopping cart toward the cart corral. He'd seen far too much of life for a boy his age.

She hoped he knew how much he was loved. That he had a family he could depend on now. She hoped he knew how lucky he was to be part of the proud Taylor tradition, and how proud she was that he had become a part of that tradition.

A dark figure hurtled between two parked cars and slammed Martha into the side of the van. When she felt the tug at the end of her arm, she screamed.

"Shut up, lady!"

The assailant shoved her down to the pavement and snatched her purse from her pain-shocked grip. Then he was off, running into the glare of the midday sun, keeping her from making any sort of identification.

"Help! He's stealing my purse!" Her sons who were cops had told her to make a lot of noise if she was ever attacked by an unarmed assailant—draw attention to the creep. Her knees and palms burned from where they'd scraped the pavement, and her sixty-three-year-old joints throbbed from the jarring impact of steel and concrete. But her mouth and her brain and her temper worked just fine. "Stop that man! Help me! Somebody help!"

"Grandma!"

Martha crawled to the edge of the parking stall and saw Alex hurl his stocky, compact body against the taller, lankier attacker, who clutched her straw bag in his fist. The two hit the concrete with a frightening thud.

"Alex!"

A kaleidoscope of images bombarded her senses. Black gloves. A stocking cap. The crack of a fist against a jaw, a spew of foul curses.

Urgent hands reaching down to help Martha stand. A kind voice. "Ma'am? Are you all right?"

The space-age tones of a cell phone being dialed. "I'll call 9-1-1."

Squealing tires and the stinging odor of burned rubber as a dingy white pickup truck skidded around the corner and screeched to a halt beside the two men rolling on the ground. Alex had the purse-snatcher in one of those neck-holds he'd learned on the wrestling team. He pulled him to his feet. He had the upper hand. He was reaching for her purse.

"No!" Fear churned in Martha's stomach. Her bravado evaporated in an instant as the driver of the pickup threw open his door and ran around the hood of the truck. He, too, wore gloves and a stocking mask. "Alex!"

But her warning came too late. The second man punched Alex in the kidney. Martha flinched at the vicious power of the blow that arched Alex's back and freed his hold. The man with the purse spun around and slammed his fist into Alex's mouth.

"Stop them!" Martha clenched her fingers convulsively around the forearm of the good Samaritan who had stopped to help her. "Oh God. Take the damn purse! Don't hurt him."

Alex sank to his knees. The man who'd taken her bag raised his hand to strike again, but the driver of the truck snatched him by the collar of his black, long-sleeve shirt and dragged him to the truck. He shoved him inside, scrambled behind the wheel and took off at interstate speed across the parking lot.

"Looky here, *Grandma!*" The man with her purse stuck his head out the window, shouting a vile taunt through his mask. He ripped open her wallet, sending a handful of bills fluttering to the pavement. He waved the plastic sheath that held her precious family photographs, tore one of them in two, crumpled it in his fist and tossed the memories beneath the wheels of the speeding truck. As they careened around the corner onto the street, he pointed a finger at Alex—her brave, young grandson had climbed to his feet. "Watch your back next time, Taylor! We won't leave you standing!"

The driver gunned the engine and quickly lost the truck in traffic. One kind citizen tried to gather the shredded picture and money before the wind carried them off, while the man with the cell phone hurried to Alex's side.

Alex nodded at something he said, then brushed off the man's hand and jogged back to the van. "Grandma?"

"Oh, Alex. Honey." She didn't care if they had an audience. She didn't care how cool a teenager needed to be. Martha hugged the boy, hugged him tight. "Are you hurt?"

His arms squeezed briefly around her shoulders before he pulled away. "I didn't get your purse back."

A frown marred his handsome face. Blood ran from his split bottom lip. He inhaled short, hissing breaths as if the action pained him. *He* was apologizing? Maternal anger blazed pure and potent through her veins, masking the remnants of her fear. Martha pulled a floral handkerchief from her pocket and pressed it against his wound. He flinched at the pain, but she ordered him to hold still as she tended him.

"You did an incredibly brave thing. Your mom and dad will be so proud of you. I'm proud of you." She reached into the back of the van and dug out a bag of frozen peas to hold against his lip. "But nothing is worth you getting hurt. Certainly not that silly purse. It wasn't big enough to hold everything I like to carry, anyway."

Alex took over holding the icy package against his swelling mouth. She followed his glance down to the blood oozing through the serrated skin on her knees.

"But he hurt you."

"Yeah, we'll have to talk about what a tough old fart I am sometime."

He grinned at the idea of someone her age using a word like that. But the glimpse of humor quickly disappeared beneath a serious frown. "Something isn't right about what just happened."

"You mean stealing a woman's purse in the middle of the day in a busy parking lot?" She'd never believed that petty criminals were terribly bright.

The sound of sirens in the distance alerted her to approaching help. The man with the phone had rejoined them.

"I got the license number of the truck and reported it to the dispatcher. I'll tell these officers, too, when they get here," he said.

"Thank you." Kansas City was a growing metropolis, busting at the seams in nearly every direction. But it still maintained that small-town neighborhood feeling it had enjoyed since the days when Harry Truman served as the county's presiding commissioner back in the 1930s. She turned to the young mother who had stopped to help as well. "Thank you all."

"Grandma." Alex said the word and demanded she listen. "I know what it is. Those guys called me by my new name. *Taylor*."

Martha tried to grasp the significance of what he was saying. "They knew you? Were they part of a gang?"

He shook his head impatiently. "They were too old. The guy I grabbed was in his twenties or thirties, even."

She didn't laugh at his skewed conception of *old*. "They didn't call you Alex or Pitsaeli?" Though Gideon and Meghan had been his foster parents for several months, his adoption and legal name change had gone through less than a month ago. Now she was thinking what he was thinking. And hating it. "I heard *Taylor*, too. And why would he throw away money but keep pictures?"

This was something a little more complicated and a lot more personal than a routine purse snatching.

She turned to the man with the phone. "May I?"

He handed her the phone and she punched in a number she knew by heart—that of the office of the police captain of the Fourth Precinct. She kept her gaze riveted on the wise eyes of her grandson. "I'm calling Mitch and reporting this." She brushed a lock of his wavy black hair away from the corner of his bruised mouth. "And then we're going to the hospital."

Chapter One

Something wasn't right.

Maybe it was him.

Cole Taylor looked through the limousine's tinted window and watched the muddy, gray-green waters of the Missouri River rush beneath the arched steel and concrete bridge. The dual highway took them north from Jackson County into Clay County, leaving behind the congestion of interstate traffic and expanding commercialization for the scenic rolling hills and lush farmland of rural Missouri.

He was alert, but not afraid. He'd numbed himself long ago to the fear and danger he lived with every day. Ignoring his emotions was a matter of survival. Giving in to them meant madness or death. Or turning.

Some days he wondered if he'd gotten so good at his job that he *had* turned.

Truth and justice had once sustained him, driven him. But those ideals had blurred as he'd made enemies into friends, and a few friends into enemies. He'd ignored his conscience and turned his back on everything he'd once held dear. As the car picked up speed toward its destination, Cole admitted that this day—like so many others in these past few weeks—was more about surviving than caring why he was here.

Two years working under deep cover for KCPD and the

DA's office had whittled the scope of his day-to-day living down to nothing more than that. Survival.

It was a damn cold-blooded way to live.

He was the good cop gone bad, selling out his colleagues and his soul for big money and a chance to dispense justice on his own terms. That was the story that had gotten him here. Only the story was beginning to feel a whole lot more real than the life and loves and friendships he'd left behind.

"You seem antsy this morning, Cole—"

Years of training kept him from starting at the indulgent voice of the man sitting beside him on the black leather seat of the limo.

"Is something wrong?"

Cole pulled himself from his worrisome thoughts and turned to the white-haired gentleman. "Just a feeling." He reassured his boss with an expression just short of a smile. "I wish you'd let me check out this private hospital before driving out here. You want me to be in charge of security, yet you insist on taking foolish risks like this." He nodded toward the unlit cigar clenched in the other man's arthritic hand. "And you know the doctor is going to tell you to give up those things, too. How many times have we had this discussion about your impulses?"

The older man laughed. "My wife, rest her soul, was the only one I ever let criticize my choices. Now you're nagging at me."

At six-four, with a muscular body and well-honed skills that made him a deadly fighting machine, no one would mistake former KCPD Detective Cole Taylor for anyone's nagging wife. Yet Jericho Meade patted Cole's knee and scolded him as if Cole were his nurse, not his bodyguard.

"I'm not nagging," Cole insisted, hating these fond, almost familial feelings he had for his employer. "I'm laying it on the line. You make my job harder than it needs to be."

"Keeps you on your toe—" Meade's laughter wheezed into raspy puffs of air. He pressed a gnarled fist to his chest as a fit of coughing seized him.

Cole squeezed a supporting hand around the man's bony shoulder. "Jericho?" The old man snatched at his left jacket pocket, desperate to retrieve what was inside. But twisted bones and rattling coughs kept him from succeeding. "What is it?"

"His mint." The robust man sitting across from them leaned forward. Paulie Meredith's thin strands of black hair barely covered his scalp, making it impossible to hide his deep wrinkles of age and concern. He reached into Jericho's pocket, pulled out a foil-wrapped piece of candy, opened it and slid it into his friend's mouth. "It soothes the cough."

Cole frowned. "You're sure he won't choke?"

Sinking back into the plush upholstery, the seventy-six-year-old patriarch waved aside Cole's concern. "I'll be fi—" Another fit seized his chest, ruining the reassurance.

"Jer, old friend, you have to take it easy." Paulie wore the trappings of his wealth in a half-dozen gold and silver rings, and the paunch of his belly that pulled at the buttons of his designer suit. "There are hundreds of doctors in K.C. Good ones. I don't know why you insist on seeing this Kramer guy way out here."

Jericho's chest shuddered in and out, indicating just how difficult it was for him to catch his breath. But the firm command in his steely blue eyes brooked no argument, even from his oldest and closest friend.

"First of all, Paulie, never call a sick man '*old friend.*'"

The teasing fell on deaf ears. "You're not dying."

"The hell I'm not." Jericho's breath whistled in his throat as he gasped for air. But then, through sheer will, it seemed, his breathing regulated to a raspy but even rhythm. And though his pasty skin didn't regain its healthy color, he smiled. "Dr. Kramer said he could run the diagnostic tests at his private research clinic with few questions asked and no publicity. My heart and lungs may be going, but I don't want anyone outside the family to know about it. Not until I find Daniel.''

Find Daniel? Cole discreetly looked away at the mention of Jericho's son. It was the one aspect of his employer's personality he didn't know how to handle.

Paul Meredith was more direct. ''Daniel's dead, Jer.''

''We don't know that. I'm not selling the business, no one's running me off, I'm not naming a new heir until…'' He couldn't say it. He couldn't bring himself to speak of the gruesome task he'd given Cole. *Find my son's body and bring it to me. Then I'll know he's dead.* The shallow wheezing became a moan of pain. But it wasn't physical. ''He's still with me, Paulie. I feel him. I know he's trying to reach me. He wants me to find him. He wants to tell me something.''

The pallor of Jericho's skin alarmed Cole more than did his boss's ramblings. ''You need to take it easy.''

''You should be lookin' to rip out the heart of the man who did that to your son,'' Paulie advised, talking the way a strong, healthy Jericho Meade would have talked months earlier, ''not pretending he's still alive.''

''Paulie,'' Cole warned. There was honesty, and then there was cruelty.

Jericho's blue eyes clouded. ''I'm not pretending. I know what I've seen and heard. If it's not Daniel, it's his damn ghost.''

''It's obvious you need some kind of treatment, Jer. I want you to be in a place where they have the best staff and equipment.'' Paulie slicked his hand across his ruddy scalp. ''How do you know we can trust this Kramer guy?''

How could a man like Jericho Meade, who had destroyed so many lives in his half-century-long quest for wealth and power, ever trust anybody?

Cole watched the old man steel his will and battle past the grief that consumed him. He was considerably calmer, if weaker, when he spoke.

"I'm paying Dr. Kramer enough money to ensure his loyalty. He'd better work a damn miracle."

"Maybe you should check yourself in to Kramer's clinic, then." Paulie was sounding like a gentle, lifelong companion once more. "I can run things for a while. Get yourself out of the house. Forget the business right now. Worry about yourself."

"I *am* the business." Jericho's voice was firm. "I wanted Daniel to become the business too. Until I understand what he's trying to tell me, I intend to hang around."

Paulie shrugged. "What would a voice from the grave be trying to tell you?"

Cole had asked the same question the first time Jericho had pounded on his door in the middle of the night, sobbing and disoriented, claiming his son had been in his office and left a message, begging his father to listen.

"Maybe the name of whoever killed him," replied Jericho.

The answer still didn't make much sense.

Jericho pressed his tattered cigar into Cole's hand and closed his eyes on a weary sigh. "Now you two shut up and let me rest. And tell the driver to kill the air-conditioning. He knows I don't like it this cold in here."

Paulie quickly spun in his seat and knocked on the partition window that separated the driver from the back of the limousine, to do his boss's bidding. Cole tossed the cigar onto the car's drink console before settling back into his corner. Then the three men fell silent and tuned in to their own internal musings.

Cole had been there four months ago, the night the un-marked package was delivered to the estate. After screening the box for any trace of explosives or chemicals, Cole himself had opened the box in front of Jericho, Paulie and a handful of family members. He'd nearly retched at the sight of the dismembered finger. Jericho had identified the ring he'd given his son and then collapsed in his chair.

Amidst the tears and curses that filled the room that night, Cole had read the attached, computer-generated note.

Jericho—
I thought a deal was a deal.
You took what was mine, so I'm taking what's yours.
Without an heir, the days of your empire are numbered.
Start counting.

Jericho Daniel Meade Jr. had never come home, and his father had never recovered.

Cole watched the gray ribbon of highway pass by in a blur. He'd taken this assignment two years ago with the intent of destroying Meade's criminal world from the inside out. Now, someone was trying to do the job for him by killing Jericho's son and driving the man toward madness. Leaving every part of Jericho's world in chaos until he named someone new to take over the family business—or someone moved in on the weakened patriarch and simply took what they wanted for themselves.

It was a lose-lose situation as far as Cole was concerned. He knew the likely successors Jericho might name. Every one of them would continue his reign of violence and intimidation under the guise of civilized gentility. And if an outsider was behind this takeover threat, a retaliatory mob war unlike anything Kansas Citians had seen before would leave the streets strewn with innocent victims. Battles for drug turfs would ensue. Good men and women would be cheated out of their livelihoods. Children would live in fear.

Cole felt the heavy weight of fatigue and responsibility down in the marrow of his bones. He had to keep Jericho alive until he was ready to name names and turn over state's evidence and end an era of terror before a newer, less certain one could begin.

His deep sigh fogged the glass, obliterating his view. Waking himself from his own murky thoughts, Cole wiped the window clear with the side of his fist. He pulled at his ponytail before glancing across at the dying old man he was destined to betray.

Dozing with a peaceful expression on his wan face, Jericho Meade resembled any self-made multimillionaire who'd lived long enough to enjoy the power and profits of his labor. Tall and slender and wizened as any much-loved grandfather might be, he wore his distinguished cloak of respectability like a second skin, giving no hint of the ruined lives and deaths and addictions that could be attributed directly to his position as one of the Midwest's most powerful and feared crime lords.

Meade's empire might include legitimate forays into the oil and natural gas industry, real estate, the restaurant business and numerous charities. But it also included arms and drug trafficking, murder, witness intimidation, money laundering and any other number of crimes on which Cole had been assigned to uncover and deliver information to the District Attorney's office.

It galled him that he should feel any sort of sympathy for a man like that. Whatever pain or danger or heartache Meade faced now had been brought on by himself and the greedy, ruthless habits that made the man a name on every federal, state and local most-wanted list.

But dammit, he did pity Jericho. Cole blinked his eyes and turned back to the sporadic traffic outside. Hell, he almost cared about the old man.

Probably because he'd been separated so long from the people he did truly love that Jericho's dependence on him felt like something more substantial. It didn't matter that their relationship was based on a lie. Cole had done his job well, starting as a bouncer in one of Jericho's clubs and working his way up through the ranks to become the boss's personal bodyguard. He'd immersed himself in this assignment so completely that turning Jericho over to the Feds or the DA, and testifying against him almost felt wrong.

He clung to that *almost* like a lifeline, using it to salvage whatever was left of his conscience and soul.

But any guilt, confusion or wishful thinking vanished as the limousine slowed and turned onto the outer road. Cole voided all emotion whatsoever and tuned into the survival instincts that had gotten him this far.

As they drove along the long, horseshoe-shaped driveway, he noted that each of the tall, ancient oaks that shaded the sloping hillside was painted white, four or five feet up the trunk. A sharpened sense of vision looked beyond the immaculate grounds, scanning the shadows behind each tree and evaluating the condition of the three redbrick buildings perched at the top of the hill.

Two of the twentieth-century buildings appeared abandoned, judging by their boarded-up windows and crumbling facades. Not good. Any busted window or broad tree trunk would provide ample camouflage for an enemy. Construction scaffolding and canvas drapes obscured sight lines even further.

Cole shook his head. For a kid, this would be a primo location to play hide-and-seek. For a man of Jericho Meade's reputation, this remote place was the perfect setup for an ambush.

Despite the new sign that labeled this former nursing home a medical complex, it appeared that only the main building had seen any sort of renovation. Freshly painted black wrought-iron work framed each door and window, and stood out in sharp contrast to the sandblasted brick.

Through the modern double-paned windows, he could see the bright lights and sterile decor of the foyer and waiting room. Inside, a handful of patients and an attentive bustle of men and women in white lab coats and colorful scrub uniforms were clearly visible, even from a distance.

Every one of them made an easy target.

Jericho would be no different.

His bones radiated with an unspoken warning, an uncanny survival instinct that, combined with his unique, formidable skills, had kept him alive when other men would have ended up dead. Cole trusted that instinct the way a newborn babe trusted his mother. There was something in the air. Something waiting.

Automatically, he patted the Glock 9mm that hung beneath the hand-tailored cut of his suit coat and adjusted his pant leg to cover the smaller Beretta strapped to his ankle.

Feeling the easy possibility of an attack like a personal threat, Cole wrapped his hand around Jericho's arm and nudged the older man awake. "You don't go anywhere without me or Paulie right by your side. Understood?" He made the demand as if he was the one in charge.

Jericho smiled at his audacity and nodded. "Your concerns are duly noted, Mr. Taylor." He turned away in curious anticipation as the car came to a halt in front of the double front doors and the driver hurried around to open the door.

Cole was already there when Jericho climbed out. He stood several inches taller than his ailing boss, making Cole an ample shield and giving him a clear, 360-degree view of their surroundings. With the driver leading the way and Paulie bringing up the rear, they formed a protective triangle around Jericho and walked him into the clinic.

A young man, barely out of his teens, greeted them with an articulate, guttural accent. "Right this way, Mr. Meade."

After several furtive glances, the waiting attendant sat Jericho in a wheelchair and guided them at a brisk pace past the admissions desk and down a newly tiled hallway.

Cole couldn't tell if the young man was new on the job, nervous about working with a patient of Jericho's reputation, or just plain intimidated by Cole's imposing size and demeanor. Whatever the cause might be, his rabbitlike movements only heightened Cole's suspicions about the place. He took note of the attendant's name tag. *Joe Barton.* Yeah, right. Not with that accent. Cole planned to run a few tests of his own while Dr. Kramer evaluated Jericho.

All the doors along the corridor stood open, and the rooms were apparently empty. *Strike that,* Cole amended, as a chin-high stainless-steel cart, packed with fresh, folded linens, rolled through a doorway just before they reached it. Instinctively on guard, he pushed Jericho's wheelchair and the attendant against the wall and positioned himself between their entourage and the cart. His hand was inside his jacket on the butt of his gun when the cart swung around and he got his first look at the man on the other side.

''Whoa. Sorry, pal.'' Stooped over in green scrubs and a white lab jacket, the orderly barely made eye contact before pushing the cart on past.

Cole's breath eased out between tightly compressed lips. He nodded to the attendant to keep moving, but remained behind to cool an edgy pulse that was still firing jets of adrenaline through his system. He breathed in deeply, a new plan forming in his head before he followed Jericho into an exam room. The green clothes and shuffling walk were different, but the orderly's scraggly brown mustache and beady black eyes behind the glasses were the same.

Lee Cameron.

His contact with the DA's office.

Something was up.

TEN MINUTES LATER, Jericho was secure in the exam room with Dr. Kramer, a nurse and Paulie. The driver had parked the car and returned to stand watch at the door. The nervous attendant had been sent back to the main foyer and Cole was plugging change into a vending machine and waiting for a can of soda to fall through.

Lee Cameron leaned against the wall beside the vending machine, facing Cole's direction without actually looking at him. He looked for all the world like a worn-out clinic worker who needed every bite of the candy bar he was munching on to sustain him to the end of his shift.

"You're not looking nearly as dapper as when we met in the bank last week." Cole's words teased his fellow investigator, though he pretended a rapt fascination with the ingredients on his can of soda.

"Budget cuts hit me in the fashion department." Lee chewed a mouthful of chocolate and peanuts. "You might give me fair warning next time you change plans. I could have scrounged a tie and posed as a doctor instead of borrowing these from the laundry."

"Meade usually sees a doctor named Lyddon, east of the Plaza." Cole popped open the soda. "I didn't know we were coming here until this morning. If Powers is pressing for something new, I haven't got it."

Assistant District Attorney Dwight Powers could be a real hard-ass when it came to an investigation. But what the man lacked in personality he made up for in courtroom performance. Powers got convictions that were rarely overturned. When he sent felons to Jeff City or Potosi, they served their time.

But it was up to men like Cole and Lee to find the ammunition to make Powers's big legal guns work.

Lee scanned the break-room area and ran through the usual questions. "We're ready to serve the warrants on the drug trafficking tip you gave us. Nothing on the new money laundering scheme?"

Cole moved to the candy machine and studied his choices. "I haven't gotten anything on the new accountant. Except that Chad Meade hired him, not Jericho." He dug some change out of his pocket and made a selection.

"Chad's the nephew, right?"

"Heir apparent." Cole pulled the candy bar from the bottom bin. "He doesn't have the brains Jericho or even Daniel had, so if he's up to something, you can bet he's not in it alone. I'll keep digging."

"No news on who ordered the hit on Powers's family?"

That was the ADA's one suspicion he'd found no evidence to corroborate. Powers's obsession for the truth bordered on vengeance.

"Nothing I can prove yet. The timeline fits. Powers was gearing up to prosecute Jericho's son. Two large sums of money were withdrawn from the Meade accounts that same week. But I've got no phone record, no eye witness to place Jericho with the hit man."

"And we've got no hit man," Lee added.

Cole nodded. "I'm still waiting for someone in the Meade camp to let something slip. But I haven't heard anything concrete yet."

Lee wadded up his empty wrapper and shot a basket in the trash can. "I'll pass the word along, but you know Powers wants every loose end wrapped up before we pull you in."

Cole shrugged his shoulders and took a drink. The few minutes they'd been conversing would start to draw attention soon. Lee Cameron was his one link to the DA's office, Cole's only safe channel of information in or out of the game. Lee wouldn't risk making contact with the UC operative just to shoot the breeze. "So I've got nothing new, you've got nothing new. Why are you here?"

Lee shifted position. The subtle tensing of his posture was

enough to make Cole glance his way. "It's personal," said Lee.

"Me or you?"

"Your mom."

Cole's fingers dented the can in his grip. "Yeah?"

"Yesterday morning she was assaulted in a grocery store parking lot. Had her purse stolen."

Forget anonymity. Cole stared right into Lee's intense black eyes. "Is Ma okay?"

Lee gestured with his hand at his side, warning Cole to look away. "She's fine. Scrapes and bruises. But your nephew Alex—I guess he tried to defend her—he got some stitches at the E.R. and was released."

Cole let the anger surge through him, then forced it to dissipate into mere frustration. His mother had been attacked. Not only had he not been there to help, he hadn't even known she'd been hurt.

"He's a good kid from what I've seen. Probably did some damage himself. They catch the guy?"

"Not yet. But they got a plate number. Stolen vehicle. No surprise there. But we're trying to track it. And she called in your cousin Mitch."

A police captain on a routine purse snatching? His concern ratcheted up a notch.

"The captain doesn't believe it was random. He seems to think they were attacked because they were Taylors. He wanted me to remind you to watch your back."

If laughter wouldn't have drawn attention, Cole would have given in to the irony of the situation. Warning an undercover cop to watch his back? "Every damn day."

"I think Powers would understand if you wanted to come in off the job."

"The hell he would. I'm right where he needs me, and my work's not finished yet." Cole tossed the untouched candy into the trash. Worrying about his mother wasn't a distraction he could afford right now. Jericho's examination would be over soon and he didn't want his absence questioned. Still, the guilt wouldn't go away. "Keep me posted?"

Lee grinned behind his glasses. "That's why they pay me the big bucks."

Though he couldn't say he knew Lee well enough to claim him as a friend, Cole appreciated his go-between's efforts to keep him connected to the real world. "Use it to buy some new clothes. I'll contact you the usual way when I find out something on the new accountant or where the money's going. Tell Ma I love her. And if there's anything I can do to help…" But there wasn't. They both knew there wasn't. "Just tell her I love her."

COLE DISPOSED OF THE SODA can on his way out the door and headed down the long, empty corridor where he'd left Jericho with the doctor. Empty. Completely.

His smooth stride stuttered as his tension shifted in a new direction. The doors were closed now. Every one of them. Efficient cleaning crew? Or cover for hidden adversaries? And where the hell was the driver?

His bones were screaming at him now.

He unhooked the holster beneath his arm and hastened his step. He knocked and shoved open the door to Exam Room 6. "Where's Jericho?"

Paulie Meredith swung around, his large girth not a handicap when it came to defending his oldest friend. "Jeez, Taylor, you about gave *me* a heart attack. What's wrong?"

Cole glanced toward the inner door. "Is he in there?"

"Yeah. Doc Kramer's giving him the lowdown. It doesn't look good." The pinched lines around his mouth deepened. "Something happen?"

"Where's the driver?"

Now Paulie was glancing around, looking equally suspicious of their surroundings. "I sent the new guy out to bring the car around while Jericho changed."

Kramer's office door opened and Jericho himself filled the doorway. He acknowledged the tension in the outer room with a nod, but his stoic expression never changed. "Call me as soon as you know the results of the bloodwork," he said, saluting the black-haired doctor, then he reached out to link his arm through Cole's. He patted Cole's arm and rested his weight against him, suddenly acting old beyond his years.

"Your bones bothering you?" he asked.

Cole understood the reference. "This place is locking down tighter than a prison. We're leaving. Now."

Paulie zipped ahead to open the door and check the corridor before moving out. "All clear."

"Go." He hurried Jericho along with as much urgency as the old man's tired steps allowed. Cole's head swiveled back and forth in 180-degree arcs as he kept an eye on each door. He'd take a crowded hospital any day over this abandoned tomb of waiting danger.

"The doctor can't figure out what's wrong with me." Jericho kept talking, more confident in Cole's abilities than oblivious to any unseen threat. "He's prescribed inhalers and steroid treatments to help my lungs, but says my heart isn't showing the blockage or deterioration he expected. I told him it was just broken."

Cole supposed a murdered son could aggravate any existing condition or trigger psychosomatic symptoms, even hallucinations. He listened with one ear and tuned the other to the sounds of the clinic. Or lack thereof.

He wasn't the only one on guard against the eerie emptiness of the main room. He gave a passing nod to Lee Cameron, who had parked his cart in the opposite corridor. *Get out!* Cole wanted to yell. *Something's going down.* But he couldn't risk audible communication with the detective.

Cole turned Jericho toward the door. He could see the limo outside, the driver striding up the front walk— The young man pulled out his weapon just as the receptionist at the check-in window behind Cole screamed.

"Gun!"

Cole whirled around. She wasn't alone.

The nervous attendant, armed as well, rose from behind the counter and shoved her aside. "For the glory of the homeland!"

"Get down!" He pushed Jericho to the floor, and the next few seconds ticked by with time-altered clarity.

Caught in the crosshairs of the well-orchestrated hit, Cole dove for the cover of a row of chairs and dragged Jericho behind him. Paulie was there a second later, shielding Jericho with his own body, as an explosion of gunfire shattered glass and popped stuffing out of the upholstery and ricocheted off stainless steel.

Shots rang out from a third direction and the driver fell.

Cole palmed his Glock and fired. Once to move the shooter to the edge of the desk. Twice to nail him in the chest and throw him against the back wall.

The seconds returned to real time as the attendant sank to the floor, leaving a trail of blood on the wall behind him. Cole rose to a crouch to assess the man outside—dead or dying, his gun out of reach. Keeping his Glock trained on the front desk, he stood, bracing his hand on Jericho's shoulder to keep him down and out of the line of fire.

"Everybody in one piece?" Cole asked, hearing the gasps and wails of the receptionist as she huddled inside the break-room doorway.

Jericho trembled beneath his hand, shaking off Cole's concern. "Dammit. I never should have hired that lowlife. Couldn't drive worth—"

"I'm good," Paulie answered, climbing to his feet. He

wielded his gun as well. He scooped a hand beneath Jericho's arm and helped him stand. "Let's get out of here."

"Take him." Cole pushed Jericho toward Paulie and the door, and rushed to the desk. He knelt down to check the attendant. Dead. *Damn.*

For the homeland? That didn't sound like a typical hit. Where was this guy from, anyway?

He'd have Lee run the guy's face and prints through the computer. If they could ID the hitman, chances were they could track down whoever ordered the hit. Maybe tie it in to a lead on Daniel Meade's death.

"Cole!" Paulie urged.

The receptionist stared at Cole in openmouthed shock. *Call the cops,* he mouthed, hoping his insistence was enough reassurance for her to believe he wouldn't kill her as well.

There were voices in the halls now, as if someone had conducted a fire drill and the evacuated staff and patients were just now returning to the building. Cole stood and hurried toward the front door. But the fallen man near the linen cart caught his attention.

"God, no." He dashed to Lee's side and rolled him onto his back. Cole swore, every last vicious, damn-the-universe curse he knew. He smoothed the scraggly hair off the investigator's forehead, revealing the bullet wound that had taken his life. Lee had taken out the driver, but somewhere in the melee, he'd gone down in the line of duty.

A mist stung the corners of Cole's eyes. *Damn. Damn. Damn.* Lee still held his gun in his frozen grip. His badge was peeking out of his front pants pocket. Respect and regret swamped Cole. He didn't even know if Lee had a family…. This wasn't right. It wasn't any damn way to live— or lose—a life.

A stroke of divine fortune had him pushing the shield

down into Lee's pocket and hiding it an instant before he felt the tugging at his sleeve. Paulie.

"We go now, Taylor."

"Yeah. Yeah." Cole rolled to his feet and followed Paulie out the door. Jericho was already in the back of the limo. Cole climbed in beside him while Paulie got in behind the wheel and floored it.

The painted trees passed by in a blur, as did his conversation with Jericho. Yes, he was all right. Pissed off. Sore. But all right.

Cole had done his job. Followed his instincts. Made his shot. Put his life on the line for the man to whom he'd sworn his loyalty. He couldn't protect his own mother and nephew, but he'd kept these murderers alive. The gall of it burned in his throat and chest, as Jericho promised a substantial bonus and a thorough check into Kramer and his clinic.

And as they sped down the highway toward the river— with Jericho on the phone to Chad while Cole checked his gun and holstered it—another, even more disturbing realization churned the bile in his throat.

His contact was dead.

He had no connection to the real world now. No backup. No lifeline. Nowhere to go for safety. No one to call for help.

He was on his own.

The surrounding danger and guaranteed death that such a deception could cost him didn't bother him as much as it should have.

It was the madness that scared him. Knowing just how easy it would be for him to turn now. To forget who he really was. To never find his way back to life and love and the reasons he'd agreed to this assignment in the first place.

He'd killed a man today. He was more Meade than Taylor now.

Chapter Two

Victoria Westin sweated.

Let the upper-crust grande dames like her mother perspire or *glow* like a lady. When Judeen Westin wanted to improve her appearance, she had something lipoed or lifted or nipped and tucked. When she wasn't feeling good about herself, she got a new boyfriend.

When Tori wasn't feeling good about herself, she ran. As she started her last mile, the coolness of the June morning was rapidly dissipating as a canopy of river town humidity set in for the day. But she didn't mind. The rhythm of her feet hitting the rubberized track drowned out the memory of last night's phone call with her mother.

"You really should make peace with your grandfather, Victoria."

"Is something wrong? Is he ill?" That momentary flash of concern that snuck around her hardened defenses should have warned her. If she didn't care, she couldn't be hurt. But once her emotions kicked in, she made an easy target. And her mother rarely failed to hit the bull's-eye.

"No. But he'll die someday. When your father died unexpectedly, we never had a chance to say goodbye. This isn't just about your inheritance, but about living with a clean conscience. I know you have your work as a diver-

sion, but I'd hate for you to be all alone and dealing with the rift between you two. You really should plan ahead.''

Father. Inheritance. Alone. Three direct hits.

''Mother, I'm a little busy now. And we've covered this ground before. Is there another reason you called?''

Though her mother believed Tori's work at the Nelson-Atkins art museum was her life, it was her real job as a federal agent that gave her a sense of purpose and accomplishment. But she couldn't tell her mother that. For a variety of reasons, she'd never been able to tell her mother much of anything. Already stung by the mention of her father's death in a plane crash twelve years ago, she wasn't surprised as the conversation continued to spiral downhill.

''Have you thought again about having your breasts augmented, dear? I've met the most delicious cosmetic surgeon here in California. He says there's a procedure that—''

''Mother.''

''I've always thought you'd have the most lovely figure if…''

It was the damn *if* that always stuck with Tori. No matter what she achieved with her life, that *if* never seemed to completely fade from the back of her mind.

What if her father hadn't died?

What if her grandfather wasn't one of the wealthiest men in Kansas City?

What if she'd been born the son her family had always wanted instead of the daughter who never quite measured up?

And so she ran.

Tori worked damn hard to stay in top shape, to replace skin and bones with endurance and muscle, to toughen up the outside in an effort to toughen up the inside, too. Running was her escape. It had been the saving talent that a too tall, too skinny, too smart high school girl could master while other girls got dates and her world fell apart.

Now, as a twenty-seven-year-old woman, it was vital to her job and mental health to exercise regularly. Running was almost as good as coffee ice cream with chocolate sauce. It was almost as rewarding as bringing down the bad guys. After wrapping up her most recent investigation and providing the key evidence to indict a gang of drug smugglers who'd used shipments of paintings to transport cocaine across the country, she should be feeling pretty good about herself.

If…

She sprinted her last lap at her high school alma mater, the Pembroke Hill School, slowed her pace and turned for home.

Maybe if she had a new case to dive into right now, her mother's biannual chat wouldn't bother her so much. Maybe if her date the night before hadn't been such a dead end, her mother's insinuation that Tori wasn't as pretty or perfect as she could be might not have a ring of truth. Ken Burford had told her that her greatest asset was her red hair. But she'd read between the lines of his tedious conversation— her greatest asset had always been her grandfather's bank account.

Tori jogged north, up along Rockhill Road, toward the art museum and her renovated condo. Traffic was getting heavy with Kansas City's lunchtime rush, and the sun had popped through the clouds to warm the bare skin of her arms and the pavement beneath her feet. She stopped at the red light and jogged in place, pressing two fingers against her pulse and checking the second hand on her sports watch to monitor her heart rate. As cars and pedestrians gathered at the intersection around her, she ignored curious glances and…something else.

One particular look she couldn't ignore.

Though she couldn't immediately place the source, Tori felt the thorough, personal scrutiny like a tap on the shoulder. She curled her fingers into fists and slowly dropped them to her side. Someone wasn't just scanning the crowd, giving a second look to the tall, slender jogger. He was watching *her*. Intently.

Professional training, which she trusted more than personal intuition, kicked in. The light changed to green, the flow of traffic switched, and Tori jogged out ahead of the slower walkers. She inhaled deeply through her nose and lengthened her stride, her face fixed straight ahead, her eyes scanning the street from curb to curb.

Black car. Four o'clock position. Approaching from the rear. Local plates. She slowed her pace and watched it pass by. Two men. Unknown to her. She paused beneath the shade of a tree as she reached the parklike area of the museum grounds. Unzipping her fanny pack, she pulled out a bottle of water and took a long, quenching drink, using the opportunity to verify her impressions of the vehicle.

She'd seen it parked at the school. The men inside just happened to be leaving at the same time and taking the same route as she? When the teak-skinned driver pulled into the museum parking lot, she was certain they'd been following her.

Amateurs.

Tori replaced the bottle and tucked the wisps of her straight copper hair back into her inch-long ponytail. She jogged in place until the driver and passenger climbed out. Both men wore suits and ties and gloves. Driving gloves she could excuse without alarm. But gloves on the passenger? In another couple of weeks it'd be summer, for crying out loud. He'd better be doctoring a rash inside those things.

She waited a few seconds longer, until Rash-man glanced her way and the two men nodded to each other. Time to go. She cut out across the museum's thick, green lawn. The detour around the building would add an extra half mile to her run, but she had a feeling she was going to get a thorough workout no matter what route she took.

She grinned as the two men gave chase.

Tori didn't take chances when it came to her own personal safety, but she wasn't afraid to confront danger when it ran into her path—or, in this case, ran after her. She doubted they wanted to rob her. She'd allowed them to see the contents of her fanny pack. And a rape in broad daylight wasn't unheard of, but these guys had had a better chance of nabbing her at the school.

She had a feeling this pursuit was related to work. Or family. At least the danger she faced on the job served a useful purpose. The family connection could be a little trickier. But whether these two *Lethal Weapon* wanna-bes were the good guys or the bad guys remained to be seen. Wearing them out in a footrace would give her the advantage, either way.

When she neared the copse of trees and low wall surrounding the modern statue of a giant shuttlecock, she seized her opportunity. Tori jumped once, up onto the wall. Then she jumped to the ground on the other side, crouched low behind the statue and stilled her breathing. The would-be Riggs and Murtaugh came scrambling over the wall, the dark-skinned one puffing from the exertion. The shorter one with the blue eyes reached inside his jacket. "Lady?"

Fat chance.

Without waiting to see what kind of weapon he'd pull out, Tori sprang to her feet and charged. With her hands fisted, her leg braced, she kicked out and knocked the weapon from his hand.

"Son of a—" He grabbed his wrist and shook his hand as if his fingers had gone numb.

"Lady, wait!" The driver wanted his turn. "Miss Westin, we're—" She spun and kicked, forcing him back into the wall. He plopped down on his rump and threw his hands up in the air in surrender. "We just wanted—"

"How do you know my name?" she demanded. She was guessing family business now—of the worst kind. Only she couldn't imagine any of her grandfather's enemies hiring two bad-boy wanna-bes like these guys to come after her. And if they *were* with the Bureau, they needed to revisit basic training. When he started to get up, she thrust her palm toward his face and he scrambled back to his seat to avoid the blow. "Why are you following me?"

"Victoria Westin, right?" he confirmed. "FBI under-cover task force? You're Frank Westin's granddaughter?"

She kept him pinned with the proximity of her fist. "Who are you?"

Feeling had apparently returned to the shorter man's hand. He was adjusting his gloves now. "We don't have to deal with this kind of crap, Brady. Let's take care of this ourselves."

"Backer!"

Take care of this? Ignoring his partner's warning, he advanced on Tori from behind. She shot her elbow back into his solar plexus. "Stay away from me," she warned.

"Hey, lady." The shorter man stooped over, holding his gut. His words were barely a whisper as he struggled to find his breath. "We know you know martial arts, already. Give it a rest. I swear, we just want to talk."

"Talk?" She moved aside, keeping both men in her sights. "You chased me."

"You ran."

"I was out jogging—"

"This should help." The dark-skinned one named Brady interrupted the debate and unbuttoned his suit jacket, show-ing her the interior lining.

"Stay away from that gun." She recognized the Sig-Sauer, government issue, strapped to his belt.

"It's okay." With a silent warning for his partner, Backer, to stay put, he used his thumb and forefinger to pull a slim leather wallet from his inside pocket. He closed his jacket and flipped the wallet open to reveal a badge and ID. "We're with the Customs Department. I'm Agent Bill Brady. My hotheaded partner here is Agent Bill Backer."

"Let me see your badge." She silently nodded to Backer, who picked up his wallet from the ground and displayed it. That was the item he'd been pulling from his pocket. She wasn't sure whether to feel embarrassed, amused or irritated by this unusual introduction. But the badges looked legit. The photo IDs matched. Customs agents. Tori lowered her hands to her sides and took a deep breath. "You're both Bill's?"

If this was a decent con, they'd have changed their names.

"Confusing, I know." Brady laughed and pocketed his badge.

Backer sat beside him on the wall, rubbing his sore stomach. "Jeez, lady, you're tougher than you look."

"I told you she'd be right for the job." Agent Brady took on an almost fatherly tone. "Your credentials are impeccable, Agent Westin. So's your spin kick."

"Thanks." Now she was a little confused. "Why didn't you introduce yourselves right away?"

Backer grimaced. "Did you give us a chance?"

Tori crossed her arms and canted her hip to the side. These guys were harmless. "You should have used the telephone or stopped by my office. Following a woman who's on her own in the big city is hardly a reassuring way to approach her."

"Sorry," Brady apologized. "We wanted to keep this out of normal channels, for secrecy's sake."

Intriguing comment.

"You have a degree in art history, right?" he asked.

More intriguing. ''One of my degrees is, yes.''

''And you're Frank Westin's granddaughter?'' Backer seemed more impressed with that relationship than she was.

Not like she'd claim the man. But she supposed wealth and power and shady connections got one's name mentioned in certain circles. ''We've already established that. What do you want?''

''Have you heard of *The Divine Horseman?*''

Damn intriguing. She loved a good mystery. And, as far as she was concerned, *The Divine Horseman* was one of the biggest.

Tori could have run through the extensive mental catalog of Middle and Eastern European art she'd memorized from years of interest and study. But this was one rare, beautiful piece she knew by heart. The legend surrounding the sculpture had fueled adolescent fantasies about men and heroes that reality couldn't match. ''Jewel-encrusted statuette of a knight on horseback. European. Dates back to the Crusades. Stolen from a museum in New Orleans a year ago. Hasn't surfaced at any public auction or private sale since. The diamonds, rubies and gold alone are valued at over a million dollars. The history of the *Horseman* makes it priceless.''

Agent Backer grinned. ''She *does* know her stuff.''

Despite her earlier annoyance with these two bozos, their friendly banter and inept efforts at covert action were growing on her. And her curiosity was definitely piqued. ''What about *The Divine Horseman?*''

''We've talked to your superior at the FBI and have gotten permission to recruit you to assist us. Your expertise in the art world, your Bureau training and your family connections make you the perfect choice for this mission. I have your orders here.''

''Orders to do what?'' she asked, excited at the prospect of what they were asking of her, but leery of why the Westin name had to be a part of it.

"Word is, the current *owner* plans to sell it to a foreign investor and ship it out of the country. All under the table, of course. Before that happens—" Agent Brady pulled a sealed envelope from his pocket and handed her the assignment "—we want you to get it back."

Two weeks later

"WAIT HERE." The taciturn butler who'd introduced himself as Aaron Polakis opened the thick walnut door and pointed Tori into the library. His cropped blond hair had receded so far that the points of skin gave him a devilish expression which rivaled the friendliness of his personality. Maybe his thick Middle European accent was an indication he didn't know the language very well. Or maybe he was just an economist when it came to words. He paused before closing the door on his way out. "Sit."

Clearly, he hadn't been hired to make guests feel welcome. She wondered what his real job was here at the Meade estate, and whether the gun holstered beneath his uniform jacket had something to do with it.

Tori felt comparatively naked without her Glock sidearm strapped to her waist. But then, art historians rarely armed themselves. This afternoon she was Victoria Westin, associate professor of antiquities, not Tori Westin, FBI agent. Indiana Jones aside, she needed to come off as book smart and boring, not armed and ready for action.

Bearing that in mind, Tori smoothed the legs of her taupe linen pantsuit and perched on the edge of the brocade wing-back chair to await an introduction to her new employer. Her mother would tell her the color of her suit was drab and clashed with her rich surroundings. But the understatement fit the role she was playing. Besides, she was here to do a job, not snag a husband. Brains and resourcefulness were the requirements of the day, and Tori had those in spades.

She rose to her feet, intending to make the most of any unguarded time in the house by inspecting every room until she could narrow down the search. And, judging by the turrets and wings and widow's walks she'd seen driving up to the front steps, she had plenty to search.

The Meade mansion was an historical testament to Victorian architecture, with its red brick and dark wood and ornate moldings. Heavy velvet curtains and gilt trim bespoke power and money.

But there was a chilly heaviness to the air, as if the weight of too much opulence and too many secrets had grown too great for the walls to bear. Tori pushed aside the fringed drapes and gazed out at the ominous clouds that gave a dusky cast to the afternoon sky and threw long, fingerlike shadows across the lawn and driveway below.

A few miles to the north, above the downtown skyline, the air was still clear and sunny and blue. But like a tail she hadn't been able to shake, the clouds had rolled in and darkened and followed her south. Now, they seemed to linger overhead, thickening in strength, churning in an ongoing battle within themselves.

Tori knew it was only the results of winds and ions and barometric pressure, but a sudden, almost panicked need to feel the heat of the sun had her reaching toward the sky, splaying her fingers against the cool glass and holding her breath.

On the next, saner breath, she curled her fingers into her palms and pulled away from the window. She wasn't prone to panic attacks or silliness of any kind, but the sensation of being trapped in a world of darkness had tapped into some whimsical notion from her childhood, when she'd still believed in fairy tales and mythical monsters.

Time to bring herself firmly back into the modern, real world she could control.

Activating the electronic sensor on her Cartier watch, she scanned her surroundings. A single hit. The blinking readout indicated one listening device. She let her eyes find it first, then crossed over to the bookshelf, ostensibly to inspect the leatherbound collection of French classics, while she evaluated the design and capability of the bug. Audio only. Good to know.

No camera, no problem with leaving a guest unattended. Apparently, she could snoop wherever she wanted as long as she was quiet about it. Smiling at her good fortune, Tori closed *Les Misérables* and replaced it on the shelf. Jericho Meade's library spoke more of privilege and culture than of the top-notch security fortress her briefing had led her to expect.

Cole Taylor was the name she'd been given—warned about, in fact. A former cop with KCPD, he'd been seduced by enough money to turn his back on Meade's illegal activities and become the reputed crime boss's personal bodyguard. Backer and Brady had said there hadn't been one successful break-in or attempt on Meade's life since Taylor had taken over the job. No one in law enforcement on the local, state or national scale had been able to make a dent in Meade's criminal empire since Taylor had taken over security.

Tori frowned. This notorious Taylor must have a secret weapon he relied on, because she'd seen little evidence of anything top-notch since she'd driven up to the main house.

True, getting here hadn't been easy. The feeling of isolation had probably been planted in her subconscious mind as she'd wound around secondary highways and back roads to find it. Secluded on seven acres near the Kansas City Zoo and Swope Park, the Meade estate was surrounded by a forest of oaks and maples and leafy undergrowth—some of it landscaped, more of it left to grow wild and create a natural barrier that separated the redbrick mansion from the park, the road and the rest of civilization.

Yes, there'd been a guard at the wrought-iron gate. He'd searched her shoulder attaché and scanned her with a metal detector. But at the house itself, she'd seen nothing beyond a routine electronic alarm system at the exterior doors and windows, and Aaron Polakis, who seemed to have lost interest in keeping an eye on her. If this was Taylor's idea of security, then she was overqualified for the job.

But she wouldn't claim an easy victory just yet. She couldn't help wondering what else the two Bills at the Customs Department had been misinformed about. They had little hard evidence that Meade had actually stolen the statue—only his affinity for rare art and business trips that put him in New Orleans at the time of the theft. Maybe the intercepted communiqués to a mysterious Sir Lancelot weren't talking about the sale of the statue at all. The *horse* in the memos Bill and Bill had shown her could be referring to anything. A shipment of drugs. A thoroughbred. Another work of art.

If the statue was here, though, she'd find it. She owed that much to the memory of her father.

A knight in shining, golden armor. A lone warrior on horseback. *The* Horseman *will always ride to your rescue,* her father had told her. He'd first shown her *The Divine Horseman*'s picture in a museum magazine when she was fourteen, and, in her adolescent heart, Victor Westin had seemed every bit as handsome and heroic as that fabled knight. He'd promised to take her along on his next business trip and show her the real thing.

But her father never came home again. Except in a box for his own funeral.

"Focus, Tori," she chided herself in a whisper, slamming the door on those tender memories of Victor. She was here to complete a mission, not to reminisce about what might have been.

Hidden at her sides, Tori's fingers stretched and curled in a balletic display of controlled dexterity. She wasn't nervous so much as steeped in adrenaline. She was far more comfortable taking action than biding her time.

The Westin name had gotten her in the door. Her credentials as an appraiser would give her access to Meade's reputedly extensive collection. Then there'd be time for plenty of action.

She settled back into the chair, easing the anticipatory energy from her posture. Thoughts of her father and foolish schoolgirl fantasies were firmly tucked away. Agent Westin was in control once more. Correction, *Professor* Westin was in the house. She was good to go.

"Ms. Westin—?"

Tori shot to her feet at the male voice, tinged with a hint of arrogance and a full dose of down-home charm.

"Or should I say Professor? Doctor?"

"Victoria's fine." She extended her hand to the thirty-something man in the crisp white tennis outfit. Six feet tall, maybe. Compactly built. Not one strand of his light-brown hair looked out of place. This wasn't the white-haired patriarch from the Customs Department briefing file.

"Victoria, hmm?" He savored her name as if he'd taken a sip of pricey champagne.

Too smooth, too handsome, for her tastes. Definitely more her mother's type.

He folded her hand up in his and smiled. "I'm Chad Meade. Jericho's nephew."

The grip on her hand tightened when she would have pulled away, and she could have sworn the stroke of his thumb was an intentional caress. A shiver of revulsion skittered along her spine, dredging up an instant sense of distrust.

Fortunately, he misread the confusion that must have shown on her face. "He's resting right now. But since I manage the estate and oversee the acquisition and donation of his collection, I thought we should get acquainted. I want to help any way I can."

"I see." Tori pulled her hand away, resisting the urge to wipe it clean against her thigh. "I hope Mr. Meade isn't ill. I was looking forward to getting started with cataloging right away. It's exciting to think he has so many pieces, he can't keep track of them all. Who knows what I'll discover."

"Admirable work ethic. He'll like that." He gestured for her to retake her seat and crossed to a tray of ice and drinks in the corner. "Can I get you anything?"

At two in the afternoon? Tori crossed her legs at the ankle and feigned a relaxed pose. "Nothing for me, thanks." To his credit, Chad bypassed the decanted liquor and filled a tall glass with ice and sparkling water. "Will I be reporting to you, then?" she asked.

"That remains to be seen." He turned and raised his glass in a toast. "How closely would you like to work together?"

She didn't plan to have anyone looking over her shoulder, especially this starched and tanned loverboy. Tori pulled her reading glasses from her bag and put them on to emphasize the bookish, I'm-not-here-to-flirt role she'd come to play. "I tend to be pretty independent. Since the list I was given is out-of-date, it might be easier if I go from room to room to document items as I go. The job can be tedious and time consuming, and it sounds like you're a busy man. I'm content—and more productive—when I work alone."

Seemingly undaunted by a pair of wire frames, Chad took a drink and crossed to the desk. He leaned against the edge of the dark cherry wood immediately in front of her, forcing her to tilt her chin up to maintain eye contact.

"Keep in mind, Victoria..." He nodded to a line in the

paneling that ran parallel to the edge of the redbrick fire-place. She'd already spotted the hinges on the bookshelf marking a hidden door. "This old Victorian monstrosity is filled with secret rooms and passageways a stranger could get lost in. We had a new maid here once who went down to the cellar for a bottle of wine and ended up missing in the catacombs for two days. Needless to say, by the time we found her, she wasn't inclined to return to work, so we let her go. For your own safety—as well as protection of Jericho's artifacts—until our chief clears you, you'll be restricted to certain areas of the house."

"But I'll need access to every room, even the hidden ones, in order to do my job completely."

"True, my uncle's taste in fine things goes through the entire house. Nonetheless, there are restricted areas throughout the estate. I doubt the chief would look too favorably upon finding you where you shouldn't be." He flashed a smile as white as his shorts, then stood and circled behind her chair. He traced his fingertips along the sleeve of her jacket, marking a trail from wrist to shoulder. "Of course, I, too, have an appreciation for fine things. Perhaps I could personally show you some of the more valuable items we keep behind locked doors."

Tori stared deep into the grain of the desk, resisting the urge to clench her fists at the unwelcome touch. She had a feeling breaking and entering, and risking the wrath of Jericho Meade would be preferable to spending time in close quarters with this lothario.

"The chief?" she asked, keeping her voice even. "You mean Mr. Meade?"

Irked by her lack of interest in his offer, the charm bled from Chad's voice. "Our chief of security. Cole Taylor." Chad stalked to the drink cart and splashed some brown liquor into his water. He drank half the glass before speaking again. "He used to be a cop. Lost his badge on a corruption charge.'' The rest of his drink disappeared in another long swallow and he refilled the glass, ignoring the water this time. ''Taylor saved the old man's life one night, and now he's the golden boy. He guards Jericho and all that's his with the devotion of a damn puppy. He's the one you really need to worry about.''

So she'd heard.

Chad's smile was firmly back in place when he faced her again. But she'd glimpsed the chink in his plastic exterior. Was it jealousy over Taylor's quick rise in the family hierarchy? Contempt over *golden boy*'s qualifications for the job? Mistrust because Jericho had let an ex-cop into the fold?

Tori didn't push. Curiosity aside, she wasn't here to investigate crime family disharmony—unless she needed to use it as leverage to achieve her own agenda.

''So when can I meet Mr. Taylor?'' Though she'd have a hard time feigning respect for a man she knew to be a crooked cop, she had to play the protocol game, or risk her cover. ''The sooner I get started, the sooner I can have the estimates for your uncle.''

''Why are you so anxious to get to work, Victoria?'' Chad bolted his drink and strolled back to the desk.

''Because it's the job Mr. Meade hired me to do?''

He, apparently, didn't appreciate flippancy. He sank into the chair behind the desk. Neither of them was smiling now. ''*I'm* Mr. Meade,'' he stated, emphasizing his claim to authority while sounding for all the world like a petulant child. ''I'd think you'd want to be making a better impression on me. My uncle is in his late seventies. His mind and health are failing and he's tired all the time. *I'm* the one who arranged to have you hired. We're trying to avoid a legal nightmare with insurance claims and make sure his wishes are carried out after his death.''

The library door opened with a quiet *swish* across the carpet. "Don't write me off just yet, Chad."

A wizened old man with a shock of snow-white hair and clear blue eyes entered the room. The gnarled fingers of his left hand clutched an unlit cigar and rested on the arm of a plump man with slick, thinning hair. Though the men were similar in age, there was an unexpected frailty about the white-haired man.

Despite the added lines and yellowish pallor, Tori recognized Jericho Meade even before Chad rose from his seat to acknowledge him.

"Uncle."

"Mr. Meade." Tori stood and extended her hand. "Victoria Westin. It's a pleasure to meet you."

Releasing his grip on the sturdy anchor of his aide, he moved forward to shake hands politely. "So, you're Frank's granddaughter. I haven't seen that old coot in years." A single, sliding glance sent Chad scrambling from behind the desk. "Aren't you late for your game with Lana? It's not wise to keep your fiancée waiting." Jericho's smile turned back to include Tori. "Especially to flirt with another beautiful woman."

Ah, so schmaltz ran in the family. Tori forced herself to smile at the indirect compliment. "Thank you."

Reluctant to be dismissed, Chad paused beside the portly man she'd identified as Paul Meredith. "Just one thing before I go. I'm curious, Victoria. The university recommended you as an experienced consultant with whom they've worked several times. I've attended several university and museum fund-raisers. How come we've never met before?"

The dare in his eyes and voice made her wonder whether he was trying to score smart points with his uncle or show her up as a fraud because she'd rebuffed his advances. She'd dealt with power-hungry men like Chad all her life, and had learned to walk a fine line between asserting herself and placating their egos. ''I'm dedicated to my work.'' That wasn't a lie, but she wasn't about to elaborate on her real profession. ''My mother's the fund-raiser in the family. My talents lie more behind the scenes. With graduate school, research and travel, I've really had little time for socializing.''

''There. You see, Chad?'' Jericho held on to the desk and guided himself to his chair. ''She doesn't waste her family's money or her time partying—''

''I work damn hard. If you're insinuating—''

''I believe your uncle dismissed you.'' Paul Meredith turned and blocked Chad's path back to the desk. ''Lana will be upset if your tennis match gets rained out because you kept her waiting.''

Chad cocked his head and glared at the bigger man. ''You think he's going to leave any of this to you, you old buzzard?''

''Chad.'' Frail though he might be in appearance, there was no mistaking the authority in Jericho's voice. Or the warning. ''Because I loved my brother dearly, I've raised you like a son. But my patience is wearing thin.'' His tone said the discussion was over. ''I expect to see you and Lana both at dinner. Enjoy your game.''

Tori snuck a peek over the top of her glasses. A stiff, tawny lock of hair had actually fallen out of place across Chad's forehead. He smoothed it and his temper back into place as he faced his uncle.

''I don't presume to take Daniel's place in your heart, Uncle. But he's gone. I could run this business if you'd give me a chance.''

Jericho's eyes glazed over at the mention of Daniel. He did nothing to acknowledge that Chad had even spoken. Finally, accepting his uncle's dismissal, Chad dipped his chin in a curt nod to her.

"Victoria. Until dinner."

Tori and Paul watched him leave. She made a mental note to steer clear of family politics unless she could find a way to take advantage of it. She could ill afford to side with the wrong person too early in the game. The whole idea of undercover work was not to draw too much attention to herself. And she didn't want to alienate anyone in the household who might have the answers she needed.

"Jer?" Paul Meredith's gentle prodding brought Jericho back from whatever distant place he'd drifted off to.

The patriarch blinked, then grinned. "Take off your glasses."

"Excuse me?" Tori turned to see the old man watching her intently from across the desk. Though curious at how quickly the confrontation with Chad had been forgotten, she complied, pulling off her reading glasses and folding them in her lap. She boldly returned his scrutiny, and he smiled.

"Yes, I see the resemblance in the eyes. Sometimes it's easier to remember what happened years ago than what happened yesterday." Jericho's voice wavered with a hint of his age and illness now. "But I know those eyes. That deep, true green must be a strong Westin family trait. Though I must say they look prettier on you than they ever did on Frank."

"I see some men are never too old to flirt." She smiled on cue as he'd meant for her to, though it had been a long time since she'd considered having more in common with her grandfather than a name. And she wasn't interested in exploring any family history. It was enough to know the two men had once done business with each other. Her smile never wavered. "You know what would really impress me?"

"What?"

"Show me some of your etchings?" The line might be trite, but it had the intended effect.

The old man laughed. "You flatter me, girl."

Whatever was happening to his deteriorating mind and body wasn't affecting him now. He leaned on the desk and pushed himself to his feet. Paul Meredith was right there to support him, but Jericho waved him aside. "If you'd let an old man hold on to you, dear, I'd love to show you some of my favorite pieces."

Tori's pulse thrummed in anticipation as she tossed her bag over her shoulder and stood. Lax security. The distraction of a power struggle within the family. Approval from the boss.

The Divine Horseman was as good as hers.

Chapter Three

Tori hadn't really thought Jericho would take her straight to a vault filled with stolen goods. But she had hoped he'd do more than point out the Borglum bust she'd already seen on display in the entryway or the George Caleb Bingham painting over the mantel in the living room.

There were no fewer than six archways off the foyer, and she'd been shown through only two. They were both public areas—places to entertain guests. She hadn't seen anything remotely resembling a safe or secret room. Or an office. The Meades owned buildings in downtown Kansas City, but there had to be a nerve center for an estate this size. A place to run a business, hold meetings. Keep records.

Stash stolen artifacts.

Jericho did own an impressive collection of art. But, recalling the list supplied by the two Bills, she knew everything she'd seen thus far had been legitimately purchased.

There was no golden horseman in sight.

If she was going to find it, she'd have to gain access to the restricted rooms of the house and open a few of those locked doors. With or without Jericho's or Cole Taylor's permission.

Forty-five minutes after the tour had started, Paul tapped his watch. "It's time for your medication, Jer. At least an hour before dinner, remember?"

"You're as fussy as an old woman," Jericho grumbled. "Call Aaron," he ordered. With a reluctant sigh, he patted Tori's hand and excused himself for a chance to rest.

Tori stood alone in the foyer for several minutes. It was long enough for her to study the paintings on the wall, making mental appraisals of each one's value and working her way closer to the restricted wing of the house. She was close enough to reach for the knob of one of the French doors recessed in an archway when Aaron Polakis suddenly materialized behind her.

She traced the ivy vine carved into the walnut molding framing the doorway. "This house has beautiful woodwork, don't you think?"

He didn't care about her opinion. "This way, Ms. Westin."

His accent was even more pronounced as he replaced each *W* with a *V* sound. For a moment, she thought he might have been spying on her, that he'd seen her looking into places she shouldn't and was going to call her on it. But then she realized he was more worried about something else.

He was slightly out of breath. And the instant her gaze fell to the open front of his jacket, he quickly buttoned it, then pulled down the cuffs of his shirt at the end of each sleeve. The adjustments were brisk and methodical, but done hastily enough to make Tori think he'd just changed his clothes and run in from somewhere.

The man had been out of uniform and out of touch. But whether he'd been taking a legitimate break and had been caught unawares, or he'd been caught off guard, period, was hard to tell. Another flaw in Cole Taylor's half-baked security system.

"We go now." Aaron led her directly to her room on the second floor. "There—" he pointed out the tall, antique armoire where her clothes had been hung "—and there."

He opened the door to the adjoining bath. "Dinner is at seven in the dining room. Down the stairs. To your left."

"Thank you."

His dark eyes swept over her with something like disdain before he closed the door. Maybe he was anxious to get back to whatever had detained him, or just afraid she'd report him for dereliction of his duty. She certainly hadn't made a friend there. But she did appreciate the silent reminder to watch her back while she was here.

After throwing open the drapes and sheers in a futile effort to bring some much-needed light into the room, Tori dropped her bag onto the chenille bedspread and picked up the monogrammed notecard lying on her pillow beside a piece of wrapped candy. She unfolded the card and read the dramatically scrawled message written inside.

Miss Westin—
    Welcome to Meade Manor. Looking forward to our time together.
    Enjoy your stay.
    J.D.M.

"Nice touch." Her host was definitely old school, like her grandfather. But she had a feeling that his polite, gentlemanly manner, like Frank Westin's, was just a facade that hid a ruthless, driven man who cared more about profit than people.

Tossing the card onto the bed, she popped the candy into her mouth. She winced at the strong taste of bitter mint inside the chocolate and spit the nasty thing back into the wrapper, then tossed the whole thing into the trash.

"I prefer a caramel on my pillow, thank you very much." Speaking her real opinion out loud, even on a topic as mundane as candy preferences, reminded Tori that she was playing a role for the next several days. Professor Westin could talk freely. Agent Westin needed to be on guard every moment she was undercover. With her mind firmly in business mode, she conducted a thorough search of her room and the white-tiled bathroom. She found one listening device on the lamp atop the correspondence desk, but her sensor picked up no cameras. For a passing moment, she considered disabling the bug. But no sound from a room where someone intended to eavesdrop would raise suspicion.

"Let's see, what shall I wear?" The mundane comment covered her as she ran her fingers along the joint where the walnut armoire butted against the wall. The tall antique with its flowery cornices rested flush against the rose-patterned wallpaper, not even separated by the width of the baseboard. One of the lovely eccentricities of Victorian manor houses was the scarcity of built-in closets. Architects and designers of any era rarely attached furniture to the wall itself. So that meant…

Tori opened the door and hauled out her suits and blouses on their hangers and dumped them onto the bed. She pulled a penlight from her bag and, reliving a favorite childhood book, climbed right up into the armoire itself, searching first with her eyes and then with her fingertips for any kind of latch. She'd almost given up in disappointment that she wouldn't be transported into another world when she spotted a set of four odd marks imprinted in the dust on the back panel.

"*Curious,*" she thought, holding her right hand up beside the marks. The size was greater than her own hand, but the pattern was the same. Other than an odd span between the third and fourth spot, they lined up in the perfect imprint of four fingers. *"I've had company."*

And she didn't think it was the lost maid.

Even a forensic specialist would have a hard time recovering usable prints once a layer of dust had settled over them. But four out of five was a significant number. It should be easy enough, through casual observation, to find out who in the house was missing the ring finger on his or her right hand.

But it wasn't the *who* so much as the *how* that interested Tori right now. Placing her own hand beneath the telltale prints, she pushed. And smiled at the answering *click*. A spring-loaded door. She backed out of the armoire as the panel sprang open, then stepped inside for a closer look.

"Ooh." She shivered as she stepped into a pocket of cold air. Every follicle on her arms and legs puckered into a sea of goose bumps. Who ran air-conditioning inside the walls of a house? But as she took another step in, the chill passed. Tori's skin and heartbeat returned to normal. "Curiouser and curiouser."

Her light revealed a handle on the opposite side of the door for pulling it shut, a two-and-a-half-foot-wide passageway framed by the exposed studs and cross-beams of unfinished walls, and dozens of footprints trampled in the dust on the floor. She peered deeper into the passage, following the well-used path with her eyes. But the prints and her small light were swallowed up by the distant darkness.

"The guest room must be a popular destination."

But for whom? And why?

Thunder rumbled in the sky like the distant hoofbeats of a galloping herd, shaking the foundations of the house itself. Tori squeezed her toes inside her shoes and refused to read anything more into the sky's trembling and the house's response than spooky coincidence. As well-maintained as the mansion might be, it was an old structure, susceptible to sound waves and atmospheric changes.

Her affirming sigh stirred the dank air and she sneezed as a spiral of dust motes tickled her nose. Was this part of Cole Taylor's archaic security measures? Sneaking through the house and spying on guests? Were these hidden passageways a conduit for clandestine sexual liaisons? Or, were these catacombs the perfect hiding place for stolen artifacts?

Chad had hinted that secret rooms and passages cut through the entire mansion. *The Divine Horseman* could be stored anywhere inside this maze, transported in and out by visitors—known or otherwise—to this room. And though fanciful thoughts of knights and maidens and secret rendezvous tempted her to explore, Tori was practical enough to realize she should eliminate more obvious hiding places for the statuette before she went combing through the innards of the house.

She wrinkled her nose against the next wave of sneezing and climbed out of the armoire, quietly closing the door behind her and re-hanging her clothes to cover it. As much as Jericho loved his pretty things, he'd be more likely to put *The Divine Horseman* on display in a private room where he could look at it whenever he wanted. Besides, she had a hard time picturing an arthritic old man sneaking through the narrow, dusty catacombs. She'd be smarter to start her search in one of the locked rooms downstairs.

Smarter and cleaner.

As another spate of sneezes burned her sinuses, Tori noticed a soft spring rain falling outside her window now, punctuated by rumblings that foretold a more violent storm in its wake.

The gloomy weather was the least of her concerns. She stripped and stepped into the claw-foot tub with a pull-around curtain for a quick shower. She'd have a hard time explaining a stuffy nose and cobwebs in her hair if she showed up for dinner after poking around the secret passages.

One thug, one bug and a secret entrance to her room… Just enough security to keep her on her toes, but not enough to worry her. Yet. Maybe it was time to challenge this unseen Cole Taylor, she thought as she dried off. If he was the loyal protector Chad had made him out to be, then these amateurish efforts to safeguard the Meade mansion were intended to put her and any unwelcome guests off their game. But she'd been tested before; she wouldn't let him lure her into a false sense of confidence.

"CLASSICAL MUSIC, HMM?" Cole was a rock-and-roll man himself, but the sudden blare of trumpets brought him from his desk to the bank of monitors that gave him visual access to key parts of the estate, and audio access to nearly everywhere else.

She had cranked the music in her room—the art professor with the fiery red hair. Now she was zipping around the guest room, wrapped in a white towel that covered her from armpit to thigh. She crossed to the far side of the room to retrieve something from the dresser, giving the camera a wide-angle shot. Cole started unrolling the sleeves of his shirt and buttoning the cuffs, watching the screen and enjoying his work for a change.

They didn't make towels long enough to cover *those* legs.

Professor Westin had passed his background screening, the security check at the gate, and—other than those few minutes alone in the library—had been under constant surveillance by Aaron or someone else in the house. But their newest guest had shown an inordinate amount of curiosity in her surroundings. He supposed intellectuals were like that, always poking around, eager to learn something new. His brother Mac was a forensic scientist who never missed a detail. Mac could read a crime scene with all five senses, and with a little help from chemistry and computers, piece together the who, what, where, when, and sometimes even the why of the crime.

Cole's powers of observation lay in reading people.

The professor had first caught his attention when she climbed into the wardrobe. Odd. But he'd seen stranger stuff in this house. When she disappeared into the bathroom, he'd gone back to his desk to finish up some paperwork. But now, as he watched the hurry in her movements, he realized her curious eccentricities served a purpose. What, he didn't know yet. But she was up to something. Dinner wasn't for nearly an hour, and she showed all the signs of a woman who was late for an appointment.

He hooked the last button on his cuff and unbunched the oxford cloth sleeves beneath the elastic and leather brace of his shoulder holster. He missed the days when he could just toss on a pair of jeans and… He froze with his hands at the knot of his tie.

She'd dropped the towel.

A better man might have turned away, but Cole couldn't. Slim and delicate from the nape of her neck down to the heel of her foot—with miles of smooth, milky skin in between—Victoria Westin didn't look like any professor he knew. Even in black and white, she was tall, lean and sexy. His pulse quickened. His lips parted to accommodate the sudden heat inside that sought escape.

She'd pulled on panty hose, a slip and a plain green dress before he forced himself to blink and look away. He retreated all the way to his desk to grab his suit coat from the back of his chair and slip it on, needing the physical activity to work off the tension that made him edgy and horny and frustrated as hell. He needed a long workout in the gym or a stiff drink. He didn't need to be dreaming up scenarios about slender redheads doing stripteases.

He was in one screwed-up mess, sitting on a time bomb. He'd uncovered dates and codes and had no clear idea whether they were legit or not, without outside verification. He hadn't heard boo about his mother's recovery from being attacked. And he was certain that someone in this house suspected he was a traitor. They might not know he was a cop, but he or she saw him as a threat.

How else could he explain the influx of invitations to sit in on every meeting? Not just with Jericho, but with Chad and his fiancée. Paulie. Aaron, too. Supervising deliveries, consulting on stock options, hiring accountants. Strategies for dealing with a relentless district attorney who'd published yet another interview about his determination to rid Kansas City of organized crime. He'd never been so popular.

What did they want him to say? That he knew the assistant district attorney personally? That ADA Dwight Powers believed Jericho Meade had gotten away with murder?

Someone was trying to keep Cole very busy, and feed him lots of misleading information in an effort to trip him up and reveal his connection to Dwight Powers.

"What the—?"

Victoria Westin had just slipped something inside the lining of her jacket. Cole moved closer to watch. She smoothed lipstick over her lips and smacked them together, studying her appearance in the mirror. The luscious shape of her mouth interested him almost as much as what she did next. Instead of replacing the cap, she unscrewed something from the bottom of the tube and tucked that into her jacket as well.

"What are you up to?" he whispered to the image on his screen.

Cole buttoned his jacket as she opened her door and peered into the hallway. He typed in a command and switched the view to the one from the upstairs hallway camera, and caught her slinking along the railing toward the landing's sitting area.

"That's beyond curious, lady. Who are you?"

Instincts borne of too many years on the job transformed his suspicion into a defensive awareness that radiated through his skeleton and sharpened every sense. He looked past her to the bigger picture on the screen.

Where was Aaron? Polakis was supposed to be watching her until dinner.

A nosy guest. A missing guard.

Too many unanswered questions.

When Ms. Westin peeked over the top of the banister before tiptoeing down the stairs, a plan took shape in Cole's mind.

It was crazy. It was desperate.

But it was a plan.

WITH RIMSKY-KORSAKOV filling the room and the ear of whomever might be listening on the other end, Tori slipped out her door and made her way to the grand staircase.

Through the window overlooking the landing she spotted Aaron outside. He was smoking a cigarette in the gazebo at the end of the garden path and trading words with a platinum blonde who wore a thigh-baring tennis dress and his rain-spattered jacket across her shoulders. That must be the infamous Lana, who hated to be kept waiting. Had they been caught in the rain together? And where was Chad?

Aaron hadn't struck her as the kind of man who'd go in for the gallantry of offering a woman the warmth of his coat. Nor did he seem to be at a loss for words with Lana, judging by his angry gesticulations. Hmm. Five fingers on his right hand, she idly noted.

But as long as he was occupied, Aaron wasn't her immediate concern. Counting his trouble with women and weather as a stroke of good fortune for her, Tori hurried down the main stairs, ducked through one of the unexplored archways in the east wing and broadened her search.

This was more like the two Bills' report. A rotating camera hung at the end of a short, empty hallway. There were two heavy walnut doors on either side, all trimmed with polished brass and new locks. She could tell from the understatement of the decor that this was a suite of offices.

What was housed inside them, she couldn't say, but the word *Private* on one of the doors was all the invitation she needed.

It took her only a few minutes to time the sweep of the camera. Once her pathway was clear, she placed a dime-size dampening module against the lock to prevent the disruption of any electronic alarms, then quickly picked her way inside.

Closing the door behind her, she leaned back against the shoulder-high walnut paneling and breathed deeply, silently, orienting herself to her surroundings. Steady tremors of cloud-to-cloud lightning provided all the light she needed to see. A desk sat at one end of the room. Heavy and ornately carved, it was the style of furniture that touted a man's power and virility. But it was the file cabinet recessed into the wall and the computer sitting on top of the desk that got her pulse racing.

Information heaven. She mouthed the words in triumph, conscious of the presence of listening devices in the room.

Moving without a sound on her two-inch heels across the oriental rug, she circled the room, taking note of the two seams in the floor-to-ceiling bookcase that marked another hidden door. Everything was neatly dusted in here, making it difficult to tell whether the passageway had been opened recently. The switch would be hidden behind a book, or maybe inside one of the lacquer boxes displayed on the shelves.

Though curiosity begged her to search for the way inside, to see if it connected to her room, this was a reconnaissance mission. She needed to explore all her options as quickly as she could, then return to the main part of the house before she was missed.

Lightning flashed outside the window and a clap of thunder galloped closely on its heels, warning of the worsening storm. The wind picked up and tree branches drummed against the panes like impatient fingertips. Dark house. Big storm. Tori clutched the edge of a chair and carefully identified each sight and sound, refusing to be unnerved by the weather or her own inexplicably fanciful mood. Then a second flash lit the room.

Her startled gasp was drowned out by the answering thunder.

The end wall held a nearly life-size painting of Jericho Meade and a man who must surely be his son, Daniel. They shared the same lanky build, the same sharp nose. And though the younger man's hair was golden and Jericho's snowy white, they shared the same cold blue eyes.

Tori shivered at the creepy feeling of those painted eyes watching her every move. Oils and canvas couldn't hurt her, though the real thing could.

Determined to meet her fear head-on, she lined her cheek up against the wall to inspect the gilt-edged frame. *Pay dirt!* The hanging cord above the heavy portrait was a fake. The back of the picture was anchored by a spring-loaded hinge, an indication that a safe was hidden in the wall behind it. Anticipation danced through her, soothing her jumpy nerves. She would definitely find her way back into this room.

With restored perception, she approached the desk. She noted the cut-glass bowl of foil-wrapped mints similar to the one she'd spit out earlier. Someone had strong taste buds or—she smiled—used the bitter taste to cancel out another bad habit. She stroked her fingers across a nineteenth-century humidor, then lifted the wooden lid to sniff the pungent aroma of the cigars stacked inside. A hint of the same fruity tobacco smell had clung to the material of Jericho's suit. There was no questioning whose office she'd entered.

The job didn't get any better than this.

But she wouldn't solve this case in a day. Tomorrow, she'd find time to sneak back in to unlock the desk and file cabinet to locate inventory lists, bills of sale or transit, even a combination for the hidden safe.

Unless, of course, Jericho happened to keep something like that on his computer. She was the one who'd romanticized the secret doors and passageways as gateways to stashes of stolen goods. Maybe Jericho was more modern when it came to doing business.

She wasn't late for dinner yet.

Tori spared a few seconds to flip on the computer. She held her breath as the machine beeped softly and came to life. It made no other sound as the software loaded. Still, that single mechanical tone, jarring against the natural symphony outdoors, was enough to set her on edge. The glow from the monitor seemed inordinately bright, and steady as a spotlight compared to the periodic bursts of electricity from the storm. A vague sense of imminent danger shifted Tori on her feet and she automatically looked to the watchful eyes of the portrait. They seemed to blink on and off, open and shut, with each streak of lightning.

But, of course, there was no movement except the row of icons popping onto the screen. Tori crouched behind the desk and read through the file names.

C. Donations. Charitable donations? A possibility for listing art acquisitions. But stolen ones?

PM. Paul Meredith? Prime Minister? Afternoon?

Tori flexed her fingers as a dozen ideas filled her head. She needed uninterrupted time to play on Jericho's computer, to bypass possible encryptions to open files and evaluate the information stored there. This was just an introduction to all the possibilities that could aid her search.

Layout. She liked the looks of that one, hoped it meant house plans.

Daniel.

Daniel? She mouthed the question and frowned. What

records would a man keep on a computer about his deceased son?

Lancelot. Tori's heart leaped in her chest. Naw, it couldn't be that easy. Maybe she could spare one more moment, just to click on the icon—

"Bang. You're dead."

Lightning flashed and Tori jumped at the low-pitched voice from across the room. Someone a hell of a lot scarier than a lifeless portrait was watching her. And he was no figment of her imagination.

She slowly rose, silently cursing the seconds when she must have dropped her guard. Then silently cursing the man closing the door behind him. She *hadn't* dropped her guard. She'd been outmaneuvered.

With her eyes adjusted to the room's sporadic light, it didn't take her long to assess the well-cut suit that clung to massive shoulders and masked the sleek bulk of a weapon holstered at his side. Or the long, dark hair pulled back from carved cheekbones and hanging past his starched white collar. Or the eyes that pierced the darkness and condemned her long before she ever spoke.

This guy had "Don't fight, don't run, don't even breathe funny" written all over him.

An unfamiliar, nervous energy shimmied across her skin, and she curled her fingers into tight fists at her sides. Tori couldn't tell if it was acknowledgment of a worthy adversary, a surge of ill-timed sexual attraction or an uncomfortable combination of both that had her emotions scrambling for cover.

She straightened her fingers and stiffened her spine, pushing aside her initial reaction. She wouldn't surrender her mission to an attack of nerves. Nor would she let an unexpected rush of hormones sway her from her purpose. "Let me guess. You're Cole Taylor."

"And you're trouble."

She supposed that was confirmation enough of his identity. He strode across the room, moving as stealthily as she had. God, he was even bigger up close. And she was a tall woman. Way too much man for her peace of mind. She curled her toes inside her pumps to keep from retreating. Those deep blue eyes scanned the room without ever losing her from their line of sight.

"Breaking into the boss's office? Accessing files. There's a reason it says *Private* on the door."

Tori didn't bother denying the obvious. "What gave me away? No one followed me. Any sound I made was muffled by the storm. And I bypassed the door sensors."

The subtle curve at the corner of his mouth could be a smile or a sneer. "The computer."

He reached across her to shut off the machine. Tori turned her nose to the side to avoid contact with the crisp scent of pressed gabardine. He paused, giving her time to inhale the subtler tang of the man himself. It was far less personal than Chad Meade's touch had been, yet far more potent. Taylor knew he was too close to be polite; he dared her to be afraid.

"I rigged an alarm program that alerts me in my office. If you don't type in the right code within ten seconds of the screen boot-up, I pay a visit."

She rolled her gaze up to meet his, boldly refusing to be intimidated. "Clever."

"Clever enough." He pulled his arm away and stepped back. "You're Victoria Westin, the art lady."

"Art historian." She let a little huffy indignation creep into her voice. She was an invited guest, after all—even if the invitation didn't extend to this private room. Maybe she could bluff her way past Cole Taylor's censure. "I'm here to appraise and catalog Mr. Meade's collection for estate purposes."

"Bull." A flash of lightning punctuated his opinion.

So much for bluffing.

"You're Frank Westin's granddaughter. Westin and Jericho Meade were business partners decades ago. Frank claims he made his fortune on the straight and narrow. Rumors say he gets infusions of cash from, shall we say, less honorable means. Word in the city says he's expanding his real estate holdings and he's a little strapped for cash right now."

"Word in the city?" Tori faced him head-on, age-old hackles rising in self-defense. "I work for the museum, not Frank. I resent your implication. And how do you know so much about my family?"

He leaned in, ignoring the whole idea of personal space. Tori tilted her chin and held her ground.

"I make it a point to know everything I can about everyone I meet. You here to help out Grandpa? Maybe sweet-talk your way into a loan from Jericho? Or do you have something else in mind?" He opened his palm and showed her the tiny dampening device he'd pulled from the lock. "I've never seen technology like this used in any museum. Unless you're planning to steal something."

"First I'm a con artist, and now I'm a thief?"

He'd grabbed her wrist and lifted it, thrusting her watch toward her face. "I've got cameras hidden around here that this baby can't pick up."

"Get your hands off me." Tori had managed to twist free, but she had a feeling he'd simply let her go.

"Where'd you get the hardware?"

"It's none of—" The buzz of voices in the hallway diverted her defensive temper. "Afraid you can't handle me on your own?"

The alertness that put Tori on guard against the threat of discovery paled in comparison to the exponential energy that suddenly suffused every muscle in Cole's posture. He seemed to swell in height. A vein ticked along his jaw and something reckless flickered in his midnight-blue eyes.

Harsh and demanding undertones riddled the bone-deep pitch of his voice when he suddenly reached for her. "Take off your jacket."

"What?" Tori darted back a step. He followed.

"Strip, lady," he ordered, cornering her at the edge of the desk.

A key slipped into the lock but didn't turn. There was laughter as a third voice joined the conversation outside. Tori glanced over her shoulder at the door, not sure which enemy proved the greater danger at the moment. But when she felt the hand at her breastbone, she knew.

"Hands off, buddy."

She wound her fingers around his wrist and pinched, a sure move that had taken down others. The big man grunted a curse at the pain she'd inflicted, but instead of going down, he twisted out of her grip and pinned her arm behind her back, crushing her thighs with his own against the desk.

"Hey—" was all she got out before a taut hand muffled her mouth.

He leaned in close enough for her to feel his hot breath against her cheek. "I'm trying to save your life."

Then his fingers were on her buttons again, undoing them to the background noise of joking voices just outside the door.

Tori pulled at his hands. "You're trying to get in my pants." She struggled, unable to get a good line on his instep or crotch. "This is some perverted form of sexual harassment."

"So report me," he challenged.

Tori stilled, her eyes locked on his, mere inches from her own. Her deep, defiant breaths pushed her breasts against the warm hand that branded her through only a few layers of silk. The heat that zapped her with each unintended caress was as fierce as it was foreign to her.

"You're the one who broke in," he reminded her in a succinct, hushed tone. "You're the one snooping. And you aren't any damn art historian."

"I have a degree—"

"Save it for someone you can fool. Now take it off."

Clearly overpowered and out of her league, she needed to think of an alternative tactic to get this crazy man off her case and out of her space.

Leaving his thighs and other parts of his body pressed intimately against hers, he freed her hands with the expectation that she would finish unbuttoning her jacket. She did, buying herself time to mollify him. "Why are you doing this?"

The voices outside grew louder. She could identify them now. Jericho. Paul Meredith. And a woman.

"Faster," he ordered, "or you're dead." Ignoring her question, he reached behind his collar and freed his hair from its band. He sifted his fingers through the sable mass, stirring a Samson-like cascade that fell around his shoulders.

"Can't get a woman any other way?" she taunted.

The key turned in the lock.

The urgency Cole exuded hummed between them. "Trust me."

"To do what?" He was chief of security. He thought she was a crook. This was blackmail. "Hey!"

He swept aside a lamp and pencil caddy and lifted her onto the desk, pushing her legs apart and moving boldly between them, sliding her jacket off her shoulders and baring her arms to the elbows, cinching them at her sides. "There are only two reasons to explain why you got caught in Jericho's office. One of them will get you killed."

He tunneled his fingers into her hair, forcing her head back as he pulled her to his chest. "The other is this."

He smothered her startled yelp with a kiss, just as the door swung open and the overhead light flashed on.

Chapter Four

The storm raging outside was nothing like the battle of wills going on in Jericho Meade's office.

Cole clutched Victoria's long, writing body as tightly as he dared to prevent her escape. He stopped up her mouth with his own to bring to life an illusion that had come to him in a moment of voyeuristic inspiration—or maybe a moment of madness brought on by two weeks of utter isolation.

He was a healthy, mature male. Beneath a veneer of respectability he was a product of the working class, rough around the edges and streetwise to the core. He might not be the smoothest guy on the block, but he'd never had any complaints. She was an adult female, albeit one with that classic sort of touch-me-not beauty belonging to aristocrats and pageant queens. Their paths would never cross in the outside world.

But she was female.

Catching her dead to rights, breaking into Jericho's office, gave him the upper hand.

The ruse should work.

He'd had no time to explain, only to act. And though their position on top of the desk would appear intimate enough to anyone passing by, a closer look would show that this embrace was all one-sided. And he hoped to hell he was the only one who could tell the sounds humming from between the art lady's stiff, defiant lips into his mouth were protests, not lustful sounds of pleasure.

As he captured her mouth beneath his, he bore into her emerald gaze, willing Miss High-and-Mighty to cooperate. Maybe she didn't understand how easy it was for Jericho to punish anyone who broke the rules—and she'd already broken several—or how serious, how permanent, that punishment could be. She clearly didn't understand his efforts to save her alabaster hide.

Or his own considerably tougher one.

Using the overhead light as a cue, Cole moaned in his throat and shifted his mouth over hers in his best rendition of a kiss.

The buzz of voices gave way to a beat of silence—a silence that ultimately registered with the woman he was kissing. Victoria went still in his arms. Her startled lips caught a gasp of air from his mouth.

Come on, lady, he silently urged, gentling his kiss. *Play the game with me.*

Then something happened. Lightning outside flickered like a strobe light throughout the room, charging the atmosphere with electrons and standing the hair of his arms on end. The universe shifted on its axis and Cole's well-guarded world was thrown into chaos. Seconds ticked by into aeons, as if counted down on an arrested clock. The three interlopers standing in the doorway, staring with an assortment of expressions, faded into the decor.

Electrons weren't the only thing charging through his system.

The woman was kissing him back.

And it looked—and felt—damn real.

Lush lips softened their paralysis beneath his and his whole body flamed in response, abruptly awakening from its self-imposed sleep to the scents and softness and shape of her.

Though he'd allowed her arms no room to move, she'd twisted her fingers into the ends of his hair, sending tender prickles across his scalp with a series of urgent, questing tugs. The perfume she wore was something light and elegant that drifted past his nose with the shift of her body as she arched against him, lifting her mouth into his.

Good God. She wasn't wearing a bra. Her nipples stood at pert attention as she rubbed against him, and Cole unwittingly hardened in response. She might give a visual impression of cool gentility, but he was discovering a hidden side to Victoria Westin that matched the fire in her coppery shock of hair. Built long and lean, there wasn't much to her in the curves department. But everything about her was sleek and toned and crackling with an energy that tingled along his skin.

Cradled between her silky, thoroughbred thighs, everything about him that was male lurched at the heat he felt there. He softened the assault on her mouth, let her take the lead as her tongue darted out to touch his. Her lips traveled a cautionary expedition at first, then grew bolder, as if testing the sincerity of his unexpected and overwhelming desire. Then accepting it. Matching it.

Her fingers clenched in his hair, dragging him closer. Her mouth opened, hot and moist and seeking beneath his. She squirmed against him, right *there,* crumbling walls of self-preservation with an intense fiery pleasure that was building to the brink of no return inside him.

Cole battled the urges of his hungry body at her brazen response. He wanted to free her hands to touch him at will, but couldn't risk it. He wanted to stroke those thighs, caress that skin, but he didn't dare release her.

It had been forever since he'd allowed himself to think about a woman in a sexual way. Weeks since he'd reacted to anything except the threat of danger. Now, his crotch seemed to be leading all his thinking regarding this fire-and-ice woman.

But the needs of survival were too deeply ingrained to be completely ignored. Passion distracted. Lust betrayed. This kiss was for show, he reminded himself. No matter how good, how real, it felt. It served a purpose that had nothing to do with his libido. He was counting on Victoria Westin to save his life. By blackmail, if he couldn't gain her cooperation any other way.

But like a hungry man set before a banquet, he couldn't seem to make himself stop.

TORI IGNORED THE WARNING siren going off in her head. There was something crazy wrong with this picture. She was kissing this man. She should be going for his gun or his groin and her freedom. Instead, she was soaking up his passion the way the parched earth craved the rain. She was reveling in his attention, coming on to him as if his caveman seduction technique had been some kind of turn-on instead of an insult to every feminist bone in her body.

The Bureau hadn't trained her for this. Growing up a skinny tomboy in her mother's fussy society world hadn't trained her for this. But here she sat clinging to a man who smelled like money and danger. A man who was solid and warm and incredibly strong beneath the tactile layers of nubby wool and starched cotton. A man whose unspoken hints of genuine need shot around her icy defenses and melted her down to a puddle of untapped femininity.

She felt fluid inside, prickly outside. Every touch was both torment and reward. There was a wildness to this embrace that matched the storm outside.

She'd played the role of femme fatale a time or two, had acted as girlfriend or decoy on assignment. She knew things to say to a man, knew how to tease. But she didn't know about this. This all-consuming fire. No one had ever demanded passion from her like this. And she'd never risked offering it.

When Jericho Meade's chief of security had caught her and called her a thief, she'd known a moment of panic at the possible repercussions. The danger of revealing her identity. The ignominy of failing her mission. The frustration of being bested by a man.

Fear had turned to anger. Anger to indignation. And when he moved between her legs, self-doubts had turned it all back into fear again. But with the demand of his handsome mouth—as if he had every right, every wish, to touch her like this—Cole Taylor had turned all those volatile emotions into passion. He seemed to want nothing less from her.

Maybe it was the challenge she couldn't resist. Maybe Cole Taylor was simply the first man in too long a time who registered on her sex-starved radar.

Or maybe she would always be that idiot who never learned to read the difference between a man who wanted her and a man who wanted something from her.

"Stop," she whispered, or perhaps she only thought the word. She sensed his withdrawal an instant before the memory of past mistakes dashed her to her senses.

"Please, stop," she breathed against his lips. Passion waned as surely as the heart of the storm's fury was subsiding into a dark, steady rain.

She'd heard voices earlier, somewhere in the haze of hormones run amok. They had an audience. And though she couldn't see them, she could feel their curious stares from the doorway behind her.

First, she'd been caught trespassing. Now, she'd been caught…what exactly did she call this out-of-control response to a virtual stranger?

Someone cleared his throat. *Great.* Heat radiated through

her cheeks. She had a sinking feeling this piece-of-cake mission had just become very, very complicated. And she had no one to blame but herself.

"If it was anyone else, Cole Taylor…" The gravelly voice from the doorway reprimanded them with indulgence. She heard a tongue tsking against teeth. "Anyone else."

Jericho Meade.

Not good.

Untangling her fingers from the mahogany silk of Cole's hair, Tori flattened her palms against his chest and forced herself to breathe. One deep, stuttering breath in through her nose, one shaky, cleansing breath out between her sensitized lips.

Though he still had her perched on the desk, Cole, too, was making a visible effort to slow his breathing and ease his grip on her. He peppered her face with tiny kisses, drawing out the last sparks of her combustible reaction to him.

He rested his forehead against hers and sighed with audible regret. "I guess we got carried away, hmm?"

After all their whispers, the normal volume of his voice jarred loudly in her ears. Tori lifted her questioning gaze to that sea of deep, dark blue in his eyes. They focused intently on hers, demanding a comprehension that finally dawned on her.

Not good at all.

He wanted something from her. He wanted to be caught in a compromising position. With her. But why?

Humiliations, past and present, cleared her head as nothing else could. Tori sorted her thoughts and calculated possibilities, trying to regain the upper hand, which she feared she'd lost for good. She raised an eyebrow and challenged his high-handed behavior.

"I don't know what kind of kinky game—"

"Believe me, sweetheart, this is no game." His deep voice dropped back to a whisper for her ears alone. He smoothed his palms up and down the bare expanse of her upper arms, raising goose bumps and placating her for the benefit of the witnesses behind her. He brushed the warning against her ear under the guise of yet another kiss. "Follow my lead and we'll both walk out of here."

Tori's entire body went rigid with protest. "You want me to pretend—? You're threatening me?"

"Better than Jericho killing you." She clamped her mouth shut beneath the final press of his lips. "And I expect you to be a very good actress."

Jericho's hoarse cough demanded attention. "Someone want to tell me what's going on?"

Cole took a measured breath and looked beyond her shoulder. "Mr. Meade. Paulie. Lana. Did you need me?"

"I came to *my* office to get a cigar for after dinner. Why are you here?"

"We needed a little privacy." Cole's hand slid to her knee in a possessive grasp. Was that part of following his lead? Or just another way to keep her trapped? Either way, the sudden suffusion of heat where his palm branded her skin was a distraction she didn't intend to fall prey to again.

Tori primed her nails to attack Cole's hand. But when she saw how many inches of silk-clad thigh were showing beneath her hiked-up dress, she shoved at his chest instead. He retreated a step, helping her down with the panache of a gentleman. Needing room to think as much as to reclaim her modesty, Tori swatted his hand away and scooted some distance between them. She faced the trio at the door.

"I'm sorry, Mr. Meade," she said, smoothing the hem of her silk dress to a line just above her knees and buttoning her rumpled jacket. *Oh damn.* Tori clutched at the jacket's slack lining. Her picklock! "Mr. Meredith." She scanned the carpet, visually retracing her path to the doorway as she acknowledged the bulky man looming like a shadow behind Jericho's right shoulder. She cringed at the unabashed humor in his grin. She hoped he wasn't laughing at anything more than a little indecorum.

Where the hell did I lose—? Thank God. She spotted them on the desk. Scattered among the pencils were the two toothpick-size gadgets of stainless steel that worked in tandem to override a locking mechanism. They must have fallen out when Cole stripped the jacket from her shoulders. Or pulled her into his arms. Or… Hell, if he'd held her at gunpoint and turned her over to Jericho, she couldn't be more rattled.

It was just one stupid kiss!

Paulie was teasing Cole about something now. Tori made a show of bending over to adjust her heel, gripping the desk for support. She stretched her fingers, slid the tools off into her hand and stood. Both men laughed at some remark. Clenching the pick in her fist at her side, she breathed a cautious sigh of relief.

A large hand closed around hers and Tori tensed behind the smile she'd plastered on her face. *Dammit.* Did the man have eyes in the back of his head? Cole thrust his thumb between her fingers and pried loose the lock-pick, his strength overpowering hers, all under the guise of holding her hand.

"Do you know everyone here, babe?" he asked, the sappy endearment a mild irritant compared to the riptide of impotent anger surging through her.

To hell with blind obedience. Tori wanted to know what the security chief was up to before she started playing by his rules. She'd sacrificed enough pride by kissing him. She wouldn't sacrifice her mission as well. She jerked her hand free.

"I know this doesn't look very professional, Mr. Meade. I can assure you it won't happen again."

"That depends on whether or not you're wearing that same perfume, sweetheart," Cole drawled, teasing her with a lover's tone. In one smooth move he dipped his head and nuzzled the hollow beneath her ear, and slipped the pick into the pocket of his slacks. "I'm not willing to make any guarantees."

Tori's cheeks flooded with heat that was half temper and half fear of the flutters of awareness that radiated along each nerve at his sensuous touch. "Mr. Tay— Cole," she said, catching herself. She pushed against his shoulder and chest. "We need to stop now."

"You didn't want me to a minute ago."

He had the nerve to bend his head to kiss her again, but she stiff-armed him, digging her fingers around the strap of his holster through layers of wool and cotton. It afforded her a solid grip, but it also reminded her that her own weapon was locked up at home in her bedside table.

Everything about Cole Taylor was hard and dangerous and sexy and controlled.

And she was at his mercy.

Ooh! One kick. To something vital. That's all she asked for, a chance to even the playing field against the stealthy giant who'd forced her into the untenable situation of not being able to defend herself without risking her cover. Jericho was clearly upset by their presence here. But claiming she and Cole meant nothing to each other would raise even more questions. If she wasn't here to seduce the chief of security, then what was she doing in the office? They might question why she was at the Meade mansion in the first place. Tori pulled her hands away and seethed in silence, refusing to acknowledge Cole's taunting smile.

"Isn't this cozy?" The third member of their audience, the platinum-blonde Tori had seen arguing outside with the butler, had a proprietary arm linked through Jericho's. In diamond earrings and an evening suit of silver satin, she looked as cool and sophisticated now as she'd been hot under the collar earlier. "We'll have our discussion about rescheduling the European shipments at another time and place, Jericho. Seems the new girl is making herself right at home. I guess she's, uh…familiarizing herself with security protocols.''

New *girl?* Familiarizing? And what shipments? To Sir Lancelot?

Already bristling with tension, Tori jumped at the brush of Cole's fingers against her back.

''Easy, babe,'' he crooned. ''You're among friends here. I'm sure Lana didn't mean to imply anything.''

Yeah, right. She wasn't anybody's *babe,* and nothing about this confrontation felt friendly. But the pitch of his voice soothed each frayed nerve ending, calming the instinct to fight or flee. And though she resented his ability to shift roles from blackmailer to champion so quickly, Tori realized she'd already foolishly responded to it. Her charging heartbeat had slowed to a manageable pace. She wasn't just reacting, she was thinking. And reluctantly playing her part.

''We haven't had the opportunity to meet yet, Ms. Shepherd. I'm Victoria Westin.''

Cole flattened his hand at the small of her back. The stamp of possession felt unexpectedly like unspoken support. But she didn't know him well enough to judge whether he was a consummate actor, or if there really were a few good-guy cells beneath his blackmailing exterior.

''Lana manages several of Mr. Meade's investments and she's engaged to his nephew, Chad. Victoria's an art historian. She'll be spending the next week or so with us.''

''How nice for you.'' The gleam in Lana Shepherd's brown eyes wasn't the warmth of welcome. It wasn't even amusement at Tori's expense. It was the look of a territorial female sizing up the competition.

Great. So she shouldn't plan any late-night girl chats over ice-cream sundaes to get acquainted and learn the secrets of what they were shipping to Europe. First Aaron, now

Lana. Tori was quickly alienating potential sources of information. Of course, she could always take Chad up on his offer to get *really* well acquainted, but she had a feeling Lana would have something to say about that, too.

Engagement ring or not, apparently the platinum-blonde had staked her claim on every man in the household. Including Cole.

"If I'd known you had a thing for redheads, I'd have dyed my hair and gotten a few lessons on security myself."

Dead silence filled the room as Cole and Lana exchanged enigmatic glares. There was something going on there—past love? thwarted lust? bad blood? And who was the injured party? Tori had no desire to fight with Lana over any man, especially one as insufferable and unpredictable as Cole Taylor. And the only property she wanted control of in the house was one particular gold statuette. The blonde was welcome to him—except Cole was still holding *her.* And he'd kissed her like…like…

Oh hell. Definitely time to switch to a less personal topic.

Tori directed a grateful smile at Jericho. "Thank you for the card, Mr. Meade. It was a lovely gesture."

The white-haired man frowned. She'd caught him daydreaming. *Preoccupied* was more accurate. He seemed to have a hard time dragging his gaze away from the portrait at the end of the room. "What card?"

"On the pillow in my room this evening. 'Enjoy your stay,' that kind of thing. I appreciate the welcome."

The lines on his forehead deepened in consternation. "I didn't write any card."

"Oh." Now Tori was the one frowning. "It was signed 'J.D.M.' I assumed…"

The color drained from Jericho's face. He sagged against Lana's arm. A hard, painful breath raled in his chest. In an instant, Paulie was there supporting him from the other side.

"Easy, Jer."

Cole shifted beside her, and Tori got the impression he wanted to run over and help the powerful man, who looked ancient and frail as a fit of coughing seized him. "Did I say something wrong?" she asked.

"My son..." Jericho wheezed and answered before Cole could. "He signed papers with his initials. *J.D.M.* Jericho Daniel Meade."

His supposedly dead son? Tori had read more about Daniel Meade's disappearance in the papers than she had in her mission briefing. Though the police had no leads, his blood type at the site where Daniel was last seen, a missing body and plenty of enemies had the press speculating he'd been the victim of a gangland hit.

"I'm sorry. Maybe he wrote the card for another guest who left it behind." It was a lame excuse. Her name had been on it. "Maybe I just misread the initials."

"He wrote it." Jericho clung to Lana and Paulie, but his voice was emphatic. "I know he did. He's contacted me, too."

Was he implying that a ghost sent that note?

Distant thunder rumbled right on cue, and Tori frowned. As a child, her father had filled her head with legends and ghost stories. He'd told her that the Horseman had been a simple knight, fighting for his king and God in a foreign land. When the enemy overtook the European stronghold, many knights fled through a secret passageway to the sea and escaped, abandoning the noblewomen who'd joined the Crusade as missionaries and companions. The Horseman stood his post and was killed.

But through divine intervention, his brave soul was given a second chance. Brought back to life as the enemy stormed the gate, he led the women to the safety of the last ship and died a second time, fighting valiantly to ensure their escape. Story had it that the ghost of the Horseman would return whenever there was a soul in need of protection.

Did *she* need protection?

Had the search for one legendary ghost awakened the interest of another?

For a few heartbeats, Tori let her imagination make the fanciful connection. But then the practical, well-trained agent in her took over. Dead men, whether criminals or heroes, didn't write messages or send warnings. And *she* took care of herself. She was either the victim of an unfortunate coincidence, or the unwitting ally in a cruel joke on a grieving father.

"There must be some mistake," she apologized. "I'm sorry I upset you."

Cole's fingers closed around her arm, offering support or shutting her up, she couldn't say. His grip tightened and he bent low to whisper into her ear.

"I want to see that card."

Surely Cole Taylor didn't believe in ghosts.

Jericho ended the conversation by shooing away his support and hobbling across the room to the bookshelves. The furious determination of his painful pace made his agitation clear. "Cole, you should know better. Until certain issues are resolved, I won't tolerate any mistakes in security."

Issues? Mistakes? Tori's instincts buzzed on full alert.

Jericho picked up one of the lacquer boxes and cradled it between loving hands. He lifted the lid, peeked inside, then breathed a sigh of relief before gently closing it.

Tori took note of the box's lapis-blue color and inlaid scrollwork. Whatever was inside was precious to Jericho. He'd been worried that the contents had been disturbed or stolen by her or Cole. Or a ghost? Was it an artifact? A key? Family photos? Visual reassurance that it hadn't been touched seemed to drain the anger right out of him.

She'd definitely be back to find out what was hidden inside.

"Nothing happened here that's anyone's business but

Victoria's and mine,'' Cole argued. ''Trust me, those concerns of yours are well in hand.''

The two men traded a warning look that could have meant anything. ''Are they?'' asked Jericho, carefully replacing the box on its shelf, letting his hands linger atop its lid.

He'd been jovial and charming at their meeting this afternoon, a sweet old man who liked to show off his wealth and do some harmless flirting. But there was something almost mad in his eyes as he turned and stared at the father-and-son portrait again. His gaze came back to the box, then hardened as it settled on Cole and Tori.

Jericho's tight-lipped disapproval told Tori that she might have hit the jackpot by choosing this room as the place to search for clues to the missing statue. Or maybe there were other secrets he was worried she might uncover here.

But being right didn't make her feel better. Jericho looked right at her, through her, deep inside her, as if somehow she'd been made. As if he could see the lies on her lips or a badge tattooed over her heart. Or something else entirely…

''Did Daniel speak to you?'' he asked. ''Did he tell you to come in here? Is that what the note said?''

TORI WAS TOO SHOCKED by Jericho's questions to do more than form her mouth around one word. ''What?''

She slid her gaze up to Cole and took note of his grim expression. Lana's pink mouth had dropped open and Paulie was shaking his head. But Jericho was still staring at her, looking for answers to questions she didn't understand.

Tori shrugged. ''No, it wasn't—''

''Tell me everything!'' Jericho's face blazed with rage as he stumbled toward her. He smacked her collarbone as he made an awkward grab at her jacket.

''Mr. Meade—?''

"I know he was in that room with you. That's where he meets all his women. He sent you here, didn't he." *Meets?* Present tense? Tori retreated a startled half step as the frail man spat an accusation at her.

"He told you who murdered him—"

"I swear—"

Cole's big hands wrapped around Jericho's fragile wrists and pried his shaky fingers from Tori's collar. "She's in here because of me." Cole's voice was firm, paternal even, as if explaining facts to a confused child. "Not Daniel."

Jericho's rheumy eyes narrowed, then shifted to Cole. He seemed so confused. "Are you sure? Don't try to protect an old man. I hate when people keep things from me."

After a tense moment, Cole released him and slipped his arm around Tori's shoulders, snugging her to his side. She held herself stiffly against the hard wall of masculine strength, but didn't move away. There was something too wild, too pathetic in Jericho's expression to risk creating any more of a scene.

"We're not keeping anything from you. Do you know how hard it is to get a few moments of privacy in this house? I invited Victoria here to be alone with her."

The bald-faced lie slid from his lips as smoothly as his hand slid down to her hip. Tori bit her tongue to keep from twisting away from the possessive, palm-size brand of heat.

"Besides a few pencils and my pulse rate, I assure you nothing's been disturbed in here."

Tori had no idea whether she was about to be thrown out of the house or shot for trespassing, or if Cole's defense had just saved her life and her mission. But there was something quiet and sincere in the tone of Cole's voice that had the same calming effect on Jericho as it had had on her.

Cole Taylor was an anchor in a storm of catty words and angry threats and unpredictable actions that just didn't make sense. It was all too easy to feel herself relaxing her defensive posture, absorbing some of the strength and self-assurance he wore with the same true fit as his gabardine suit.

Jericho seemed to feel his influence, too. The old man's eyes closed, and when they opened again, they were a clearer blue. "Forgive me," he sighed, as if just now recognizing the strangeness of his attack. He pulled his shoulders back a fraction, standing taller, looking tougher, taking charge of his emotions once more.

"Maybe I'm old-fashioned." Jericho limped to the desk. Cole's hip brushed against Tori's as he subtly angled himself between her and the approaching man, as though he was prepared to take the brunt of whatever Jericho might say or do. "I understand young men and women and their assignations. I don't begrudge this match. I rather like the notion of the two of you hitting it off, in fact. But there are rooms in this house where I conduct business. And rooms that are reserved for…entertainment."

Tori held her breath, awaiting judgment. And though his calm facade revealed nothing, she sensed Cole was starting to feel the tension, too. Every muscle in his body braced.

Jericho pocketed a mint from the dish on the desk. He repositioned the humidor, opened the lid and pulled out a stogie, taking his time to run the rolled tobacco beneath his nose and savor its richly aged scent. He tucked the cigar inside his coat and patted the pocket. Then he pointed a gnarled finger at Cole. "And there are rooms where no one is allowed without my permission. This is one of them. Do I make myself clear?"

"Yes, sir."

Meade's finger shifted to Tori. "Do I?"

"Yes."

Satisfaction crept into Jericho's expression. He'd made his point. Hanky-panky between the art consultant and the chief of security was fine as long as it was discreet and didn't interfere with his business. And as long as it didn't take place in any room that—for professional or private reasons—he held dear.

Jericho reached out and laid his hand against Tori's cheek. His fingers were cool to the touch and knotted with age. Yet there was a possession to that loving grasp that alarmed her in ways his violent outburst hadn't. It required considerable control to stand still and not jerk away.

"Cole has an important job to do for me. I trust you won't keep him from his work?"

"No, sir."

"Good." Jericho flashed a smile as if nothing unusual had just occurred. No breaking in. No making out. No detours into the Twilight Zone. He chuckled with the delightful charm he'd shown her earlier in the day and pulled away, dismissing Tori and giving Cole a good-ol'-boy wink. "Well then, let's gather for dinner."

"Yes. I'm starved." Lana hurried to his side and tucked her arm through his, sparing a look for Tori that reminded her *Lana* hadn't upset the boss today. "We can discuss that information leak I mentioned over brandy and coffee afterward. You'll join us, won't you, Cole?"

Instead of feeling snubbed, Tori was relieved that she hadn't been included in the invitation.

Jericho answered for him. "Of course he will— Shall we?"

Lana spared Cole a smug look before showering her full attention on Jericho. "I think I've got the problem solved."

"You?"

"I told you I could handle it."

Shaking his head, Jericho turned toward Paulie, who held open the door for them. "I don't question your abilities for one minute, Lana. But I thought I asked Chad to see to that. Where is my nephew, by the way...?"

Their voices faded down the hall. Paulie waited in the

doorway. "You coming?" It was more of an expectation than a question.

Tori didn't need to be asked twice. Her quick reconnaissance of the house had been a major bust. She was lucky she still had a job and a chance to regroup and replan her mission. She pulled free of Cole's grasp and hurried to the door. But Paul Meredith's bulk filled the exit.

"What possessed you to meet in here?" Paulie looked over her shoulder at Cole. "You know how he is."

She felt Cole's heat as he came up behind her.

"It's getting worse every day. This room is practically a shrine to Daniel. But it was close by." He folded his hands around Tori's shoulders and pulled her back against his chest. "And how could I resist her?"

You have to make yourself irresistible to men, Victoria. Maybe we could tone down your hair....

Tori twitched and looked at the rug, trying to block out the intrusion of her mother's voice. She hated when it sneaked into her thoughts like that. No matter how many awards she'd won, how many cases she'd solved, how many lives she'd changed, in Judeen Westin's eyes, she would always be a work in progress. And a man couldn't want her because of all the things she was and wasn't.

Too smart. Too competitive. Too physical. No figure. No feminine frills. And Cole thought he could make a fake relationship work with her?

Fake was about all she *could* handle.

"Don't be so modest, sweetheart." Tori forced her way past the undermining self-critique, lifted her gaze and smiled. She reached up and patted Cole's hand at her shoulder. "You're the one with the irresistible animal magnetism."

Her touch and smooth line surprised Cole, judging by the sudden squeeze and quick release of his hands. But Paulie laughed, buying the lie of their affair. He rubbed the top of his balding head and winked at her.

"Well, you two have fun. Just be more careful where you get carried away next time."

As soon as Paulie moved, Tori dashed from the room, eager to leave Cole and her confused sense of purpose behind. But there was no escape. Out in the hallway, he snagged her by the elbow and pulled her aside.

"It's okay." He reassured the other man with a grin. "I have something to discuss with Victoria. We'll be in the dining room in a minute."

Paulie locked the door and grinned. "It's about time you got a life, Taylor. All work and no play, you know. You watch yourself with this guy, Ms. Westin." His dark eyes teased her as he thumbed over his shoulder at the office behind him. "You get into another 'discussion' like the one you were having in there and we won't see you until dessert."

"I'll keep that in mind."

Tori held a smile until Paulie disappeared around the corner. As soon as he was gone, she freed herself from Cole's grasp and whirled to face him. "What do you want from me now?"

He sized her up with a hungry, suggestive look that kindled those unwise longings inside her all over again.

"You can stop doing that. Our audience is gone."

"Oh, but there are eyes just about everywhere." He glanced up at the security camera as it pivoted toward them. In a deliberate move, he tunneled his fingers into her hair and cupped the nape of her neck. "Even ones your little high-tech devices can't detect. Did you enjoy your tour of the wardrobe?"

"You saw—?" Tori went rigid. But he already had her backed against the wall and she had nowhere to go except through him. "I undressed in that room!"

"Don't worry. I sent the guard on his coffee break while you were changing."

"But *you* watched?" Someone had been in her room, had used the secret entrance. Setting up a camera? Leaving friendly notes that sparked chaos?

Ignoring the self-preserving instinct to keep her distance, she grabbed his hands and held them up for a quick inspection. One, two... Five fingers on each hand. Long, sturdy fingers, with clean, trim nails and smoothed-off calluses. Her breath eased out on a sigh that held more confusion than relief.

"Looking for something in particular?"

When she saw questioning blue eyes laughing at her through ten splayed fingers, Tori released him and rattled off the first sarcastic thing she could think of. "How about a sense of decency?"

His teasing vanished behind an unreadable veil. "It was a private show, sweetheart. And don't worry, there's no camera in the bathroom."

As if that concession to privacy made it all right! He'd been spying on her, watching her, lying in wait for her to break into Jericho's office so he could...what? Catch her? Kiss her? Discredit her?

"You knew I was in there before I turned on the computer. You set me up."

"I did." He tunneled his fingers into her hair again and leaned in closer, creating a pose that could pass as a secret exchange between lovers. But the fall of his dark hair masked the truth from the camera. She read the suspicion in his eyes, felt the warning in the grip at her nape. "I needed to know if you really were a threat, or were just overly curious. I'm still not sure what you're up to. But it can't be good for Jericho."

"So why not turn me in?"

His nostrils flared as he inhaled deeply. "That really is killer perfume you're wearing."

What kind of answer was that? Even if the camera was wired for sound, she'd be the only one to hear the husky compliment. If she could only learn to read a man's signals in that department. If she only knew which messages to trust. The lustful words or the controlling actions? She dug her fingertips into the coarse grain of the wallpaper and clung to rational thought as his mouth traced the line of her jaw without actually touching her skin. But his heat touched her, shamelessly awakening her senses.

This was crazy. *She* was crazy for wanting this criminal to kiss her again. "Mr. Taylor."

"We can't talk here," he whispered against her neck. "But you do owe me for saving your hide. Meet me in my room at ten o'clock tonight. There are no bugs or cameras there."

"I'm not going to bed with you."

He pulled back just far enough for her to see the speculative grin that creased his mouth. "You haven't been asked." But his eyes danced with possibilities that mocked the heat blooming in her cheeks. "Yet."

What the hell was this man up to? It might be worth the peace of mind to give him what he wanted and hope that meant finding answers and getting on with the job she needed to do.

"Fine." But Tori was too smart to be caught in a compromising position twice. No way would she give him that kind of advantage over her again—whether his intentions were business or sexual or something even more bizarre. "But on neutral ground. I'll meet you, but not in your room behind a closed door."

He seemed skeptical that she should agree to his request at all. His eyes narrowed with an unmistakable threat. "Don't play me. You turn on me and you're done here."

The idea of being blackmailed stuck in her craw. But the opportunity to learn more about Cole and the secret job he was doing for Jericho, to explore his connection—if any— to *The Divine Horseman,* made playing his game a little easier to swallow.

She curled her fingers into the lapels of his jacket, sending a few mixed signals of her own. "You hold all the cards, Mr. Taylor. My job and my reputation mean a lot to me. I don't intend to steal anything that belongs to Mr. Meade. I don't know what that poor man's afraid of but I don't intend to hurt him. But since you won't believe that, I guess I'll have to meet you."

She clutched her hands into fists, drawing him a half-inch closer. Her gaze fell to his lips. So close. So tempting. So off-limits. She tilted her eyes to his. "But under my conditions. We meet in a public place. And you keep your hands to yourself. That's the deal."

The seconds passed like minutes as his eyes locked onto hers and he considered her offer. She didn't realize she'd been holding her breath until he slowly unwound his fingers from her neck and splayed them on the wall beside her ear.

"Deal."

He still stood just as close. His shoulders were just as broad. His eyes were just as blue.

You rat. He could concede to her wishes and still make her feel as if he had the upper hand.

He wasn't touching her, but she was still holding on to him. Frustrated by her inability to focus on the problem instead of the man, Tori snatched her hands away and ignored his knowing grin.

"You like moonlit strolls?" he asked.

"I'm here to do a job, not conduct a romance."

The last time she'd tried to combine the two, the results had been disastrous. She'd paid a high price to salvage that mission. And her attraction to Ian Davies hadn't been anywhere near as volatile or potent as the chemistry that sizzled between her and Cole Taylor.

"Meet me in the park adjoining the estate, just south of here. On the observation deck at Lake of the Woods." Cole's directions were as crisp and businesslike as the atmosphere cooling between them. "The rain should be done by then, leaving everything wet and muddy. Maybe there'll be a wino or two who hasn't been chased out of the park yet. Is that unromantic enough for you?"

Tori glared. "The park is fine."

"Be there. Or I'll come looking for you. And I will find you every time."

"Is that another threat?"

"Don't make it one. Just show up."

He took his sweet time to dip his mouth beside her ear and create the illusion of a kiss for the camera. He never touched her, but she inhaled his bracing scent and shivered at his consuming energy just the same.

"And don't tell anyone where you're going."

When he pulled away, her breath rushed out as if she'd been doused with cold water.

"It'll be our little secret."

She had a feeling it would be one of many.

Chapter Five

JDM

Cole studied the heavy scrawl, remarkably similar to the handwritten notes that used to come across his security desk. *I'm having company tonight. Unlock the gate and keep Lana occupied.* That company was usually female and Lana was usually pissed. Lana must have a masochistic streak, putting up with Daniel's philandering throughout their engagement, then moving on to Chad. Maybe she had a high tolerance for cheating men—as long as marrying into a fortune remained a possibility.

Cole turned over the card Victoria had delivered to him. He could verify that the stationery, at least, was authentic— the same business stock used by father and son alike. He flipped it over and read the generic message again, shaking his head. This was a new twist in an ongoing mystery that refused to make any sense.

"I'm no expert. But it looks like Daniel's handwriting."

He'd love to get it to the crime lab for analysis because he knew damn well that ghosts didn't exist and dead men didn't write notes.

"Is it possible Daniel Meade's still alive?" Victoria jogged in place beside him. "Maybe he's trying to get a message to his father."

"Daniel wouldn't voluntarily walk away from the millions he stood to inherit.'' Cole thought back to the severed finger that had been delivered to the house. Daniel wouldn't voluntarily give that up, either. And the Daniel he'd known was more likely to retaliate with violence when threatened than to play these crazy mind games. ''This would be easy enough to forge. Jericho hasn't thrown away any of his son's things. There are plenty of writing samples around the estate and downtown offices to copy.''

''So what's the point? 'Welcome and enjoy' is hardly a threatening message.'' Victoria finally planted both feet squarely on the concrete observation deck that overlooked Lake of the Woods. She dabbed her forehead with the sweatband on her wrist and smoothed aside a stray lock of hair that clung to her skin. ''Unless you think Jericho wrote it and just forgot?''

Jericho might be sad and ailing, but Cole didn't think he was senile. ''He hardly writes a word anymore, the arthritis in his hands is so bad. If he did manage to put this many words on paper, it'd be illegible.''

The idea that someone would forge a message to take advantage of his boss's grief didn't sit well with Cole. But it would play in to some of the crazy things Jericho had told him. Things like hearing his son's voice at night, believing that Daniel was trying to tell his father who his murderer might be.

''Then I guess I just have a secret admirer with a twisted sense of humor.''

Cole didn't like that idea, either. Damn, he was tired of fighting this battle. Maybe he was making too much of the note. More than ever, he needed to get out of this assignment before it sucked his soul dry. With a sigh that echoed right down to his bones, he tucked the card inside his suit jacket and returned to more pressing business.

''Any questions about what we discussed?'' Cole watched the thin bead of sweat at the hollow of Victoria's neck catch in the moonlight and spill over to create a glistening path down to the scooped neckline of her fitted running top. From the moment she'd jogged out onto the deck, using the excuse of a late night run to meet him, he'd been unable to keep his eyes off her for more than a few seconds at a time. "I need to know you can handle it."

"Having second thoughts about blackmailing me?"

He was having second thoughts about everything.

Why the hell she hadn't driven to meet him on this isolated stretch of road he'd never understand. A woman alone at night was putting herself in unnecessary danger. His own sister, Jessie, had been on her own that night in Chicago when she was abducted. Tortured. Raped.

Hell.

Cole squeezed his eyes shut against a fiery rush of impotent anger. He hadn't been there to protect his sister then. He hadn't been there to protect her when her kidnapper returned to finish what he'd started, either. He hadn't even been around to hold her hand or listen to her fears the way he had so many times growing up together.

But Jessie was okay now. The man was dead. She was moving on with her life, planning a big wedding to the FBI agent who *had* been there to help her.

Cole was missing that, too.

He loosened his tie and unhooked the top two buttons of his shirt. The evening rainstorm had passed, leaving the air sticky rather than refreshed. He took a deep breath anyway, but couldn't find any calming reprieve. Opening his eyes and turning toward the polished surface of the lake, he sought the cool-headed detachment he needed to make this work.

"Just answer the question. Do you understand what I'm asking you to do?" He was definitely screwed on this undercover op if he kept paying more attention to details like sweat and moonlight and endless stretches of creamy skin than to whether she'd agree to his plan. Not that she had any choice. But it'd go a long way toward assuaging his guilt if he didn't have to bully every bit of cooperation from her, and if he knew she'd be more sensible about keeping herself safe.

"I get it, already." Victoria's chest heaved with even breaths while she pressed two fingers to her wrist, checked her watch and measured her heart rate. "Set up a meeting with your cop friend. Deliver a message and bring the response back to you. Be prepared to do it more than once. And remember that no one will be happy if I get caught because I'm surrounded by bad people. Does that cover it?"

Her version seemed to make light of the danger she'd be facing as his courier, but her facts were straight. "Yeah." He gripped the deck's black iron railing in a nonchalant pose but angled his face toward hers, letting his expression convey the depth of his warning. "But make that *very* bad people. My last courier was killed two weeks ago."

She seemed to absorb that piece of information with a little more gravity. Even shadowed by night, her furrowed brow couldn't mask the sudden darkening of regret in her eyes.

"I'm sorry. Was he a friend of yours?"

A friend? Cole stared hard into her eyes, trying to gauge the sincerity of her compassion. He'd never even shaken Lee Cameron's hand. The closest he'd come to paying his respects was reading the obit in the *Kansas City Star*. But Lee had been a fellow cop and he'd been Cole's lifeline to the outside world. Both were reasons enough to mourn his passing.

"Sort of" was as much as he'd admit to caring. "More of a business associate."

"Was he killed *because* he was your courier?"

Smart question. Cole had thought about that one since the moment he drove away from the clinic. Lee hadn't been the intended target of that hit. But he wouldn't have been in the line of fire if he hadn't been there for Cole—to tell him about the attack on his mother and nephew. And now Cole was putting Victoria in the same line of fire. He really had sunk to the level of the men he was trying to destroy.

Knowing he couldn't give an answer that either one of them would like, he said nothing.

"Forget I asked." Victoria's eyes glittered with checked emotion as she tilted them into the moonlight. But her sarcastic tongue was still firmly in place. "And here I thought extortion was just your lame idea of a pickup line."

Cole almost laughed at that one. Sharp as a pin popping a balloon, she diffused the tension coiling inside him. But he'd denied himself the luxury of uninhibited responses for so long that he couldn't quite get the sound out of his throat. "Masquerading as lovers will be our cover to exchange information. An easy excuse for you and me to meet regularly."

"And privately. Isn't it convenient that your bedroom is the only one without a hidden camera."

She swung her right leg up onto the railing, then leaned forward, touching her nose to her knee and stretching with the controlled flexibility of a ballet dancer. Plain gray leggings and a functional fanny pack suddenly became as sexy as silk lingerie framing the sleek swell of her hips and butt.

"How do I know you won't take advantage of me again?"

"Take advantage?" *Damn.* Blindsided by his body's instant flare of interest in the flex of her derriere, Cole's temper shot through what was left of his cool reserve. For a lying thief, Ms. Can't-Touch-This sure had a mighty self-righteous opinion about getting it on with the hired help. "Your short-term memory must be on the fritz. I wasn't the only one who forgot that kiss wasn't supposed to be the real thing."

The seamless flow of athletic grace hitched with an awk-ward jerk, and her right foot plopped to the ground. He'd struck a nerve. Her fingers twitched, snaking and curling in a dexterous display before clamping into fists she planted on either hip. Cole crossed his arms and faced off against whatever excuse she was going to throw at him now.

"Flatter yourself all you want, Taylor. You didn't leave me any choice when you staged that seduction. I could ei-ther play along or lose my job, which I am not going to allow to happen. You've blackmailed me into a business partnership. I just want assurances that that's as far as it's going to go between us."

"You call that playing along?" Cole breathed in deeply, feeling the sting of her accusation in every guilt-riddled bone in his body. He'd never forced himself on a woman in his life. Hell, he'd never spied on one in her bedroom without an invitation. Until tonight. With the clock ticking and danger closing in all around him, he'd cast aside the last of his values.

The similarities to an unknown man going after his sister haunted him.

Maybe he needed a few assurances of his own.

He studied the defiance in her expression. And caught a glimpse of that something not quite so tough she couldn't completely hide. That was the part that got to him. The part that had whispered a desperate *"Stop."* The part that fed his regret and made him wish they were just a man and a woman who had the time and the chance to get to know each other, instead of a cop and a crook who'd been forced into an alliance.

For one risky moment, he thought like the man. With a single finger, he reached out and caught a loose strand of copper hair, grazing the smooth angle of her cheek as he lifted it off her face. "I'm sorry if I scared you in Jericho's office. Acting before asking, I mean. But can you honestly tell me you don't like at least some of what's going on between us?''

He had the fiery silk tucked behind the shell of her ear before she flinched away.

"I don't scare easily, Mr. Taylor." Back to business. She turned, braced her left leg on the railing and resumed her stretching. "So we share a few public kisses, then meet privately to promote the idea that we're having an affair."

Cole almost smiled with relief that she hadn't ended the contact sooner. Whether she wanted to admit it or not, the attraction between them was mutual. His conscience eased a fraction. This was more about pride or bad timing than about fear or revulsion. She hated being at any kind of disadvantage. He could relate to that.

Leaning his hip against the railing, Cole sat back and watched her fill the night air around them with her amazing energy. For both their sakes, he focused on business, too.

"The private part is key," he cautioned. "No one else can know about this. You won't have regular contact with anyone in the house but me, except at breakfast and dinner, and you'll be gone in a week. That's why you're perfect for the job."

"Lucky me." She stood on both feet again but never really stopped moving. Now she was rolling the kinks out of her neck. No wonder she was built like a streamlined sports car. There was always some part of her that seemed to be in motion.

"As a guest, you have more freedom to come and go from the estate than I do. Obviously, I can't be seen hanging out with a cop. But it wouldn't raise suspicion if you were to meet with him." He pulled a slip of paper from his pocket and handed it to her. He hoped he still had at least one old friend out there he could count on. "Once you're away from the house, call this number and ask for A. J. Rodriguez."

"Rodriguez," she repeated, tucking the paper inside her fanny pack. "Am I supposed to know him?"

"He'll know me. Give him my name and he'll talk to you. I'll give you the specific message tomorrow. We'll see where we go from there."

She adjusted the pack around her waist. "Lana mentioned an information leak. Does she know it's you?"

Did Victoria pick up on every detail in a conversation? That kind of awareness was a trait Cole admired. It was also a trait to be wary of.

"What makes you think I'm an informer?"

"Don't insult my intelligence. Get a secret message to the cops? Maybe Lana wants you so bad, she can't see it. But you're playing both sides. Trading information for a lot of cash, judging by that restored '65 Mustang you're driving and the Gucci suit you're wearing. Everyone at the house talks like you're the man. Chad's jealous of you. Jericho thinks you're gonna save the day."

Not bad. She'd been at the estate fewer than twenty-four hours and she already had the family pegged.

"You're selling them out," she added.

Selling out. Cole plunged his hands into his pockets and straightened. It hadn't been an accusation so much as an observation. She had *him* pegged, too. As far as the world knew, he'd sold out his family, his fellow cops, even his hometown to work for Jericho. Two years of living the lie had blurred his memories of the truth.

He did love the vintage cars and the slick suits. But he'd loved his family and friends more. He'd loved being a detective. He'd been trained by his former partner, A. J. Rodriguez, the best UC man on the force. Now Cole was so damn good at blending in with the bad guys that it felt as if he was betraying both sides of the law.

And now he was using Victoria to do it.

"You call it selling out. I call it survival." He turned

away and grasped the railing to peer out into the night. The trees were thick beyond the water's edge, broken only by the stone picnic pavilion on the far side of the lake and the road that wound through the park. "Jericho's sick. He wants me to do two things before he dies. One is find out who murdered his son. The other is find out who's killing him."

"*Killing* him? As in ongoing?" Her body stilled. Then she joined him at the railing. "That doesn't make any sense." The sarcasm was gone. This was real curiosity, real concern talking. "You know someone is plotting to kill him? I read about a shoot-out at a private clinic up in Liberty a couple of weeks ago. Jericho's chauffeur, a suspected hit man and an orderly were killed. Do you know who's behind it? Is that what you want me to tell Rodriguez?"

Cole had no desire to relive that particular morning. He wondered if he was sharing too much, if he was foolishly giving this woman more inside information than he held over *her* head. But the park was empty, the night was calm, and the only sounds were the lapping of the water against the concrete pylons beneath them and Victoria's strong, steady breathing beside him.

The moment almost felt…real.

Separated from the world by moonlight and shadows, he felt as if he could slide his hand across the railing and hold on to hers. As if he'd find solace taking her in his arms again. As if, like any normal man, he had a woman, a partner who wanted to listen, who wanted to comfort. Who saw something worth loving inside him.

The man in him, who'd been separated too long from the real things in life, kept right on talking. "The doctor at the clinic did some bloodwork. Jericho's being poisoned. Something slow-acting but cumulative in his system."

"Like lead or other heavy metals that build up to toxic levels?"

Her knowledge impressed him. "Exactly. Except this is

something new. Undetectable until he'd ingested enough to damage his heart and lungs. We can treat the symptoms, but the doctor says it's too late to reverse the deterioration of healthy tissue.''

He could feel her looking at him now. He imagined her polite curiosity was compassion.

"How long does he have?"

Not long enough. If Cole did manage to bring down Jericho, the old man wouldn't do any time—he'd probably be dead before the arraignment was over. And the hell of it was, Cole was half afraid he was going to miss the guy when he was gone.

Maybe she misread his heavy pause, mistook confusion for sadness. Whatever the cause, her soft sigh was like a balm to his shattered soul.

"It's that bad?"

"A matter of weeks, days maybe…who knows. It's a synthetic toxin, one the doctor hasn't seen before. Probably from out-country. He's working on an antidote, but…'' Cole had a feeling that looking at Victoria would involve the urge to touch her. And without an audience to justify putting on a show, he didn't want to risk spoiling this tenuous truce between them.

So he was half glad when a nondescript black sedan rounded the corner and splashed through a puddle before pulling into the pavilion parking lot across the lake. It was too far away to get a bead on the license plate or passengers. Since he didn't recognize the car itself, he didn't overreact. He pushed away from the railing, checked the Glock at his side, and kept his eye on the car until it disappeared from view.

"Once I expose the killers, I'll be a marked man. I thought I'd be smart and try to have the law on my side to protect me. Once Jericho's gone, I won't have an ally to trust inside that house."

"Someone in his own family is poisoning him?"

Cole nodded. He'd restricted Jericho's activities enough to narrow the source at least that much. And there was certainly no shortage of motives when it came to taking over a multimillion-dollar empire. Beyond that, he'd need access to a lab to pinpoint how the poison was being administered.

"Now do you see why I need your help?"

Victoria looked him straight in the eye, the mood broken. "How do you know you can trust me?"

He didn't. It was more a case of ruling out everyone else he knew he *couldn't* trust. "My gut, sweetheart. And a little bit of logic. You're after something. Something you want badly enough that you're willing to do this for me instead of being exposed as a fraud."

Her fingers flexed and coiled into fists. She was moving again. "I'm not sure *willing* is the right word. But I'll do it."

"Good." He fell into step a few paces behind her as they headed back toward the parking pull-off near the entrance to the deck. Nice view. Side to side. High and tight. He'd liked it naked, too. Of course, the ultimate turn-on would be to see it live and naked. *Lowlife*. Cole could think of a dozen worse names to fit his perverted obsession with Victoria Westin.

He tipped his face to the stars and shook his head, calling down some bad-ass attitude to replace the tender cravings and provocative fantasies that were wreaking havoc on his common sense.

"If word of what we've discussed tonight gets back to Jericho or anyone else—"

"I've got your back." She halted abruptly. "I'm assuming you'll guarantee the same—"

"Whoa—" Cole skidded, unable to stop himself from plowing into her as she spun around. Automatically, his hands shot out to grab her arms above the elbows to keep her from falling.

Her startled gasp blended with his hasty apology. Her hands landed on his biceps as slingshot momentum carried her back into him. Her grip tightened convulsively and she caught herself just shy of making full contact. A wisp of her hair fanned across his chin and that light, fresh scent she wore filled his nose. It was pure sex and all lady and damn appealing. They froze in that mock embrace, her gaze riveted on his mouth with the same longing she'd denied in the hall outside Jericho's office. Her pupils dilated and every yearning instinct in Cole's body wanted to give her exactly what her sweetly parted lips silently asked for.

He heard his own voice as a husky whisper in the night. "I've got your back, babe."

They stood close enough to feel the heat of her searing his chest and arousing points well south of his belt buckle. Cole wasn't inclined to move away.

But she was. A quick shove and she was beyond his reach. Her abrupt retreat was as effective and insulting as a slap in the face.

"My legs will cramp up if I don't keep moving. Good night, Mr. Taylor."

Man, she had burn-hot-and-blow-cold down to an art form. If she bolted every time that flash-fire chemistry ignited between them, they'd never fool anyone with their charade. Forget the havoc it was playing with his ego, his conscience and every male hormone in his body.

She'd already reached the sidewalk, putting a good fifteen feet between them.

"Victoria!" She turned and jogged in place. He wished he knew the magic words to wipe that arrogant smirk off her face. But then, he didn't suppose he'd earned a friendly smile. "At least let me give you a ride."

"No."

"It's late. Let me drive you so I don't worry."

"Your worry is your problem, Taylor."

"It's Cole," he corrected, wondering if she got some kind of thrill out of butting heads. "You'd better get used to saying it so you don't slip in front of an audience."

"I won't slip. And you should call me Tori. Keep your *babe*'s and *sweetheart*'s and worries to yourself."

COLE WATCHED TORI JOG around the arc of the lake, fading into the shadows and reappearing like a wraith as she passed through each circle of light from a street lamp. When his weary thoughts turned to what else those strong, toned legs could do, he knew it was time to hit the road.

He climbed behind the wheel of the cherry-red Mustang and started the engine. The prowling hum of the motor reminded him of one extremely stubborn redhead. Though Tori's confident pace would get her back to the house in fifteen minutes, an echo of his mother's voice from years past played in his head: *"You see that girl home, Cole Taylor. It's what a gentleman does. And I expect all my boys to be gentlemen."*

Whether Tori would appreciate the effort or see it as some other means of spying on her, Martha Taylor's training had been ingrained long before he'd become a cop or a mob boss's bodyguard. He hadn't been able to protect his sister, but this woman he could help. Whether she liked it or not.

With no traffic to speak of, Cole shifted into gear and followed her at an unobtrusive distance. He'd shadow her until she hit the main road to the estate, just in case she tripped or landed in a pothole, or some other fool tried to take her on. When she was safely in range of the front gate, he'd zip on past, giving her the distance from him she so obviously craved.

Cole tapped on the accelerator when she disappeared

around the bend in the road. The pavement forked left into a private drive and to the right out of the park. The moonlight shone between the trees, reflecting on the moisture that frosted the long stretches of asphalt. It cast shadows everywhere else.

He didn't see Tori anywhere.

Fatigue vanished in a heartbeat. Alarm surged through him, clearing his mind, sharpening his senses. "Where'd you go?"

He spotted her to the right, cutting through the trees toward the pavilion parking lot. A shortcut? At this time of night? "Where the hell did you learn your survival skills?" he muttered, speeding up to keep her in sight.

She ran past the black sedan in the parking lot and dashed out of sight beyond the shelter's stone facade. The black car's dark interior suddenly flashed as the front doors opened and two men climbed out. Dark clothes from caps to fingertips to the soles of their feet. Furtive glances. Armed. The doors closed and they blended in with the night.

"Tori!" Cole's shout rang inside the Mustang. Potential danger had just become very real.

Cole shifted into high gear and floored it, leaving the smell of burned rubber on the road as he ninety-degree'd it into the parking lot. His headlights picked up the two men jogging around the corner where Tori had gone. Gravel pinged beneath the floorboards and spat out behind him as he sped straight across to the shelter. He slammed on the brakes, swung open the door and shot out of the car while it was still bucking from the abrupt stop.

He charged into the clearing at the side of the shelter. Tori was running toward the trees on the opposite side. The two men were nearly upon her.

Bending low to pick up speed on the slippery grass, he closed the distance. Cole was built more for playing the line, but he'd done his fair share of running down tight ends and criminals.

One of the men called out. She eased up. *No!* "Tori!" Cole shouted. "Run!"

She hit the line of trees and Cole dove for the closest man. With a flying tackle, they landed with a crunch of bone and ground and muscle. "Son of a—" Cole muttered through the jolting pain. They slid several feet and jerked to a stop in a patch of mud.

"Cole!"

There was no time to answer her warning cry. The struggle was brief. Cole rose up on his knees above the dark-skinned man and brought his fist crashing down against the guy's jaw.

His opponent sank into the grass. Ignoring the throbbing in his knuckles, Cole pushed to his feet again. The second man was pulling a gun, turning.

Cole thrust up with his hand, knocking his attacker's arm out of range and sending the gun flying through the air. Cole twisted his shoulder into his opponent's gut, lifted him off his feet and dropped him flat on his back.

Curses and moans and warnings were so much white noise buzzing in the background. Cole was on top of him now.

This guy was younger, quicker. Only momentarily stunned, he rolled beyond the reach of Cole's fist and scrambled for his gun. Cole snatched a leg, dodged a kick and—

Something hard and solid slammed into Cole's back, knocking him onto his stomach. He sprawled across the other man's legs, trapping him short of reaching his weapon.

Pain radiated from his right kidney. *How the hell did the old guy—?* Adrenaline shocked the ache into submission and Cole rose to his knees.

Another blow hit him across the shoulders. "Dammit!" He couldn't curse long enough or hard enough to short-circuit the pain and frustration spiraling through him; he couldn't spare the energy if he wanted to win this battle. He had to protect Tori. She was his ticket out. A woman alone against two men. He had to defend her.

Cole kicked back with his right leg, catching his attacker below the knees and knocking him off his feet.

"Ow!"

He spun around and leaped, pinning him to the ground. "Listen, you son of a—!"

Pinning *her*.

Cole froze. "What the…?"

Tori had been behind him. She'd delivered those blows.

Now she lay wedged beneath him, and his body leaped at the vibrant imprint of every long, svelte inch of her through his soggy clothes. Strands of red hair had fallen loose and stuck to the dampness on her cheeks and forehead. Her eyes glared deeply into his.

"I'm soaking up the mud, Taylor. Get off me."

Her ragged gasp for air swelled her chest in counterpoint to his, thrusting the delicate points of her breasts against him. His body shuddered in an instant response while his mind tried to catch up.

"What are you doing?" He pushed up onto his elbows, giving them both a chance to catch a deep breath. "I didn't hurt you, did I?"

Click. Click. He recognized the sound of a bullet sliding into its chamber. And judging by the volume so close to his ear, he knew he was target.

Something recently awakened went still and cold inside Cole's chest. He didn't spare a glance for the man with the gun; he directed every bit of his ire at Tori. "This is something I'm going to laugh about tomorrow, right?"

She wasn't smiling. There was something almost apologetic in the arch of that brow now. "I don't think so."

The man with the gun had a more direct answer. "U.S. Customs Department, pal. I want you facedown on the ground. Now!"

"I thought you were in trouble." Cole moved slowly, but did as instructed.

"I don't need rescuing. Never have, never will."

She might have been a little too adamant, but he was a little too ticked to process that observation right now.

Tori scrambled to her feet as he crawled off her and spread-eagled himself in the grass and mud. The man with the gun moved with him. She wrenched her smushed fanny pack onto one hip and rubbed the small of her back. He wasn't the only one hurting. But it wasn't slowing her down.

"He's armed," she warned the agent.

Cole inhaled the dank smell of earth against his cheek and the tang of grass stains on his suit and tie as they subdued him like the criminal he claimed to be. But it was *her* hand that reached inside the front of his coat and removed his Glock. *Her* hand that patted him down and pulled the Beretta from his ankle holster.

Steamed barely described his reaction at being played for such a fool. *He* was the professional liar. Yet he was the one who'd been set up. Ambushed. Betrayed.

Tori quickly skimmed every pocket, nook and crevice, leaving no doubt she'd done this kind of thing before. His clothes were soaked and ruined, his back ached, his legs burned with the strain of his run, and his body was heating with all sorts of inappropriate responses at every sweep of her hand.

And he'd felt guilty about taking advantage of her?

"This isn't the time or the place, *babe*." He deliberately used one of those endearments she hated. "When I said you had to be friendly in front of an audience, I didn't mean these bozos.''

''I'm not being—'' She snapped her mouth shut.

Got her. She pulled her hand away and stood, her cheeks blazing with color. It was one tiny piece of satisfaction in an altogether unsatisfactory night.

The younger bozo tried to sound tough. ''Shut your trap.''

''Bill.'' Tori's voice, though a little out of breath, was the one in control. ''Put your cuffs on him.''

''You want me to read him his rights?''

''Not yet. I just don't want him to give us any grief until we sort this out.''

Cole would have considered taking out the guy the second he fumbled switching his gun with a pair of steel handcuffs, except that the gun in Tori's hand, *his* gun, was sure and steady and aimed his way.

The first cuff pinched his wrist. There was a tug on his shoulder, the ratchet of a second steel bracelet, and then both arms were anchored securely behind his back. Cole tilted his gaze and looked hard at Victoria, admiring her victory almost as much as he hated his own failure.

He was done.

For two years, he'd survived fights, attempted hits, threats, grudges, backstabbing and loneliness. He'd been that close to breaking the case against the Meade empire.

And he'd been taken down by a skinny redhead with passion in her veins and fear in her heart.

He was beyond the humiliation of being trussed up like a pig, beyond resentment, beyond caring about any damn thing.

''So, sweetheart…'' About all he had left was the satisfaction of rattling her cage one last time. ''I'm thinking you're definitely not an art professor.''

Chapter Six

Tori secured Cole's Glock inside the strap of her fanny pack and cradled his Beretta in her right hand. The weapons still carried the warmth of his hard body. So did she.

Why couldn't she shake her fascination with him? She'd never had such confusing feelings about a man before, and she wasn't even thinking about the hypnotic voice or that incredible kiss or the fact there was just so much of him to distract her.

Which was the real Cole Taylor? The man who baited her temper and spied on her? Or the man whose desperate need for an ally spoke to some unacknowledged sympathetic spirit inside her? The man who sold out his comrades for a pricey car and a few perks? Or the man who'd charged to her rescue as if she was some sort of damsel in distress?

She could see the ulterior motive in defending her against Jericho's inexplicable attack or Lana's snide taunts. It was all part of the liar's game he was playing—the image he wanted to project to the other members of the household to mask his true objectives. But why throw his body between her and two armed men he didn't know? Why go all good-guy for her? Was there still a little bit of cop's blood flowing through his veins? Or was he just protecting his investment in her?

And why did the answer matter?

Turning her back on the source of her confusion, Tori propped her foot up on the seat beside Bill Brady at the picnic table where she'd led him. The older agent tugged the black leather glove from his left hand and gingerly moved his jaw from side to side, assessing the damage paid for getting in Cole's way. His moans cut right through her, and Tori grimaced.

"Anything broken?"

He pressed his fingertips to the mandible joint beneath his ear. "I'll live. But I have a headache that's leaking out my pores. Let me tell you, retirement's looking pretty good right about now."

"You're too young to retire." She sat down beside him and rubbed a comforting hand between his shoulder blades, wishing she at least had a couple of aspirin to offer him instead of a cautious reprimand. "Why didn't you stay in the car? I would have approached you when it was clear. Another five minutes and we wouldn't be in this mess." She let her gaze slide across to the man who had his chin in the mud, and ice meant only for her in his eyes. "You didn't spot the cherry red Mustang tailing me through an otherwise deserted park?"

With only moonlight to illuminate the distance and the darkness, she might have imagined the sudden narrowing of Cole's eyes. While she didn't comprehend the unspoken question, she'd add eavesdropping to his list of crimes. Tori dropped her voice to a more private whisper.

"There may be a way to salvage this yet."

"No." Bill's quick answer was followed by a hiss of pain. "It's too risky now. You should have let him save you and kept your cover intact. Now you've been compromised."

"He was making toast of you and Bill. I had to even up the odds." Cole's loss of contact with the world outside the Meade family had hit home with stunning clarity when she'd seen how quickly and thoroughly he was taking down her own two links to the world outside her mission.

The elder Bill patted her knee and forced a smile. "Got a soft spot for us, have you?"

Tori squeezed his hand, then removed it from her knee to maintain the professional distance she was more comfortable with. "We're a team, aren't we? I was just looking out for the team."

"Well, your *team* is the one that screwed things up. When you ran past us at the rendezvous site, we thought something was wrong."

Wrong? Like being blackmailed into a role she was ill-equipped to play? Like finding out the Meade estate was a Gothic funhouse filled with enough suspects to populate an Agatha Christie novel? What could be wrong? Tori put her sarcastic thoughts on hold at Bill's next words.

"I'm pulling you out. It isn't safe."

Failure? No way. Not yet. She could lose ground in a race, but she wouldn't quit running until she crossed the finish line. "The *Horseman* is due to ship out within a few days. If we don't get it back now, we may lose it forever." She stood to strengthen her argument. "You have to trust me. You said I was the best person for this job. I'm only getting started. Let me work."

She studied the dubious consideration in his dark brown eyes. "You're sure?" But she could see him wavering. "I don't want to blow my relationship with the Bureau by getting one of their agents killed."

"You don't want to blow your job at Customs by letting that statue get smuggled out of the country. I can do this." She emphasized her desire to succeed. She wouldn't let that golden knight and all he represented in her life go without her very best fight. She owed that much to the memory of her father. "I can handle Cole Taylor."

That part was a pretty gutsy assertion considering how

thoroughly she'd blundered the job so far, but Bill Brady seemed to buy it. "All right. It's not my first choice, but we'll give it another twenty-four to forty-eight hours with you calling the shots. What do you need from us?"

Without giving herself any time to savor the victory, Tori's thoughts were already sprinting ahead. "Run a personal background check on Taylor. I've read his KCPD service and state criminal records, but there has to be something more. If there's anything I can use to ensure his cooperation, I want to know about it."

Bill braced himself on the table and pushed to his feet. "I thought you said you could handle him."

Tori waved aside his concern. "It's a backup plan, that's all. I just want to know my options in case things get tricky."

"Trickier than they already are?" His concern gave way to businesslike efficiency. "I'll have the information for you by tomorrow afternoon."

She spared a glance at Cole, who still managed to look threatening while muddy and rumpled and handcuffed on the ground. Tori exhaled a steadying breath. With the other Bill still holding him at gunpoint, there seemed to be little chance of appealing to Cole's sense of duty or forging any kind of trust. But there was an unspoken code of honor about a man who would willingly risk his life to help someone else—no matter what his motives might be.

It was that honor she was banking this mission on. A promise for a promise. She was gambling her life that he would be as true to his word as she intended to be.

"Thanks. I'll call you on my secure cell line for the report." Tori thumbed over her shoulder. "You take care of hotshot over there in the meantime, okay? I don't think we should meet again until our prearranged check-in, day after tomorrow. If something breaks before then, I'll get word to you."

"Be careful."

She spared the senior agent one last indulgent smile. "I'll be careful enough. Now go."

Bill Brady gathered his stocking cap and leather glove and headed toward his unmarked car. Tori breathed evenly in and out her nose, centering herself on her renewed purpose before turning and striding up to Bill Backer.

She held out her hand to the younger agent, studiously avoiding any eye contact with the man lying at her feet. "Give me the keys to your handcuffs."

His blue eyes widened. "You've got to be kidding."

"Bill." She waited without so much as blinking until he fussed himself into action.

"Yes, ma'am." Acceding to her authority, he holstered his weapon, dug into his pocket and plopped the keys into her hand, grinching all the way. "I still think we should run this guy in."

"It'll be okay. *I'll* be okay." Having been raised an only child, Tori had no firsthand experience in dealing with protective brothers. But the two Bills were giving her a taste of what belonging to a caring, well-intentioned family might be like. She hoped they understood she intended to repay the favor by bringing them the *Horseman.* "Now get out of here. Go find an ice pack for Agent Brady."

Tori saluted the two Bills when they turned to give her one last, doubtful look. She felt the darkness swallow her up as they pulled onto the road and disappeared beyond the wall of trees and night.

A deep, evenly modulated voice broke the silence. "I can honestly say this isn't going the way I expected. Plan to take me out in the woods and shoot me yourself?"

Stowing the Beretta in her fanny pack, Tori bought herself a few seconds to recapture a feeling of control. "Don't be so crass. I have a little more finesse than that."

"How reassuring." The attitude in his voice was every

bit as sardonic as her own had been. "You're going to let me rot in a jail cell, instead." His hair had come loose in the fight and masked the glare she suspected shone in his eyes as he angled his face to look up at her. "No answer for that one, huh?"

"Get up." She stooped down beside him, wrapped her palm around one of those imposing biceps and urged him to stand. His arm flexed and hardened beneath her grasp, and she tried to ignore the frissons of female awareness that skittered through her each time she came in contact with the very male dimensions of his body.

"C'mon."

"Yes, ma'am." He mimicked Bill Backer's deference and rolled to his feet with enough balance and strength to make her suspect he'd only been humoring her by remaining on the ground for as long as he had.

Disregarding the unnerving impulse to rearm herself with a gun, she shoved him forward. "Let's go to your car," she ordered.

He strolled ahead of her, shaking his head from side to side. Tori followed at a cautious distance, keeping his broad back and bound wrists in clear sight.

"You know how many men have gotten the drop on me during my career?" he asked.

"How many?"

He stopped beside the Mustang's open door. The breeze off the lake caught his hair as he spun around, snagging the loose strands across his face. Tori halted, tilting her chin so that her eyes met the taunt in his.

"None."

Was that his idea of a compliment? Professional admiration? If so, it was one she was a lot more comfortable with than any lame line about her pale skin or nonexistent curves. In a surge of nervous energy, she touched his face and brushed away the strand of hair that had caught between his lips. She absently repeated the action with another strand, exploring the tactile contrasts of silky hair and sandpapery evening beard stubble.

"So I'm better than any man you've run up against?" she asked, plucking a blade of grass from his sideburn.

He dropped his chin closer, aiding her neatening up in what small way he could. "Any *adversary*," he amended. "I'd hate to stand anybody up against my brothers or sister." Before she could comment on the unexpected revelation of familial pride, she saw a teasing grin forming at eye level. "But you pet me nicer and smell better than any of them."

"Pet…?" Oh God. She snatched her fingers away. Guilt or sympathy or inexplicable chemistry had blurred the line between helping him and helping herself. "I wasn't petting you."

"You were." That grin was full-blown wicked now. "I liked it, though. Beats a kick in the back. What is that perfume you wear? It makes me crazy."

What a waste of smooth-talking charm. Angry with herself for listening to even one word of it, Tori flattened a hand against his chest and pushed him out of her personal space. "Blissful Sunrise, if it's any of your business. Which it's not. Forget the sweet talk. You're not kissing your way out of this one."

"Honey, you've kicked my ass, trashed my ego and left me with a hell of a lot of explaining to do if I want Jericho to post my bail. You have to give me credit for trying." He rolled his neck and shoulders to ease his discomfort. The massive shift of pent-up strength and barely checked ire created an invisible ripple through the air currents that raised chill bumps along Tori's bare arms.

"So, is this the part where you read me my rights and pack me into the back seat of the car? I warn you—I won't fit."

But his sarcasm was easier to handle than his seductive charm had been. "No. This is the part where you listen." She dangled the keys to remind him that *she* was the one making the deals now. "I want to let you go."

"Really." Skepticism dropped the word to a bass-deep pitch.

"Really."

Son of a bitch. Cole's breath caught in his lungs when he saw the steadfast resolution darkening her emerald eyes. She wasn't kidding.

He shifted his gaze just enough to note the repetitive clench of her fist around those keys. Always in motion. Those tender touches across his face, shyly stroking him as if he were some sort of caged wild animal, had been as much about nervous energy as denied sexual attraction.

She planned to go against the law and her training and release him from custody. Why?

He'd assaulted two federal officers. By rights, she should have kept her friends around and called for backup as soon as he was cuffed. But she was after bigger game. Lana? Chad? Jericho himself? The twists and turns of what he now realized was a dual undercover op got more complicated by the minute.

Cole tested his theory. "A Customs agent, huh? And you're just going to let me walk."

"FBI, actually. I'm on loan. And there are conditions."

"Of course." He should be relieved that somebody with a badge wanted to help him. But too many months of trusting no one kept him from reacting with anything more than wary curiosity. "What is it you're after?"

"A stolen artifact believed to be in Jericho's possession. It's a priceless statue of gold and jewels, dating to the Middle Ages. Customs has information that it's about to be shipped overseas to a foreign buyer. Someone going by the name Sir Lancelot."

She was FBI, all right. There was a confidence to her words that had been absent from their other, more personal, conversations.

"My assignment is to retrieve it and hopefully get solid evidence to implicate whoever is responsible for the theft."

"Lancelot?" That name rang a very dangerous bell. "That's the code name for a guy in Eastern Europe that Jericho does business with. He runs an arms pipeline to rebels and terrorists, buys whatever Jericho can supply him with. I don't know anything about smuggling artifacts, though."

Tori's green eyes sparkled with excitement. "Do you know who Lancelot is?"

Cole shook his head and watched the sparkle die. Good God, she was just like a rookie cop, too anxious to make a difference, primed to make costly mistakes. It was bad enough that she'd gotten mixed up with the Meades, she didn't need to be stirring up the interest of an international player like Lancelot.

"Do you know what a man like Lancelot does to people who poke around in his business? What happens to cops and Feds on either side of the ocean who get in his way?"

"I'm aware of the dangers of my job."

Aware? How about death in your face twenty-four/seven? "You mentioned the hit on Jericho two weeks ago. You want to know who I think ordered it?"

"Lancelot?" She was sparkling again.

"Yes, dammit! He probably took out Daniel, too." He chafed his wrists against their steel bands, desperate to free himself and shake some sense into her. "The shooters were foreign. They shouted something about their homeland."

Now she was frowning. Thinking. All business. Frustrating the hell out of him.

"You said someone in the house was poisoning Jericho. Do you think Lancelot has someone on the inside?"

"I've considered it."

"Why would Lancelot order a hit on Jericho if he's the one supplying him with arms? Unless he reneged on their deal—couldn't fill an order? demanded more money?" She snapped her fingers and pointed at Cole. "Maybe Jericho refused to deliver something that Lancelot thinks belongs to him. Where is this 'homeland?' *The Divine Horseman* was forged in Eastern Europe."

They were back to that damn statue. It was a good thing her cover had been compromised. It played hell with his plans to lose her, but she would be safer far away from this mess. Cole took a deep breath and schooled his patience. She liked to negotiate. Maybe she'd listen to logic.

"I don't know where he's from, or his real name. But, believe me, as Jericho's bodyguard I'm definitely trying to find out everything I can about the guy so I can stop him. I'd be happy to fill you in on anything I find out." But his hands were still tied, literally and figuratively, unless he played this right. "Is that why you're letting me go? You expect me to exchange information for my freedom?"

"I expect you to keep my secret."

Cole squinted, studying the underlying meaning of her request. "You want back in that house yourself."

"You were so determined to have us work together as a team. I can put up with your groping hands and goofy endearments to get the job done. We're both after the same guy. It seems a logical solution."

"That's your big plan?" Negotiating gave way to a burst of emotion that was fiercer and more frightening than anything he'd felt in a long time. "It'd be a suicide mission. There are a half-dozen people in that house willing to kill you if they find out you're a Fed. Not to mention Lancelot breathing down our necks."

"Then, don't let anyone find out."

He tipped his face up to the night, trying to think of

numbers to count, arguments to make, anything rational that would dissuade her from this crazy, gutsy idea of hers. "Tori, I—"

But she'd circled behind him. Her long fingers brushed against his as she reached for the cuffs. Cole ignored her willingness to free him and spun around to face her.

"Take me in," he offered. "Arrest me. I'll deal with the consequences."

"Cole."

He had her trapped against the frame of the car. Her hands came up between them, bracing against his chest. But he didn't back away. "Your friends made a mistake and I found out who you are. Someone else could—"

"Cole! Stop."

Her auburn brows angled downward into a frown—half indignant, half indulgent. If the look in those green eyes hadn't shut him up, then the gentle touch of her hand would. Folding the lapels of his suit, smoothing the stained wool flat across his heart—petting him again, soothing him—raising wary hackles that were proving useless against this woman's potent combination of stubbornness and vulnerability.

Tori's deep sigh vibrated through his bones. "You need me."

His body lurched at all the ways he could interpret that stark declaration. But his mind knew exactly what she was talking about.

"You still need a courier. You explained very clearly to me that you've taken an equally dangerous risk by selling Meade secrets to the police. If you're arrested and that information leak suddenly stops up, aren't the Meades smart enough to put two and two together? You'll be a marked man. And you know as well as I do that being locked in a jail cell is no deterrent to a hit."

"No." This was his fault. His impulsive mistake. It was

one thing to get a thief tangled up in this mess. But to blackmail a federal agent? He didn't think he could handle the death of another cop. He knew he couldn't handle another innocent woman being hurt on his watch. "I mean, yes, they might figure it out. It was a stupid idea to involve you in the first place."

"But you did. Now quit being such a good guy and think about your own skin."

Cole bristled up to all of his six feet four inches of height. *Good guy?* Man, did she have her wires crossed. What part of blackmail and shameless manipulation of her interest in him made him good? He gave it one last try.

"How do you know I won't rat you out to save that skin?"

He watched the careful consideration in her eyes, felt the soft, mindless stroking of her fingertips against his chest. When everything about her finally stilled, he braced for her answer.

"Because you're going to give me your word."

She thought his word was actually worth something? The chafing at his wrists was nowhere near as constricting as the heavy weight of hope and regret that twisted around his soul.

"My word is good enough for you? Why?"

"Because you used to be a cop. And your rescuing me when you thought I was in danger makes me believe you still think like one. Even now, you're trying to save me from Lancelot and Jericho and whatever other dangers lie in that house. As far as allies go, I could do worse."

Not much. "The statue means that much to you?"

She gave a gentle push and he finally backed away.

"It's more than a statue to me."

Cole filed away the enigmatic comment to explore later. Right now he had to think about life and death and the power of a man's word.

He studied the mud that dulled the shine of his shoes, the tiny ding in the paint behind the wheel-well of the car. He drank in the striking contrast of Tori's fiery hair against her moonlit skin. He inhaled the cooling night air and the essence of her and tried to make his conscience go away.

Victoria Westin was handing him everything he needed on a silver platter. A connection to A. J. Rodriguez and the DA's office. A solid cover story. A second set of eyes and ears in the house. Professional backup. Maybe even a few Bureau connections.

She was also giving him something to care about. Her job. Her life. Her.

His doubts wouldn't go away. But something new, something he was reluctant to even give a name to, tried to find a place inside him as well.

Ever in motion, she methodically removed the bullets from each of his guns and dropped the loaded magazines into her fanny pack. She slipped behind him again, and with a *click,* a tug and a couple of twists, he was a free man.

With the handcuffs gone, Cole rolled the tension from his shoulders and rubbed the soreness at his wrists. She stood in front of him once more, tall and tough and willing to risk everything. He wished like hell there was enough of that cop left inside him to make this all come out right in the end for her.

Tori held out the two empty guns like a down payment of her trust. "Your word?"

He took his guns, holstered one inside his jacket and tucked the other into his belt. "I'll meet you back at the house."

It was the only promise he felt qualified to make.

THE SHATTERING OF GLASS woke Sid Taylor from a sound sleep. The fact that he'd actually dozed off in the recliner in front of the television surprised him as much as did the invasive sound from downstairs. A rain delay had lengthened the ball game long past his normal bedtime. But that wasn't the surprise.

He'd done more dozing than sleeping lately, ever since his wife had been mugged in the grocery store parking lot. He'd gotten by on catnaps, watching over her with the same vigilance with which she'd protected him during his recovery from bypass surgery two years ago.

But he'd been so deeply out of it just now, he hadn't even seen the end score. Some protector.

Shaking off the groggy effects of his unnatural sleep, he sat upright, grabbed the remote and turned off the post-game show.

Muffled voices and the trample of footsteps warned him that someone had broken into his butcher shop, located on the first floor beneath the renovated condo where he and Martha lived.

Then, silence.

Alarm shot through him. In better shape in his sixties than he'd been in his fifties, Sid ran to the front door and checked the dead bolt and knob lock.

Secure.

Thank God. He breathed a little easier and went to the gun cabinet to unlock one of his hunting rifles. A shuffling noise from across the darkened room diverted his attention to the tall woman in the bedroom doorway.

"Sid, what's wrong? It's three in the morning." She pressed her fingers to the bridge of her nose. "This headache woke me up."

His healing heart thumped hard in his chest. Silhouetted as she was by the light from the bedside lamp, Martha Taylor wore an expression that was a shadowy mask as she shoved silver bangs from her eyes. But those eyes he knew to be blue would be wide with concern.

He'd married her forty-two years ago when he had nothing. Now he owned a whole building and his own business in the heart of K.C.'s City Market District. Together, they'd raised seven good children. They were working on spoiling grandkids now. But the need to take care of what was his was as powerful this night as it had been all those years before, when he'd scraped and saved just to put food on the table and keep a roof over their heads.

"Call 9-1-1, Martha." He'd never been about big romantic gestures and tender reassurances. He did what needed to be done. "We've got a break-in downstairs."

He felt pride as she hurried to the phone and made the call without questions or hysteria. Sid opened a box of shells and put two into the rifle. A vehicle door slammed outside. Tires squealed against the pavement. Husband and wife met at the window in time to see twin red taillights disappearing around the corner into the night.

"Could you make out the license?" Martha asked.

Sid shook his head, already moving toward the door. "It had to be a truck or SUV, though, judging by the height of those taillights."

Martha sniffed behind him. "Do you smell that?"

He paused. Inhaled. Crinkled his nose at the acrid scent of rotten eggs. His protective fears transformed into something closer to anger. No wonder he'd been out cold.

Gas.

"Open the windows." But Martha was already a step ahead of him.

"The appliances up here are all electric," she shouted over the banging of locks and swish of windows sliding open. The air that rushed in was warm and humid, but fresh and reviving. "The furnace downstairs must be leaking."

Or something much more deliberate. He'd turned off the heater in April when the balmy spring weather hit. It was nearly the first day of summer now.

"Stay put," he ordered, sliding aside the dead bolt and

opening the front door. The light at the top of the stairs came on when he hit the switch. But the stairs descended into a sightless black hole near the street entrance at the base of the stairs. He'd changed that bulb less than a month ago.

Sid slipped his finger inside the trigger guard and clutched the rifle in both hands.

"Here's the flashlight."

Sid jumped at the brush of a hand against his back, catching himself just before he squeezed the trigger. "Dammit, Martha. I want you to stay safe."

She wore nothing but her knee-length nightgown and slippers and a familiar expression that warned him he wasn't going to do this alone.

"Up here with the gas is safe?" She turned on the flashlight and shone it down to the base of the stairs. "I'm not sending you down in the dark with a gun and an intruder all by yourself, Sidney Cole Taylor."

Sid knew that stubborn set to her chin and conceded the argument. Pressing a quick kiss to her cheek, he nodded. "Then you're with me."

"Always."

She latched on to the back of his belt and followed him down the stairs, staying just behind his left shoulder until he nudged open the connecting door to the shop. Even with the stronger odor of gas permeating the air, after forty years in the business he recognized the smells of raw meat and freezer coils even before Martha's light swept across the destruction of his shop.

"Oh my God. Sid."

The place was deserted. But someone had been very busy.

Clutching Martha's hand in his, Sid stepped around the slabs of raw pork ribs that had been dumped in the middle of the floor and hacked and pummeled to a bloody pulp. In the back room, he shut off the furnace valve, which had been opened wide without benefit of a pilot light to convert it into heat.

They located the breaker box and found every connection to the shop turned off. Sid didn't touch it, knowing the police would want to dust it for fingerprints. Instead, he opened his toolbox and pulled out a second flashlight. Then they separated to inspect the rest of the damage.

The lock on his walk-in freezer had been pried off, the door propped open with a broom handle. Inside, every rack had been overturned, every box thrown to the floor.

Neither the cash register nor the safe had been touched. But in a display of gruesome artistry, most of his equipment had been tampered with—saw blades were stuck into a side of beef like birthday candles, plastic wrap had been wound mummy-style around light fixtures. Most of his inventory would have to be destroyed because of health codes. Meats were thawing, juices running into the drain.

"Is this some kind of gang initiation?" Martha speculated out loud, her shock and disgust rivaling Sid's. She laughed once, but it lacked her usual good humor. "A vegetarian protest?"

Sid raised his light to the "Taylor Meats" banner on the wall behind the counter. "I don't think so."

He'd found his knives. Every size and shape he owned had been imbedded through the plastic into the wall behind it, as if the Taylor name had been used for target practice.

"Sid!" Martha gasped.

He rushed to her side and wrapped his arm around her shoulders. Dammit, she was trembling. And it took a hell of a lot to rattle his girl.

"It's from my wallet. The one that was stolen."

Slowly turning, he followed the beam of her light and swore.

Centered over the entrance, a three-inch paring knife

skewered a wrinkled, faded, twenty-five year-old photograph of Martha and himself surrounded by all their children. From toddler Josh, climbing his mother's lap, up to teenager Mitch, standing tall and aloof behind Sid.

"I don't understand why." She shook her head. "Why?"

Sid squeezed her tight. He could hear the police siren and fire engine now, see the swirls of red, white and blue lights bouncing off the buildings outside. Help was coming.

"Run upstairs and get your robe on." His voice sounded remarkably calm, considering the volatile feelings churning inside him. "We'll wait for the police unit outside."

While she hurried to do his bidding, Sid moved closer to the door, silently damning the cowardly, unnamed threat to his family. He'd been in business long enough to absorb the monetary loss of such vandalism. But this felt like something else, something insidiously personal—like attacking a woman in broad daylight to steal her memories instead of her money.

Sid studied the jagged remnants of the shattered pane beside the lock. He pushed opened the door and his shoe crunched over a pile of broken glass. *Outside* on the sidewalk.

The vandals hadn't broken in to trash the place. They'd smashed the glass on their way out. To make enough noise to awaken the couple upstairs, to alert them to the destruction and violation going on right under their feet.

To make sure Sid and Martha came downstairs to feel the terror of being victimized. Again.

"I know that look." Martha was tying her blue terry robe around her waist as she joined him out front.

Sid had unloaded his rifle and draped the broken barrel over the crook of his elbow.

"You just got some bad news and you're not sure how to tell me. Out with it."

Sid tucked her under his arm again, needing her strength, offering his own. ''I don't think this is aimed at us.''

''Isn't this *your* shop? Isn't this *our* home? Somebody wants our attention.''

''Not *ours*.'' He took a deep breath and looked into her eyes. ''If you wanted to hurt one of our sons, what would be the most effective way to do it?''

It was an odd question, but Martha was a sharp gal—she had been from their first meeting forty-three years ago, when he nearly ran her down on the sidewalk, jumping off the bus on his way home from boot camp. She fingered the buttons of his shirt. The debate in her eyes had vanished. She understood. And she was just as worried as he was now.

''You'd go after his family. Hurt someone he loves.''

Sid nodded. ''I think one of our boys is in serious trouble.''

Chapter Seven

"Hey, Cole." Paul Meredith folded up the section of newspaper he was reading and handed it across the breakfast table. "These relatives of yours?"

Tori looked over the rim of her coffee cup and watched the steely control of muscles keep any reaction beyond polite curiosity from showing on Cole's face.

He read the column's headline out loud: "Taylor Meat Company Vandalized." His eyes were the only thing that moved as he scanned the article. He nodded and tossed the paper back to Paulie. "I've heard of them. It's a common enough name."

"Looks like a total write-off." Paulie shook his head in sympathy. "I hope they're insured."

Because of medical tests he'd be taking, Jericho hadn't joined them for breakfast this morning. But Chad sat in his place at the head of the table, chewing his eggs with thoughtful distraction as he tuned in to the conversation. "Aren't they located up by the river in the City Market? One of those restoration projects. They used to supply the Garibaldi Steakhouse chain, didn't they?"

"Mmm, a Garibaldi filet mignon done medium rare." Lana looked up from her stock report, apparently savoring a delicious memory. And showing off her business awareness. "As I recall, Garibaldi's bought out their supplier.

That must have made a tidy profit for Taylor Meats. Sounds like someone was savvy enough to retain the name for local business.''

Cole adjusted the knot of his yellow silk tie. He was clean-shaven this morning; every long, dark hair was pulled back into place behind his starched white collar. ''I wouldn't know.''

Paulie quizzed Cole further. ''I thought you said you grew up in the Market District. If this is a family problem, we can help you handle it.''

Tori ran a quick mental list of all the possibilities Meade *help* might entail, from dropping big money to pay for repairs to finding the perpetrators of the crime and punishing them, Meade-style.

But Cole wasn't interested in the offer. ''Like I said, Taylor's a common name.''

Was his lack of any reaction a cover to hide a more emotional response inside? Last night he'd hinted at deep pride in his brothers and sister. Or did he really not know the family who'd been victimized and who, coincidentally, shared his last name?

Aaron Polakis materialized in the dining room archway, wearing his usual scowl. His beady brown eyes made contact with everyone at the table. They lingered an extra moment on Lana, though his expression never changed. But he spoke only to Cole. ''Car's ready.''

Polakis retreated into the hallway, disappearing as quickly as he'd come. Cole tossed his napkin onto the table and stood, buttoning the front of his navy-blue suit on his way out. Tori took note of the deep wrinkles in his napkin, as if the linen had been crushed into a tight ball inside Cole's fist. Something about that article *had* rattled him.

''Excuse me.'' Tori jumped up from the table, impulsively grabbed his napkin and dabbed her lips with it, then carried it with her as she hurried after him. She wasn't sure if she was removing the clue before anyone else noticed his distress or carrying evidence to confront him with. ''Cole?''

The hall was deserted. She quickly looked both ways and spotted him closing the front door behind him.

''Cole!'' She dashed after him, swung the door open and caught him by the arm before he stepped down from the porch.

He turned and faced her. ''Jericho's waiting,'' were the only words that made it past the tight compression of his lips.

''What was that about?'' Tori whispered, conscious of the occupants of the long black limo parked in the circular brick driveway at the base of the concrete steps. She tried to find an answer in Cole's fathomless blue eyes. ''Are you okay? Are *we* okay? Is there something going on I should know about before I make a mistake and blab something I shouldn't?''

''Which question do you want me to answer first?''

''Cut the sarcasm, Taylor.'' A flurry of concerns welled up inside her. ''You haven't said boo to me since last night. Are you still going to protect my cover? What do I tell Rodriguez? Where are all your hidden cameras?''

His gaze dropped down to her hands between them. She still held tight to his sleeve and worried the napkin between her thumb and fingers. She forced herself to let go when she realized the nervous movement had betrayed her fears.

But before she could pull away, Cole reached in and swallowed up both her hands, napkin and all, between his. The warmth and strength of his calloused grip radiated through her skin, sparking alternating tendrils of soothing comfort and sensual need along her wrists and arms and deeper inside.

''Easy, sweetheart— Tori,'' he corrected himself before she got her mouth around a protest. He altered his stance, angling his full back to the limousine, holding her with both hands now. The tenor of his voice deepened. "Call A.J. as soon as you can. Ask how Ma and Dad are."

"They're your parents?" Deeply buried emotions haunted the depths of his midnight-blue eyes, giving her her answer. A kindred sympathy at his fear for his parents' safety awakened inside her. "I'm sorry. I hope they're okay."

"So do I. Someone's trying to distract me from my purpose, and my family's paying the price."

Tori's eyes widened. "You think someone here is responsible for that break-in?" She tried to switch grips and offer him the solace he'd given her.

But feminine comfort wasn't what he wanted from her. Cole released her entirely. He reached inside his jacket and pulled out a small plastic bag with her welcome note from "Daniel" sealed inside. "Give this to A.J." He bypassed her hands and tucked the card directly into the pocket of her black slacks, pulling the hem of her lilac blouse over it to keep the exchange well-hidden from view. "Have him run prints on it. It'll probably come up clean, but—"

"Taylor." Aaron's call from the far side of the limousine stopped the conversation with the precision of a Swiss Army knife. "Say goodbye to your woman. Mr. Meade is waiting."

Cole's terse sigh indicated he might have shared more if they'd had real privacy. Almost as if he'd needed the reminder from their audience that this was supposed to be a personal relationship, he pressed a light, perfunctory kiss to her lips. "I'll catch up with you later."

"I'll take care of this," she promised, subtly indicating her pocket, reassured that they were still working partners.

"Watch your back," he warned unnecessarily.

"Watch yours."

Cole took a step toward the car, then hesitated. His shoulders swelled—girding himself for some effort? resigning himself to some fate? making a decision? He whirled around, startling her with his unknown intent. His hand snaked out and he palmed the back of her head. He bent down as he lifted her onto her toes. He stopped up the nonplussed *what?* of her lips with his. Tori braced her hands against his chest for balance and held on as her world spun into a slam-bam overload of sensory images.

He kissed her hard, swirling his tongue inside her mouth and claiming her uncensored response. She caught fire as she tasted rich coffee, breathed in the freshly pressed scent of his clothes, absorbed his masculine strength and surrendered a tiny piece of her heart. But with a reluctant moan low in his throat, he tore his mouth away, ending the kiss as suddenly as he had begun it. Tori swayed on her feet, stunned by her instant and powerful reaction to his touch.

"God, Tori."

Not babe. Not sweetheart. He leaned his forehead against hers, his hand roughly massaging the nape of her neck, his heated breath caressing the tingling swell of her lips. Stars of emotion danced in his dark eyes, glittering with the same pulsing intensity of her thudding heart.

"What was that for?" she asked, embarrassed by what her breathy voice might reveal.

He swallowed hard, gathering his composure in a way she couldn't yet. "I needed to."

He needed the solace of physical contact? He needed to put on a convincing show? He needed *her?*

She wasn't buying that last theory. "Don't worry. I'm sure Aaron believed it that time."

Cole frowned. "Screw Aaron. That's not what I meant."

"Taylor!" Aaron's impatient prompt prevented further discussion.

With another pithy damnation of the audience in question, Cole brushed his lips beside her ear. "There's no camera in Jericho's office. Stay clear of the computer and the safe and you shouldn't trip any sensors. We won't be back until dinner this evening." He squeezed the back of her neck, demanding she hear *everything* he was saying. "And then we'll talk in private."

"Sure." About her meeting with A.J. "We'll talk."

"Tori?" He meant something else, something more. But she just wasn't going to go there.

"You'd better go." She was never going to be comfortable playing this sexual game. Feeling things, wanting answers. Never sure what was real or pretend. Afraid to trust instincts that had been so wrong before. She released her grip on his jacket and smoothed the lapels across the strong beat of his heart. There was no confusion when it came to doing her job, however, and the information Cole had just given her was priceless. "Thanks for the tip. I'll check out the office this afternoon."

"Call A.J."

She nodded.

"Be careful—"

"Taylor!"

"Go," she said.

"I'm coming," he shouted over his shoulder. Cupping the side of her cheek and jaw, he spared Tori once last questioning look before turning and sauntering down the steps. He took his good, sweet time crossing the drive and climbing into the back of the limo.

Amused by Cole's refusal to be ordered about by the bristly butler-turned-chauffeur, Tori watched him every step of the way—until the prickle of goose bumps crawling across her skin made her realize that she, too, was being watched.

Aaron stood at the driver's door, staring with dead-eyed intensity at her over the roof of the car. She'd been the object of displeasure and resentment before. She'd even looked into the eyes of hate. But there was something so cold, so omniscient in those unblinking eyes that Tori shivered in the spring air.

Did he know something about her and her mission? Even suspect she had an ulterior motive for working here? Did he think she'd detained Cole just to inconvenience him? Or was that accusatory stare a by-product of his surly personality?

Refusing to confirm any suspicion or grant him the satisfaction of intimidating her, Tori tipped her chin and defiantly met the enemy's glare head-on. He muttered something under his breath at her show of independence, dismissed her presence and climbed in behind the wheel.

As she watched the black limo drive away, the chill of Aaron's stare stayed with her, canceling out the heat stirred by Cole's passion. She was wrong to make too much of that kiss, anyway. He'd been worried for his parents and her safety, and her mother had told her that men often expressed their emotions with physical actions.

She'd made too much of Ian Davies's kisses, too. He'd managed to fool her as well as their audience.

Imagining herself in love with the fellow agent assigned to portray her husband in an undercover sting had been a rookie mistake. She'd fallen for Ian's smooth moves and pretty words. He'd convinced her that everything her mother had said about her shortcomings wasn't true.

But Ian had been more interested in selling information to the drug dealer they were trying to bring in. The morning after she'd finally given in to his seduction, she'd overheard him on the phone wrapping up the deal. She'd kept her head enough to play along until she could report the situation to her superior and set up an entrapment. But her idealistic view of love had been forever altered from the fairy tales her father had once filled her head with.

She'd unknowingly provided the means for Ian to achieve his traitorous goal. She'd provided a few laughs, too, she realized, once he informed her his taste in women ran to busty brunettes who knew how to please a man—hinting that she'd failed on all counts.

Heart bruised, pride battered, self-esteem beaten back to square one, Tori had received a commendation for uncovering the double agent, and Ian wound up dead in the crossfire between the Dominguez cartel and the Feds.

No Horseman—divine or otherwise—had ridden in to save her from pain and humiliation back then. No hero was going to save her now.

So she wouldn't get hurt. She was a smarter woman now, a smarter agent. Nobody could use her or hurt her if she didn't give them the means to do so. On or off the job. It was a safer, saner way to live her life.

Still, it was hard not to care when a man's family was under attack. It was hard to stay detached when a man volunteered to go to jail rather than see her risk her life. It was hard to remember this was all a very dangerous game…when Cole Taylor kissed her like that.

And she had foolishly held on and kissed him back.

Shaking off the annoying second-guessing when she had a job to do, Tori turned to go inside. But she paused with her hand on the doorknob and let common sense finally be heard over her confused emotions. In a house littered with listening devices, the best place to make a private phone call would be outside.

Not that the atmosphere felt any more welcoming out here. A stagnant, gray canopy of clouds chilled the air with the promise of more rain. Despite the lack of sunshine, she strolled down the steps as if it was a treat to sample the dreary day. Walking around to the side yard, toward the jungle-thick wall of deciduous trees surrounding the manor, Tori pulled her cell phone from her belt and Rodriguez's number from her pocket.

She punched in the number, tugged her sleeves down to

her wrists and crossed her arms against the clammy dampness that clung to her skin. The phone rang—long enough for her to stand there and note the fingers of sunlight streaming into the northern part of the city and farther west.

"Why doesn't the sun ever shine here?" she muttered to herself, listening to the third ring. She could hear an elephant's trumpet and a cacophony of chirps and barks and growls from the zoo on the other side of the trees. Breakfast was being served, cages were being cleaned. Their world was coming to life. But the air within the gates of the Meade estate was spookily still.

Still enough that she could hear the whisper of a window sash sliding open. Curious more than alarmed, she turned and studied the sprawling two-story brick facade for any sign of movement.

By the fourth ring, the phone clicked. A whooshing sound in the background made her think she'd reached someone driving in his car. The person answering waited for her to speak first.

"A. J. Rodriguez, please."

"Yes?"

There. Her room. The curtain stirred at her window. But there was no breeze. Her pulse quickened with wary anticipation. Had someone been spying on her? Going through her things? Watching her make this call?

She kept her eye on the window, looking for signs of movement that would indicate the intruder was still inside. "My name's Victoria Westin. I'm calling for…a friend." She wasn't quite sure how to define her ever-changing alliance with the enigmatic bodyguard. But she suddenly felt very much alone without him on the premises. "Cole Taylor. I have a message."

Mr. Rodriguez had little to say, but he was willing to listen. "Not on the phone. When and where do you want to meet?"

The gauzy sheers that hung at her window parted and a dark, distinct shape pressed itself to the glass. "What the hell...?"

"Ms. Westin?"

"Sorry." She quickly made the arrangements and hung up. She reached for the gun at her hip. But it wasn't there.

Tori hooked the phone to her belt and ran for the front door.

She'd seen a black-gloved hand in the window.

A hand with only four fingers.

BY THE TIME TORI REACHED her bedroom, everything was closed up tight and neat as a pin. Fresh towels hung in the bathroom, another foil-wrapped mint had been left on her pillow, and a handwritten note—signed *J.D.M.*—was lying beside it.

Tori picked up her shoulder bag and sat on the edge of the bed. *I'll see you at midnight* was hardly the stuff of which cases were built, but she'd bag it and hand it over to Detective Rodriguez with the card from yesterday. This was no ghostly invitation as Jericho had claimed, unless the laws of physics had changed. Her visitor had been the flesh-and-blood kind. The musty smell of dust and rot, like an old, dark attic—or the hidden corridor—hung in the air and tickled her nose.

The same cobwebby scent greeted her when she opened her purse to find a plastic bag. Tori pinched her nose and sneezed. Her "ghost" had gone through her things. Why? Jumping to her feet, she turned and dumped the contents out onto the bed and sorted through them, checking that nothing had been taken, nothing new had been left behind, and nothing in that bag could give her away.

Except... "Dad?" She flipped through the plastic sheaves in her wallet one more time. "It's gone." The picture of her father and herself that she carried in her wallet.

A sinking feeling that was part grief, part anger, carried Tori back in time. She'd been taking pottery lessons at the Nelson-Atkins art museum and was holding her own crude version of the *Horseman* in the photo. Her creation looked more like a dragon with a hump on its back, but her father had known it was the knight from his stories and hugged her for it.

Had the intruder seen the blob of clay and plastic jewels and recognized it for what it was?

"Idiot."

Tori snapped the wallet shut. She needed that photo back, for survival as much as sentiment.

Planting her thoughts firmly in the moment, Tori grabbed the penlight and tossed everything else back into her bag. She was going to find out where that corridor led and who was using it.

But she'd barely gotten turned around when someone knocked at her door. For a split second she considered simply not answering it. But the concealed camera left her no place to hide.

Putting away the penlight and the J.D.M. cards, she straightened her clothes, opened the door, and strained her muscles to maintain a smile. "Chad."

He posed in her doorway like a catalog model. "Remember my offer to help with your research? Today's your lucky day. My morning's free."

Oh, yeah, touchy-feely boy had impeccable timing. Tori ducked her chin to hide her frustration. She'd have to postpone her search for the intruder. Her best bet now was to ask Cole if his camera had caught the trespasser on tape. But he'd indicated she wouldn't see him again until dinner. That left an entire day to rally her patience and try to guess which member of the household had been spying on her. Might as well start with Chad.

"That'd be great." Carefully counting the five fingers on

his right hand, she tolerated the brush of them against her back as he escorted her downstairs to the office across from Jericho's.

Chad Meade's home office had a place for everything. And everything had been in its place until Tori set up shop at his desk to peruse the art inventories he kept on his computer.

Tedious as paperwork could be, though, after nearly three hours of wading through the mess of records, she'd actually made some interesting progress. She'd thumbed through pictures, bookmarked catalog numbers and made pages of notes as she verified each work of art on the database.

The system was a bookkeeper's nightmare. Someone—Chad, probably, with his penchant for order—had transferred files of handwritten notes to the computer. Each entry listed the item, its date of purchase and purchase price, its current value, and its location at the estate or downtown offices.

But the data was incomplete. There were more items in the scrapbooks than on the computer. And some of the listings were missing information—a red flag that suggested money was being secreted away by altering the values of a work or hiding its existence altogether. Of course, it could be just shoddy accounting. But Tori was certain the Meades wouldn't tolerate incompetent record-keeping when she was looking at numbers totaling well into the millions of dollars.

"Thomas Hart Benton's *Western Highway*. Seventy-five-thousand dollars." Adjusting her glasses, she traced the listing with her finger on the computer screen. "Purchased in 1984." *Blank*. She picked up a book and thumbed through it to find the photograph of the painting and its New York auction house receipt. Pulling her glasses down her nose, she looked over the top of them at Chad. "Neither entry says where the painting's located."

Willing to approach her mess if it meant an opportunity

to shine, Chad came over and perched on the arm of her chair to look at the computer screen. His hip butted against her shoulder and stayed. When Cole touched her, her skin tingled. When Chad touched her, it crawled. And while Cole baffled her limited feminine intuition, there was no misinterpreting Chad's harassing intentions. Tori rolled her eyes and leaned toward the opposite arm of the chair.

"Ah, yes, that one. Jericho owns several Benton pieces, since he was a local artist."

She was familiar with the murals Benton had painted at the Harry S. Truman Presidential Library in Independence.

"He rotates them out of his office downtown when he purchases a new one. He hasn't displayed this particular painting for several years."

"What does he do with the items he doesn't display?"

"Loans them to area museums. Gives them away as gifts."

"He gives away seventy-five-thousand dollar paintings?"

"If he likes you." Double entendre dripped from Chad's voice as he slid his arm along the back of her chair, letting his thumb catch in the strands of her hair.

Tori's mental groan quickly gave way to imagining at least three ways she could incapacitate him from this position, rendering him incapable of touching her in any way, shape or form for ten solid minutes. But since she needed the information he seemed inclined to share, she'd skip the martial arts and opt for a more subtle escape.

She set down her glasses and stood, putting several steps between them before stopping to stretch and roll the kinks from her neck. "There are hundreds of items there. Someone hasn't kept very good track of them all." She risked adding insult to rejection. "Have you always overseen his collection?"

Chad rose to his feet, his irritation obvious. He began snapping books shut and straightening piles atop his desk.

"I took over for Daniel when he became more interested in other things."

"Other things?"

"My cousin had a wonderful head for business, but not the heart for it. He could talk anyone into anything, but then he wouldn't see the project through. Jericho financed all of Daniel's whims. He'd give him money and put him on an airplane to pick up something for his collection. Then Daniel would blow it at a craps table."

And perhaps steal the item when he couldn't pay? Or hock something in storage to replace the cash? Maybe she should include Daniel Meade on her list of suspected thieves.

"Daniel would rather play with his women or place a bet than take care of responsibilities. His upbringing spoiled him, I think."

But Chad's hadn't? Tori bit her tongue. She crossed to the front of the desk and poured on the ego boost. "But you're a good businessman, I can tell. Very thorough when it comes to details."

He paused with a book in hand and smiled across the desk. She'd just scored major brownie points.

"I'm *very* thorough."

She pretended she didn't get his hidden macho message. "So you would know where those paintings and sculptures are stored when they're not on display."

Chad set down the book and picked up her glasses. "Down in the catacombs. It's cool and dark down there, the humidity's steady. Perfect for storage."

"What about mice or insects getting in and causing damage?"

"Well, we don't just lean a Frederic Remington up against a foundation wall. There are rooms that have been specially built for different purposes down there."

"Such as?"

"Storing wine, records—the phonograph kind, not papers."

Tori laughed as she was meant to.

Chad circled the desk, eager to share his knowledge. "There's even a tomb where the original owners of this house were buried back in the 1800s."

"Wow. What a great place to explore." And she intended to.

He slipped her glasses over the bridge of her nose and traced the earpieces back behind her ears. Tori gritted her teeth as his hands lingered against her hair.

"You don't want to go down there. It's dark and dusty, a maze of support walls and locked rooms. Jericho keeps the keys in his office. Daniel had a set, too, but they disappeared when he did."

Disappeared? Was a set of keys motive for murder?

"You're in charge of the art collection." Tori swallowed her pride and cooed demurely. "Couldn't I just borrow your keys?"

"You could if he had them." The throaty whine of a woman's voice joined them from the doorway. Lana.

Tori quickly backed beyond Chad's reach and tugged off her glasses. She knew she'd been caught playing to his ego, not his hormones, but a biased observer might not distinguish the difference. Judging by the shards of distrust shining in Lana's brown eyes, this one was definitely biased.

"Good morning, Lana."

The blonde raked her gaze across Tori. "Uh-huh." She closed the file she'd been reading and strolled into the room. "Chad will be running all this one day—with me at his side. But Jericho still makes him ask for the keys to the proverbial castle." She crossed to her fiancé, handed him the file and proceeded to wrap her arms around his waist and snuggle against him. Chad dropped his arm behind her back and palmed her butt, eating up the attention. "You deserve more respect. You've done so much to recoup Daniel's losses. But your uncle won't give up control of anything—even a set of keys—until we pry it from his cold, dead hands.''

''Charming sentiment, dear.'' But Chad was smiling. ''See how she spoils me, Victoria?''

''I'm just lookin' out for my number-one man.'' Lana smoothed her red-tipped fingers—five of them, Tori noted—through his perfect hair and adjusted his tie. ''Now go be your charming self, darling, and call London for me. These contracts don't contain the guarantees we asked for. Tell them that I—that *we*—'' she flashed a dazzling smile to cover the gaffe and traced her finger across Chad's lips ''—will only invest in a sure thing. If they won't pony up the money, we'll take our business elsewhere. Got that?''

''Got it.'' Chad turned his head to Tori and smiled. ''She's always pushing to make me a better man.''

A richer, more powerful one, at any rate. But Tori didn't point out the differences between position and character. ''I can see that.''

''Duty calls, I'm afraid. If I can be of any further assistance, you will let me know, won't you?''

''Of course. Thank you.''

Looking handsome as a picture and all too pleased with himself, Chad leaned down to kiss Lana. But she turned her lips to the side and offered him her cheek—maybe so he wouldn't smear that blood red lipstick she wore. Chad hesitated; his smile flat-lined.

''You don't want to keep your appointments waiting,'' Lana urged.

''I suppose not.'' He kissed her cheek with little enthusiasm. ''Til later, darling. Victoria.''

With a nod, and a wink behind Lana's back, he left.

Tori made a show of checking her watch. ''Well, I'd better be going, too. I have a lunch date.''

Despite her paint and peroxide and rarefied airs, Lana moved like a jungle cat, meeting Tori at the door and bracing her arm across the opening to block her path. "Stay away from Chad."

Making nice with Chad to ferret out information was one thing. He was easy to manipulate. Lana, on the other hand, wouldn't be fooled. Tori looked down at the shorter woman, respecting her for the enemy that she was. Honesty was easy.

"I have no interest in your fiancé whatsoever."

Except as a prime suspect in the theft and attempted smuggling of one small, priceless knight. Maybe even Daniel Meade's murder. He'd certainly had motive, means and opportunity to get Daniel out of the picture. Resentment of the "golden boy." Taking on the thankless task of cleaning up Daniel's apparent messes to protect the family's finances and reputation.

Maybe that was the threat Lana sensed.

"Like I said, I look out for him. You ask an awful lot of questions and do an awful lot of sneaking around."

And just how did she know that? "Been checking up on me?"

Lana neither confirmed nor denied the challenge. "What are you up to? Is your grandfather trying to take over Jericho's business? Are you providing him with inside information?"

It wasn't the first time she'd been accused of being a stooge for her grandfather. But Tori refused to be baited. "I'm just trying to do my job. To document and assess Mr. Meade's entire collection of art and artifacts. When I don't get straight answers, I have to find them whatever way I can."

"I wouldn't stir things up too much. There are some people in this household who like things just the way they are."

"Like you."

Lana smiled. It wasn't an expression of joy. "I'm glad we understand each other, Miss Westin. Enjoy your lunch."

Chapter Eight

"Hey, kiddo. It's me."

Cole didn't know which frustrated him more—hearing Jessie's voice on her answering machine instead of the real thing, or watching Victoria laugh at whatever A.J. had just told her over their sidewalk café table on the Plaza.

His fake mistress and his former partner made a striking couple as they drank their bottled water and waited for the meal they'd ordered. A.J.'s black hair and olive complexion contrasted with Tori's pale-skinned beauty. And with A.J.'s chameleon-like ability to blend in with any surroundings, he looked right at home in the trendy eatery with the Italian-style architecture and cuisine.

Funny how a suit and tie and the right attitude could change the world's perception of a man.

Only, admiration didn't exactly describe the unsettling emotion twisting in Cole's gut as A.J. leaned in closer to hear something Tori had said.

He couldn't be jealous of his best friend. Not over some woman who wasn't really his.

Realizing he'd left several seconds of silence on the message that would probably alarm his sister needlessly, Cole ducked back inside the toy store across the street and concentrated on the phone. "Sorry. I spaced off. I just wanted to check how you—"

A beep and a breathless voice cut him off. "Cole?" Jessie had turned off the answering machine and picked up. "We were out on the porch eating lunch. You still there?"

"I'm here." Jessie's bright, familiar voice should have picked up his spirits. Instead, it triggered a longing for the closeness the two of them had shared growing up. Only eleven months apart in age, Cole and his little sister shared an almost telepathic bond and had always been tuned in to each other's moods. If she couldn't cut through this inevitable funk he was spiraling into, nobody could. "Tell me Ma and Dad are okay."

"They're fine. No one was hurt. The shop's a total mess, though. Thankfully, everything can be cleaned up or replaced. Cousin Mitch thinks it's the same guys who mugged Ma and Alex. They found one of the pictures from her stolen wallet at the scene."

Definitely a personal attack. Most likely his fault. "Damn. Does Mitch have any leads?"

"Only that they were pros, not kids. There wasn't a fingerprint left anywhere. No graffiti or gang signs." Jessie answered his demands in a comforting tone, then turned around and reprimanded him. "You should go see them. When was the last time any of us got a good look at you?"

"I can't. I'm the bad cop folks love to hate, you know." He pushed aside the top box in a display of dolls to keep a clear view through the window on the conversation across the street. The waiter was delivering their plates now. Cole followed the young man's hurried movements, thinking back to the nervous attendant at Kramer's clinic who had died trying to kill Jericho. The similarities didn't thrill him.

"I don't know anything of the kind. We're a family, Cole. A strong one. You know we can help you with anything if you just ask." Her soft sigh recaptured his attention. "We can forgive you anything, too. Is that what's keeping you away?"

Forgiveness? If his suspicions were correct, the Taylors were being targeted because of him. A man didn't knowingly put the people he loved into harm's way and expect redemption.

He'd left Jericho resting up at St. Luke's Hospital, with Aaron standing guard, and had walked the few blocks down to the Plaza shopping and entertainment district to grab some fresh air and a bite of lunch. But then he'd spotted Tori and A.J. being seated at a café. Maybe providing an hour's worth of secret backup would make him feel a little better about using her as his courier.

The waiter left, and Cole followed him with his eyes back inside the restaurant, scanning the other patrons along the way.

"How's the Irishman?" he asked. Jessie's fiancé, Sam O'Rourke, still retained a trace of his parents' native brogue.

"You didn't answer my question."

He wasn't going to. Cole tried to think of something—anything—more pleasant than his failure to protect his family. "You know it's probably killin' Ma that you two are living together. When's he going to make an honest woman out of you?"

"We've had this conversation before. I'm not getting married until you can come be part of the ceremony."

Cole swallowed a little more guilt and returned his focus to the table across the street. Tori frowned as she slowly turned her head, searching the other tables and passersby as if some unseen person had called her name. A.J. was looking now, too. Cole scanned the street, trying to spot whatever had alerted them.

"Don't put your happiness on hold for me, kiddo." Tori's gaze swept past the toy store window, halted, then came back. *Damn.* Cole spun out of sight behind the display, nearly knocking over an aquarium filled with tiny plastic doll shoes. As he righted the water-filled sculpture, he toppled several of the boxes, capturing the attention of the other customers.

"Cole? Are you all right?"

"Yeah, fine," he answered in a tone that indicated things were anything but. He stooped to help the teenage clerk stack the boxes again.

Way to keep a low profile, Taylor. Had she spotted him? He could imagine that flame-haired temper boiling with accusations that he was getting some sort of voyeuristic thrill by spying on her again.

"Cole?"

From this vantage point, though Tori was out of sight, he could see out the window down the street. A dented white pickup drove past, slowing for pedestrians crossing the street. Something about the driver with the shaggy brown hair struck a note of recognition, but Cole racked his brain and came up empty. By the time he stood up to get a better look, the man had put a phone up to his ear, camouflaging his profile. The truck quickly rounded the corner and drove out of sight.

But he was in plain view of Tori's sharp-eyed gaze. Green eyes met blue, clear across the street. Great. Now instead of getting some honest answers about her cryptic reaction to that kiss this morning, their next conversation would be about not trusting her to handle the job or endangering her cover.

Cole didn't try to hide. With a quick apology to the clerk, he headed out the door. "Jessie, I'm going to have to call you later. Something's come up."

"Blonde or brunette?"

"What?"

That intuitive connection must be broadcasting over the airwaves. "I can tell when there's a woman on your mind. I think this one's really gotten under your skin."

She had no idea.

A.J. had diverted Tori's attention back to him, and Cole took the opportunity to survey the crowds of tourists and professionals window-shopping, taking pictures and eating lunch. Maybe Tori had only gone on hyper-alert because she sensed *him* watching her, but he didn't intend to leave anything to chance. He'd keep her safe from Jericho and Lancelot and anyone else who threatened her.

"She's a redhead." Cole smiled, knowing his sister would see through any denial, but refusing to offer any further explanation. "I'll call you when I can. Tell everyone to be extra careful. Love you. 'Bye."

He folded up the phone and clipped it onto his belt. The sidewalk radiated heat, but he couldn't shake the warning chill in his bones. He should walk away right now, and not risk drawing any attention to Tori's meeting with A.J.

But they already had somebody's attention. Cole had cheated death and skirted disaster too many times to completely ignore what his instincts were trying to tell him. It was all just a matter of spotting the perp.

"Son of a bitch."

Chad Meade, a half block away, was strolling down the sidewalk in deep conversation with a short, fair-haired man wearing tiny, frameless glasses. In a matter of seconds, they'd turn the corner by the statue of a bronze boar and the restaurant terrace would be in clear view.

Tori would be in clear view.

Cole quickly shuffled through his options and was already moving before he made his decision. Throwing out his hand to block off oncoming vehicles, he dashed across the intersection and headed straight for Tori and A.J. He let the blare of horns and the jam-up in traffic stop curious pedestrians on the sidewalk to mask his approach and buy himself precious seconds of cover-up time.

Tori saw him coming and shot to her feet. Rosy dots spotted her cheeks in a flush of emotion that could be either fear or anger. "What are you doing here? You can't be seen with A.J."

Cole swung his leg over the iron railing and potted plants that separated the terrace from the sidewalk. He pushed her back a step but kept his hand cupped around her elbow to hold her close and provide an obscuring shield of protection. "First-name basis already, huh?" He took note of the maître d' hurrying to the table and looked into the familiar opaqueness of A.J.'s golden eyes. "Never pegged you for a lady-killer, buddy." Cole nodded toward the sidewalk. "Company's coming. Get out of here."

A.J. grinned. "Good to see you, too, buddy."

Tori jerked her arm free, but kept her voice hushed to match the two men's. "I'm glad we're all buddy-buddy here, but wasn't the idea to keep your connection to A.J. secret? You don't have any faith in me at all, do you."

"I don't have faith in anyone right now, sweetheart." He put up his hand to stop the inevitable protest against the use of endearments. It had just slipped out. "You couldn't find somewhere more private? This place is crawling with spies."

"Excuse me, sir. May I be of assistance?" The maître d's greeting sounded more accusatory than friendly.

Tori intervened before Cole could answer. "We just ran into an old friend." She looped her arm through the maître d's and took him aside, charming him out of his suspicions and buying Cole a few moments with the man he'd once known like a brother.

"A white truck's already circled the block twice," A.J. whispered, his eyes scanning the streets and restaurant.

Cole nodded. "I can't place him, but he's no tourist. And Chad Meade's about to join you for lunch."

"Add in the nosy waiter and we've got all kinds of potential trouble."

"You saw him too?" The young man in question rattled

the dishes on his tray when he realized both men were watching him. He muttered something unintelligible and darted back inside. "Yep. That's not suspicious."

"I'm guessing they're not Meade's people?"

Cole shook his head. "Could be part of something she's working on. Did she tell you she's FBI?"

"Did you tell her you're a cop?" A.J. put up one hand, telling Cole he didn't expect an answer to that one. He adjusted his jacket and patted the pocket. "I'll get these cards to Mac at the lab. I'm sure we've got Daniel Meade's handwriting on file, and we'll check for prints."

These? Plural? Cole swept his gaze over to Tori. She had the maitre d' laughing now, completely distracted from the restaurant's intruder. But there was no time to ask when she'd received another message from "Daniel."

A.J. went on. "The D.A. wants to nail the shooter who took down Lee Cameron."

Cole spotted Chad and his guest at the front door through the decorative shrubs and dragged his gaze back to his one-time partner. "Tell him to get in line."

"The slug they pulled out of Cameron is a foreign job. The lab's running it through Interpol to trace the manufacturer."

"Have them focus on Eastern European sources." Tori had rejoined them. "Cross-check with the Bureau reference I gave you on the statue's original owner."

She linked her arm through Cole's, playing the couple game this time. She hesitated a moment, then lined herself up flush to his side. He felt the gentle swell of one breast, the sleek muscle of one hip pressed against him. Cole breathed out a sigh of relief at the unexpected contact. One form of tension dissipated and another, less timely sense of awareness took its place.

If she was this close, he could keep her safe. When she was this close, it felt real. He hadn't realized how much he craved *real*. Without thinking about charades or consequences, Cole laced his fingers through hers, binding them together. "You're thinking Lancelot ordered the hit?"

Tori nodded. "My guess is you're looking for a betrayed smuggler or terrorist as your contract man."

"Terrorist?" A.J. swore beneath his breath. "You never did take the easy way, did you, *amigo?*" He put his mouth to Tori's ear and intentionally whispered loud enough for Cole to overhear. "Keep your eye on this guy. He's not as invincible as he thinks he is."

"Are you still here?" Cole razzed, pushing him away. He didn't have time to debate the wisdom of having stayed with this assignment so long.

A.J. looked at a spot beyond Tori's shoulder. "Chad Meade's at your six. I'm gone." He winked at Tori. "Call me."

"Cole? Victoria?"

Startled, Tori's grip flinched within his. He gave her a *stay calm* squeeze before releasing her, and they turned to greet Chad.

"Didn't I just see you?" Tori took a stab at light, impersonal conversation. "How's London?"

"Under control now, thanks. Lana should be pleased." Chad craned his neck to look around them. "What happened to your friend?"

Cole glanced over his shoulder and hid his smile. A.J.'s reputation as the best shadow-man in the precinct was well-earned. Even his plate had disappeared from the table. He turned back around and shrugged as if Chad had been hallucinating. "What friend?"

Chad's blue eyes narrowed. He shoved Cole aside to get a clear look at a table beautifully set for one. Cole braced for the abuse about to be thrown his way.

"My uncle might believe in ghosts, but I don't. We pay you good money to guard Jericho and do as you're told.

But he's not even here, is he. I saw that man. Were you trading secrets? Does he know about the attempt on Jericho's life? Who was he?''

Tori planted her hands on her hips. ''*I* met with an old friend, thank you very much.'' She had enough miff in her tone to make it clear she felt insulted. ''First, Cole shows up and does his jealous lover routine, and now you're here making a scene, telling me I can only hang out with people who are on your list of approved friends. I didn't realize that if I wanted privacy I'd have to leave town.''

Cole pressed his smile into a firm line as Chad scrambled to do damage control with the lady. Maybe she could handle this undercover role, after all. She certainly had Chad snowed.

''I was speaking to Taylor about neglecting his duties to my uncle, not your social life. I'm very pleased with the progress we made this morning. Of course, you're free to come and go from the house and meet with whomever you please. In fact, I have someone with me now you might enjoy meeting. He runs an art gallery over on Forty-seventh. He acquired several of the more unusual pieces for us that you'll be working with.''

She tipped her nose in the air, and Chad held his breath, waiting for acceptance of his apology. She dragged out the fuss long enough to give A.J. plenty of time to blend in with the crowd. And she'd shifted Chad's focus so that he'd forgotten all about the black-haired mystery man who'd upset him in the first place. ''Well.'' She huffed out a sigh. ''I suppose I did overreact a bit. It's just that I feel like I've had someone looking over my shoulder ever since I went to work for Mr. Meade.''

Her green eyes flickered up to Cole's. Yeah, he'd been watching her from minute one. He made no apologies.

But Chad did. ''I'm sorry. We're just trying to help with your work, and we do have security measures in place we have to respect. But certainly what you do on your own time is your own business. Forgive me?''

Chad reached for her hands and carried them up to his lips, where he proceeded to kiss each one. Tori's eyes widened with a start above Chad's bent head. Something hard and territorial slammed in Cole's gut as Chad tilted his head and slyly brushed the next kiss against her jaw.

Cole clamped his hand down over Chad's shoulder and pulled him away from Tori. ''It's been fun as usual, Chad, but we were just leaving.''

Tori's eyes flashed to his, but she didn't take the hint. Correction. The arch of that auburn brow said she understood the silent message just fine. She was just refusing to cooperate.

''I've got time to meet his friend.''

She was playing a dangerous game, toying with Chad's lusty interest in the opposite sex for the promise of information.

''What's his name?'' she asked.

Chad shrugged loose of Cole's grip and adjusted his jacket, grinning as if he'd just won some kind of battle. ''Martín Lukasiewicz.''

Seeing he was the focus of their attention, the short man nodded and Tori waved. ''Lukasiewicz.'' She rolled the name around her tongue. ''Sounds Slavic or Polish.'' Her knowing gaze slid up to Cole's. ''Eastern European.''

As in *Lancelot?* Cole's muscles clenched around his bones as he imagined what she was thinking. The woman just couldn't play it safe, could she. He saw the wheels of speculation churning behind her eyes. She pulled her shoulders back and tipped her chin as if prepping for an interrogation.

''I'm not sure of his heritage, but we can certainly ask him.'' Chad's pretty, manicured fingers urged her forward.

No! The man might damn well be a representative of a

foreign crime boss. Hell, he could be a terrorist. The fact that he was a friend of Chad's made him probable scum. And she wanted to waltz on over there and play Twenty Questions?

Wasn't gonna happen.

Cole reached around Chad and snatched Tori's hand, pulling her to his side. "You'll have to do that another time. Like Chad said, I need to get back to work."

He could count on Tori to argue. "But—"

"I was hoping to hitch a ride with you to the hospital."

Those rebellious green eyes searched his face for some kind of explanation. But he couldn't very well warn her off without giving something away to Chad.

"If you'll wait a few minutes, I'll be happy to give you a ride. But I'd like to talk to Mr. Lukasiewicz."

Funny how she could articulate so clearly without seeming to unclench her teeth. He'd deal with her wrath. He wouldn't deal with her getting hurt. "I'm already late. Please?"

Chad reached for her free hand and tugged, as immune to the Taylor charm as she apparently was. "Give him your keys, Victoria. I have the Porsche. I'll drive you home."

Cole bristled at the proprietary tone. "I don't think so."

Chad puffed out his chest. "You're late. Remember?"

"Gentlemen!" Tori jerked her hands free of both men's and scolded them with the kind of glare his mother had used when he'd gotten into trouble as a boy. She didn't give either one of them a chance to argue. "You're fighting over me as if *I* were the car. I drove here by myself and I will get home the same way. You—" she pointed at Cole "—pay the bill and meet me out front. You—" she pointed at Chad "—introduce me to your friend. I can't stay long, I have work to do, too." She looked at them both. "*Capisce?*"

Quick to please the lady, Chad bowed his head with a

deferential nod. "I've always admired an independent woman," he said.

There was plenty of independent thinking to admire in this sleek redhead. "You go on. I'll be there in a minute. I need to, uh, straighten things out here, you know?"

Was that a wink? She'd wasted enough charm on Meade already, but she had the sucker wrapped around her finger and ready to do her bidding.

"Don't be long," said Chad as he retreated.

Cole tried hard not to compare the playful indulgences she allowed other men to the drop-kick and sharp tongue she used on him. When she spun around, her cheeks were flushed with color, her eyes dancing with concern.

"Do you think we diverted enough attention from A.J.? I tried to make him sound like my acquaintance, not yours. Why the hell are you here in the first place? You're supposed to be with Jericho."

"Whoa. Slow down." Maybe she didn't have everything quite under control, after all. He cupped his hands around Tori's strong shoulders, instinctively offering that same point of contact that seemed to defuse his fears every time he touched her. "Jericho's at the hospital, sleeping off the effects of one of the trial antidotes Dr. Kramer came up with."

Tori frowned. "Without the source of the poison, how can he come up with an effective antidote?"

He pulled her a fraction closer. "Finding that is on my to-do list. But right now your safety is item one. A.J.'s long gone. You covered great. Now let's go."

"Cole—" She splayed her hand across the left side of his chest, stalling his retreat.

It was one of those tentative touches of hers, the real kind that had nothing to do with public appearances and everything to do with twisting him up inside.

"I'm serious about meeting this guy. I know Lukasiewicz's reputation. He'd have the means to fence something like *The Divine Horseman*. He might be able to connect us to Lancelot. I've got to check him out. You'd do it.''

Cole considered her argument. He listened to the pleading in her eyes and the clutch of her fingertips, kneading in their ceaseless rhythm against him. The cop in him knew what the agent in her did. This was a potential lead. If a suspect like Lukasiewicz fell into his lap, he'd be asking questions, too.

But the man in him wouldn't surrender easily. He reached up and covered her hand with his, spreading it flat and holding it over the steady beat of his heart, imparting his warmth, imbuing his reluctant trust. He touched his forehead to hers.

"Five minutes," he whispered. "Any longer than that and I'm coming back in here for you. *Capisce?*"

Her upturned eyes searched his and she smiled. Cole bent down to taste the sweet curve of those lips.

But the smile vanished and she gave his chin a gentle nudge. *"Capisce."*

Maybe he'd imagined the trembling in her fingers, but she gave him no chance to press her on what it was about his kisses that she kept trying to avoid. Spinning around, she grabbed her purse and headed inside to Chad's table.

Cole kept a covert eye on the polite exchange of introductions and conversation at Chad's table while he checked the tab and tossed a couple of bills down by Tori's salad.

The spying waiter hovered in the archway leading onto the terrace. His eyes darted back and forth, settling once on Lukasiewicz, who, with a curt movement of his hand, waved aside the young man's interest without acknowledging him. The kid couldn't be more than nineteen or twenty, and the beads of sweat on his top lip were a dead giveaway that he was nervous about something. His fingers clenched and fidgeted around the tray he held.

Cole looked straight into his dark little eyes.

Something was up.

Without changing his casual posture, Cole's senses went on hyper-alert. The lunch crowd was emptying out and the stream of traffic was thinning, too. He caught snatches of conversations from passersby on the other side of the terrace railing. Business deals, tourist questions, shopping debates. The zesty smells of herbs and olive oils and warm, crusty breads wafted through the restaurant in a tantalizing advertisement for the food cooking in the kitchen. Images snapped by in slow motion. Martín Lukasiewicz shaking Tori's hand. The waiter hugging his empty tray to his chest.

The white truck slowing down as it passed by a third time.

Cole didn't see the driver's face. The only thing that registered was the semiautomatic handgun, extended to an unnatural length by a silencer and pointed out the passenger side window.

"Tori!" Cole was already charging, zigzagging, dodging the pings and splats of flying bullets and shattering debris. "Get down!"

"Gun!" She saw it, too. She shoved Chad to the floor. She flipped the table to create a shield and pushed another woman behind it. Lukasiewicz was already down.

Cole dove, coiled his arms around her and slammed to the floor, twisting his body over hers to shield her from the deadly spray of fire. Ignoring the sharp pain that scorched his left forearm, he palmed the crown of her head and tucked it beneath his chin to ride out the man-made storm.

A window exploded and rained glass across his back and shoulders. Chairs crashed as customers scrambled for shelter. Screams sliced through the air. Horns blared and tires squealed against the pavement.

And then it was done.

The smells of gunpowder and fear hung in the air. After

a beat of silence came the whimpers and foul words and prayers.

Tori stirred beneath him and Cole breathed a sigh of relief. She was alive. "Are you okay?" he whispered into the clean, normal scent of her hair.

She nodded. Her hands clutched at his chest, skimmed his flanks, reached beneath his jacket and swept back and forth. Her quick inspection mimicked the body search from the night before, but with a very different purpose in mind. "You?"

The pain in his arm had receded to a dull throb. "One piece."

"Thank God." She stilled with her arms wound tight around his waist, holding him. She buried her nose in the juncture between his neck and shoulder and clenched handfuls of the back of his shirt.

People were moving now. Good Samaritans from outside rushing in to help, panic-stricken patrons calling for loved ones and checking on strangers.

In those moments, marked by the delicate balance between life and death, Cole held on just as tightly, needing her touch and her caring more than he needed his next breath. "I know, babe. I know."

He'd have kissed her then if he hadn't sensed the immediate shift in her mood. *Babe.* Hell. "I didn't mean—"

"It's all right." She was pushing against him now, withdrawing from the impromptu intimacy of celebrated life and galvanizing into the agent she'd been trained to be. "We'd better figure out what's going on before the cops get here."

Reluctant to leave the reassurance of her warm body, Cole slowly rolled to his side and sat up, pulling Tori up into his lap. Broken glass cascaded off his hair and jacket and pooled around his hips.

She snatched at his arm. "You're hurt."

Cole shook his head at the irony of dodging a hail of tiny

bullets yet landing in someone's lunch. He plucked two long, stringy noodles from his sleeve. "It's just spaghetti."

But the skin around her lips was pinched and pale, and her cheeks were splotched with color. Seeing, hearing—feeling—her compassion for his perceived pain touched something inside him so unfamiliar that he felt like a recluse rediscovering his own humanity. He brushed a strand of hair from her eyes and let his fingers rest against the soft warmth of her cheek. It had been so long since he'd been this close to anybody who gave a damn about him. So long since he gave a damn about anything beyond bringing down the Meades.

"I'm fine."

"Really?"

"Really."

It was a silly little turn of phrase. A husky question. A deep response. And Tori breathed easier. His word. She believed in his word.

Cole found that belief in him every bit as irresistible as the creamy velvet of her skin.

But the shadows in her eyes scuttled out of sight and a new energy possessed her. The tender moments passed as if they had never happened and Cole resigned himself to the reality at hand.

"Then we'd better get to work." She braced her hands against his shoulders. "White truck?" she asked.

"White truck," he confirmed. Smart lady didn't miss a trick.

"We have to help these people." When she curled her legs beneath her to stand, he gripped her waist and gave her a gentle push to her feet. She was out on the terrace by the time he shook the dusting of debris off his coat and rose to follow her.

The rest of the world intruded back on theirs. Cole followed her outside and took the opposite point, scanning up and down the street for the truck, its escape route and any collateral damage. "Looks like the shooting was confined to the restaurant itself." He pulled back the front of his jacket and splayed his hands on his hips. Cole narrowed his gaze on her pretty secret agent face. "That means the target was someone inside. Chad? Lukasiewicz? You?"

Tori was looking just as hard at him. "Better put yourself on that list, big guy. Informers make enemies too."

She crunched through a carpet of shattered flowerpots and plates to pick up her purse and retrieve her cell phone. "I'm calling it in. Looks like he turned up Broadway. He'll dump that truck in someone's driveway or St. Luke's parking garage before the squad cars get here to take a description."

Three quick steps and Cole was at her side. He grabbed her hand and pulled the phone from her ear. "Don't sound too official," he reminded her.

She understood the warning to maintain her undercover persona. She nodded toward his chest and dropped her gaze to his right ankle. "You'd better lose your guns or get out of here."

"You're advising me to leave the scene of a crime, Agent Westin?" he teased.

Tori shushed him and inclined her head toward the restaurant's interior. "Chad already has. Go on. I can take care of this."

"That son of a—" Cole surveyed the scene. Martín Lukasiewicz was helping the woman who'd been hiding behind the table with him into a chair. But there was no sign of Chad. Every instinct told him to go after the guy and shake a few truths out of him. But whether she liked it or not, Tori had just earned his full services as her personal bodyguard. "I'm not going anywhere without you. I'll handle KCPD when they get here."

Cole's suspicions revved into overdrive as he headed inside. Chad made no secret that he saw Cole as a rival for his uncle's inheritance. But a chance meeting allowed him no time to set up a hit. Only Aaron Polakis and Jericho had known he was heading for the Plaza. Jericho didn't want him dead. But where did Aaron's loyalties lie?

Maybe Daniel Meade's killer wanted to stop Cole's investigation.

Maybe the thief who'd stolen *The Divine Horseman* wanted to stop Tori's search.

Maybe men like Chad Meade and Martín Lukasiewicz and Cole Taylor had too many enemies to keep track of.

Too many questions. Not enough answers.

He intended to find some. "Mr. Lukasiewicz." He startled the short man, who turned around and pushed his glasses up on his nose to see who'd addressed him. "I'm Cole Taylor. I work for the Meade family. Do you have any idea where Chad went?"

The older man squinted through his tiny specs and looked around. His expression seemed more confused than surprised. "No. I didn't know he was missing." His thick accent told Cole he was as European as his name. "Do you s'pose he's all right?"

"I'm sure Chad can take care of himself. Tell me, did he invite you to lunch, or did you bring him here?"

Those dark eyes seemed to hold more intelligence than the short man wanted to reveal. "He came to my gallery to ask about an arrangement I had made with his cousin Daniel. The meeting ran long and he suggested we come here to continue our discussion."

"Chad invited you here?" he repeated. Lukasiewicz nodded. If Chad had set up the hit, why would he knowingly put himself in the line of fire?

"What was your arrangement with Daniel?"

"That is a personal matter," he insisted.

"But you told Chad?"

"I only said he asked."

"How do you know the waiter here?"

He'd hoped changing the topic so abruptly would surprise an answer out of him. But there was nothing old, nothing confused, in the dark, beady-eyed glare Lukasiewicz gave him. And there was no answer he would give. Lukasiewicz pointed across the room.

"Your girlfriend is looking for you, Mr. Taylor."

Cole's aching arm grew heavier by the moment, keeping pace with his frustration. Maybe he'd cracked a bone when he'd hit the floor with Tori.

He spotted her kneeling beside the supine figure of the next man on his list to question. Cole dashed over and crouched down beside the young waiter. "Aw, no." She had two fingers pressed against the kid's neck, but he could tell she wasn't finding any pulse. "Damn."

Another dead body. Another notch carved out of his soul.

Lying in repose like this, the kid looked like he wasn't even out of high school yet. Cole made a quick inspection without moving the body. "Looks like he took a couple right in the chest. He never stood a chance. He's too damn young to be mixed up in this."

Tori sat back on her haunches, her eyes shiny with unshed tears. "But he knew the driver. He made eye contact with him both times I saw him drive by. Like he was waiting for a signal. Or giving one."

"He knew your friend Lukasiewicz, too." He glanced over his shoulder to find the small man had vanished, just like Chad. "I see he's not hanging around to grieve over the loss."

"The dispatcher said units and ambulances are en route. They took several calls." She wiped her eyes and blinked away any sign of tears. "I called A.J., too. He'll try to take lead on the investigation so he can smooth things over for you."

Cole unbuttoned his suit coat and started to shrug out of

it. Even if he was somehow responsible, the kid deserved better than dying with that frozen look of terror on his face. "If I didn't know better, I'd think you were trying to take care of me."

"I don't do relationships, Cole. Not for real." Even though she'd already revealed temper, passion, sorrow and something extraordinarily tender, she was determined to deny her emotions. "However, I do need you to stick around until I get the job done."

"What if a relationship happens anyway?" he challenged, draping his jacket over the corpse's face and chest. He knew he wasn't in any position to offer her anything she could count on, but he was damned if he was going to be the only one succumbing to this crazy chemistry between them.

"Cole!" Tori jumped to her feet, circled the body and kneeled down beside him. She took him by the hand and elbow and cradled his forearm across her knee. "That isn't spaghetti sauce on your arm." She unbuttoned his cuff and gingerly pulled the white cloth and its spreading crimson stain away from the sticky gash that bisected his skin. She picked up the sleeve of his coat and jabbed her finger into the two tiny holes—entrance and exit—he'd failed to notice. Her eyes were green and wide and full of those denied emotions when she lifted her gaze to his. "You've been shot."

"That would explain the burning sensation."

Neither of them laughed.

It was just a graze, something easily fixed with a pressure bandage and some antibiotics. But an inch one way would have shattered his arm. An inch the other way and Tori might be dead.

It had been a close call.

They seemed to be getting closer every day.

Chapter Nine

"And there's nothing else you can tell us about the shooter in the white truck?"

A. J. Rodriguez looked like a completely different man in a pair of faded jeans, thought Tori. He'd been every inch the well-dressed sophisticate when she'd met him for lunch. But with his muscle-hugging T-shirt and the twin-rigged holster he wore on each hip, he looked like unfiltered, streetwise danger. The only visible assurance that he was one of the good guys was the brass-and-nickel-plated badge clipped to his belt.

Cole rolled up his right sleeve to match the length of the left one, which had been cut off by the E.R. nurse in order to clean up the wound and tape on a bandage. "Like I said, he seemed familiar. But beyond the shaggy brown hair and Caucasian skin, I can't give you a better description."

A.J.'s partner, Detective Josh Taylor, paced the confines of the small hospital room, poking about the jars of cotton and alcohol swabs, and squeezing the bulb of the blood pressure monitor. "You sure you weren't the intended target, bro?"

Even before introductions, Tori would have guessed Cole and Josh were brothers. They were both big men with muscular builds. They shared the same chiseled jaw and deep blue eyes. Cole's were a shade darker and his hair much longer, but as he stood up from the exam table and faced Josh, she was struck by the notion that they were the blond and brunette version of the same man.

She was also struck by the cautious distance Cole seemed determined to keep from his brother. All of their exchanges regarding the shooting had been businesslike and impersonal.

"I know you're looking for a pattern with the attacks on Ma and Dad and Alex," Cole said. "You said there was a truck spotted at all three scenes. That's where I'd focus your investigation. Find the damn truck."

"We're working on it, believe me." Josh shoved his fingers through his hair, leaving short, blond spikes in their wake. "But you gotta have an idea of who's behind this."

"You want the long list or the short one?"

Josh grinned. "I want the one that says, 'Here's the guy—go get him.'" He shrugged and his boyish expression became deadly serious. "But I'll settle for knowing that you're not into something you can't get out of. I have a wife and baby now, Cole. I'd like to know your trouble isn't going to spill over and hurt them, too."

Cole's expression was equally grim. "I wish I could guarantee that. Believe me, I'm trying to wrap this deal up as quickly as I can, and keep it as far away from our family as possible."

His blue eyes deadened with so much regret that Tori wanted to go to him and comfort him. But this seemed to be a family moment, and she had little wisdom to guide her in that sphere.

"I never wanted what I do to hurt any of you," he said.

Josh walked over to his brother and did what she could not. He extended his broad hand and waited until Cole matched the gesture. With Cole's equally large hand grasping his, Josh tugged and pulled his big brother in for a bear hug. The embrace was brief—backs were slapped, shoulders were squeezed—and then they were pulling away.

"We'll secure the home front. You just get the bad guys and come home." A wide grin creased Josh's face even as he pointed an accusing finger at his big brother. "In one piece, mind you, or Ma will have your hide."

Cole threw up his hands in mock surrender. "I'll do what I can."

"What else do you need from us?" asked A.J., ending the mini-reunion and interview.

"Keep me posted with whatever you get on the shooter. I want to know if those slugs are European and if they match the bullets from the Kramer clinic shooting. I'll try to find things out on my end." To Tori's surprise, he turned to where she sat on a stool in the corner. "What about you? Need anything from these bozos?"

Grateful to be included as an equal, not mollycoddled like a damsel in distress or overlooked as inconsequential, Tori stood and joined the three men at the exam table. "Anything you can find out about Martín Lukasiewicz. His visa status, country of birth. The last time he traveled to Europe or New Orleans."

"You think he has something to do with your *Horseman?*"

Tori nodded. "He has something to do with Daniel. I think figuring out what Daniel Meade was up to before his disappearance will go a long way toward clearing up both our problems."

Cole grabbed his coat from the end of the table and turned to the detectives. "Info on Lukasiewicz, then. I'll keep you posted on anything I find out from my end."

"Do that." A.J. offered Cole a salute, then smiled at Tori. "Until our next meeting."

Josh winked and shook her hand. "Pleasure to meet you, Victoria." He dropped his voice to a conspiratorial whisper.

"Keep your eye on this one—he's always been the troublemaker in the family."

"Liar." Cole swatted Josh's hand away and laced her fingers with his own. "How many times did I bail you out, growing up?"

"Me?"

The two traded stories, and Tori couldn't help smiling at the teasing give and take between siblings. After her father's death, she'd grown up in such a lonely world. Maybe Cole didn't even realize he'd kept hold of her hand, but she did. It was at once daunting and fascinating to see the closeness within the Taylor family, and to feel like—for those few minutes in that tiny hospital room—she was a welcome part of it.

There was a palpable sigh in the air when A.J. interrupted to remind them it was time to part company. Cole grabbed his coat from the top of the exam table and pulled her toward the door with him. "Congrats on your promotion to detective, Josh. I see you're trying to take my place."

"Just makin' my own, bro." Josh grinned. It was easy to see who the charmer of the family was. "Just makin' my own."

A few minutes later, Tori and Cole were climbing into her Cadillac in the hospital parking lot. The mood had tangibly shifted into something darker and more cautionary since Josh and A.J. had departed in Josh's big red pickup.

Like her, Cole had scanned every inch of the lot as they walked along. He'd even dropped down to the pavement to check beneath her car before allowing her to unlock it.

Cole wasn't smiling anymore. As she settled behind the wheel and started the engine and air-conditioning, she wasn't smiling, either. She was starting to think of Cole Taylor more and more in a personal way, getting caught up in his family and injuries and guilt, requiring that she concentrate very hard to keep things professional between them.

He turned and tossed his jacket into the back, then stayed in that same position, facing her across the front seat. "I have something to tell you."

She kept her hands on the wheel, but angled her face to his. "That you're still a cop?"

He shook his head at her astute guess, though his amused grin never reached his eyes. "What gave me away?"

"Beyond the fact that you keep trying to rescue me and are working overtime to keep me away from the 'bad guys,' neither Josh nor A.J. questioned you once about your guns, asked to see your permit to carry, or treated you like a suspect despite your well-known ties to organized crime." She released her grip and sat back in her seat, clenching her fingers together in her lap. "Now either they're incompetent or on the take—which I doubt on both counts—or they know you're a good guy."

"Good guy?" Cole swore, one choice, pithy word. But his anger quickly dissipated. He stared at the windshield, but she had a feeling he wasn't seeing anything outside. "Technically, I still have the right to wear a KCPD badge. But after everything I've seen and done, I don't feel much like a hero anymore."

"A.J. used to be your partner, right?"

His nod was slow, his focus distant. "When I made detective, I was assigned to him. He doesn't say much, but I learned a lot about reading people and making them believe what you want them to from him. We ran a lot of successful undercover ops together."

Tori rubbed her fingers inside her palms, waiting for him to continue.

"A couple of years ago I was recruited by Dwight Powers, one of the assistant district attorneys, to infiltrate the Meade organization and bring it down from the inside. Powers is sure Meade ordered the hit that killed his wife and baby son.''

Her fingers stilled at the horrific image. She turned in her seat. "Oh my God. Have you found proof?''

Cole shrugged. "I found a trail of circumstantial evidence, but no smoking gun. I should have gotten out months ago. But there was so much more I could do. And then Jericho lost his son. He was so lost. He needed me. He became—''

"—your family?''

"Pretty sad, huh?''

Her hands were tight fists now, evidence that she was subconsciously battling the emotions churning inside her. "Two years is a long time to deny yourself contact with the people you love. It's natural to look for a substitute. It's human nature to want to feel important to someone else.''

He wasn't giving himself a break. "Not that it's mine to keep, but I am offered as much spending money a month working for Jericho as I made walking a beat a whole year as a cop. You don't see me walking away from that.''

"Cole, I come from plenty of money. That's not why you do the job. I can't believe that's why you do the job either.''

She drummed her fingers against her thigh. The movement seemed to distract him, and he turned his focus back to her. He braced his left leg up on the seat and gradually angled himself in her direction.

"I've killed people. I've lied. I've altered crime scenes and listened to Jericho confess things that'll buy him a lethal injection.''

Tori mirrored his position and pressed a fist against her bent knee. "Why did you take the assignment in the first place?''

A long silence passed as he dragged his gaze from her fist up the length of her body. When those dark-blue eyes met hers, they were almost pleading. "Some days I can't remember."

Her heart twisted with compassion. She leaned forward and urged him, "Remember now."

He laid his hand over her undulating fist and stilled its movement. When she tried to pull away, he tightened his grip. "You asked."

He challenged her to share, just as she'd challenged him to do so. His hand was warm and slightly calloused around hers. It was bigger and more tanned and shaking just enough to let her know his need for human contact with her was real.

Tori turned her hand palm-up to meet his and the trembling stopped. He scooted a few inches closer and pulled her hand over to his knee. He draped his left arm across the back of the seat and reached out to brush her cheek. It was a tickle of sensation that heated her cheeks. His eyes flickered as they studied her reaction to his gentle, sensual touch.

"Meade's people were moving drugs into the neighborhood where I grew up. Hell, they were moving them all over the city. A few innocent people took a stand against it and got beat up or terrorized for their trouble. Dwight Powers took a stand. He had Jericho nailed on some lesser charges—illegal property sales, witness intimidation. One of Jericho's lawyers got the charges thrown out on technicalities."

His right thumb was stroking the inside of her palm now, creating shivers of heat that skittered through her body from cheek to palm, waking dormant responses along the physical and emotional planes in between.

"But Dwight kept coming. Daniel Meade was never meticulous about keeping records or shy about making public threats. Dwight had him pinned and was set to prosecute, when the accident happened."

Tori's hand flinched within his. "Accident?"

"Jericho hired someone to blow up his wife's car with her and the baby inside."

"Oh God." Sensual sparks short-circuited and something deeper, more urgent took their place. She knit her fingers together with his and held on tight.

"It was an eye for an eye thing, according to Jericho. You hurt what I love, I hurt what you love." Cole abruptly pulled his hands away and cursed royally, thoroughly, rudely. "A man like that has to be stopped."

Tori slid closer, reaching for him. "We'll stop him."

Cole jerked his arm from her tentative grasp, shaking his head. "No. Too many people have been hurt." Moisture glistened in his eyes. A vein throbbed along his clenched jaw. "Now my family's being hurt. It never ends. I'm caught up in it and I can't get out. Jericho's dying and all the answers are going to die with him. And Chad or Paulie or somebody else will keep right on poisoning my city and hurting—"

"Cole." She rose up on her knees beside him and shushed him with two fingers pressed against his lips. She searched deep into those blue eyes until she was sure he was seeing her, hearing her. "You took a stand, just like Dwight Powers, two years ago, when you said you'd do this thing. That courier who was killed believed in you. A.J. believes in you. It sounds as if Josh and your family believe in you." Her cool fingers slipped to frame his jaw and absorb the heat of his skin. "You have to believe in yourself and what you're doing. You have to believe you're making a difference."

She had sunk so far into the pain in his eyes that she didn't see his hands snake out to pull her into his lap. There was only the shock of strong hands at her waist, sturdy thighs beneath her bottom, hard chest beneath the brace of her palms. She pushed to free herself from the enveloping crush of his embrace.

"Cole."

"Stay." It was a token struggle that he coaxed away with the gentle kneading of his fingers at her nape and in her hair, and the honest hunger shining in his eyes. "Please."

As his fierce grip gentled, Tori let her fingers start their own massage, smoothing the wrinkled oxford cloth and loosened silk tie against his chest, stroking the warm leather strap of his holster across his shoulders. For several moments all they did was touch and comfort, give and find sanctuary.

Tori became aware of that most masculine part of him pressing against her bottom. She was just as aware of her tiny breasts filling with pressurized heat and springing to attention.

He leaned forward and rubbed his forehead against hers, pulling loose the curling fringe of his dark hair and tangling it with hers. "The good things in life seem so far removed from where I am now. What if I never find my way back?"

"You will." Her voice came out as an embarrassingly husky whisper.

"I guess we both have secrets to keep. And demons to deal with."

Demons. Her mother's criticisms and Ian's taunts came back to haunt her. Tori pulled away and averted her face. But Cole brushed his fingers beneath her chin and tilted her face up so that she looked deep into his eyes. There was something infinitely warmer there now, something almost awestruck and hopeful.

"For a woman who doesn't do relationships, you sure make me feel like there's one happening here."

"I'm someone who can understand your situation, that's all." Tori's tongue darted out to lick her parched lips. Cole's breath caught at the tiny movement. His instant excitement rattled her own self-preservation instincts. "I'm just not any good at them. Not in the long haul. Don't invest your time and energy in me.''

"I already have.'' That sinfully deep, soft voice whispered past all her insecurities. "There's no camera, no audience here. I'm going to kiss you because I need to. I want to.'' He moved imperceptibly closer.

Caught in the spell of that voice, she was powerless to move away.

"And if you feel anything at all, I wouldn't object if you kissed me back.''

"Cole—'' He covered her mouth in a kiss so gentle, so tender, she ached at the softness of it.

Her lips parted slightly beneath his as his fingers tunneled into her hair to hold her against the sweet seduction of his mouth. Fiery frissons of tantalizing heat melted their way deep inside, building in strength around her heart and creeping outward through every nerve and pore.

Oh hell. Resistance faded beneath the need that surged within her.

Tori moved her lips against Cole's and the world shrank down to just the two of them. Man and woman. Loved and lover. Spark and flame.

He tilted her head and angled his mouth over hers, plunging his tongue inside and stoking the rising fire. Tori latched her arms around his neck and held on as his thighs rocked beneath hers, sliding her right up against his own blazing tinder. Their tongues teased and twined in a seductive dance that took them ever closer to the fire.

But it wasn't enough. Tori raked her hands into the silky cascade of his hair. She worked the band loose and sifted her fingers through its curling length, then gathered up fistfuls of it and traced the fine shape of his head, only to let the hair filter through her grasp and tease her sensitive skin all over again.

Cole skimmed his hands down her back, squeezed her

bottom, then let them skid upward again, sliding beneath her blouse to sear the bare skin along her spine. There were moans and praises, whispers and delights. Tori dipped her fingers beneath his collar, stroking the strong column of his neck. The texture of his skin, the warmth of his pulse tempted her lips to follow the same path. She touched her tongue to the vein that throbbed with the rapid beat of his heart and tasted the tang of his skin intensified by passion.

Something deeply buried and long-denied throbbed to life inside her feminine core.

"Tori." He whispered her name in that mesmerizing voice and kissed her chin. "Tori." He called to her again, brushing his lips across her jaw. "Tori." He pressed his lips to the hollow at the base of her throat, and she arched in response as a brand-new flame was kindled within her.

Cole. She tried to utter his name but couldn't speak. His hand had closed over one breast, catching the pebbled peak in the crease of his palm. He squeezed, and she jerked at the bolt of fire that shot straight to her budding heat.

"Cole." It was more breath than sound, but he gave what her needy plea had asked for. His fingers moved to the buttons of her blouse. He unhooked each one, pushed the material aside and pressed his lips to the skin underneath.

He had her undone now, the material swept off her shoulders to expose the lacy shield of her bra. The thing was more for propriety than support, a small scrap of elastic and padding. She shuddered a moment in a self-conscious flashback to every flaw that Ian Davies and her mother had so matter-of-factly pointed out.

"You're beautiful." Cole dipped his tongue to the indentation that passed for cleavage. "So responsive. So beautiful."

Those words in that voice were her undoing. When he closed his mouth over the straining bud, she bucked against the moist heat. She tipped her head back and let the molten fire rise within.

She dug her fingers into his shoulders and squeezed her thighs together. He rubbed himself against her hip, seeking the same release.

"Oh, yeah," he whispered against her skin. "Just like—"

A high-pitched chirp echoed inside the car, jarring Tori from her feverish stupor. Her eyes snapped open as a second chirp jolted her back to reality.

Cole swore. He raised his head and kissed her on the mouth. "Stay with me, baby."

"Baby?" It wasn't the endearment so much as the command that chilled Tori and withered the unsatisfied needs inside her.

"I wanted to call you something personal."

The phone chirped again and Cole cursed the interruption.

What the hell was she doing? Making love in a parked car in the middle of the afternoon. With Cole Taylor. Virile stud for hire with the delicious voice and the bad attitude.

And she was Victoria Westin.

Not Agent Westin, playing a part. Not Professor Westin, interested only in scholarly pursuits.

Victoria. Of the small chest and the bad choices and the inability to satisfy a man in bed.

She should have been blushing madly, her humiliation was so complete. But there didn't seem to be any heat left inside her. As the phone chirped again, she plucked it from Cole's belt and pressed it into his hand, pushing herself off his lap in the same jerky motion.

"Victoria?" He swiped his hair off his forehead and dropped his jaw to take a deep, steadying breath. "Victoria," he demanded.

She couldn't bring herself to look at the questions in those intense blue eyes. "Answer the damn phone."

With a snap of his wrist that nearly broke the phone in two, he flipped it open and put it up to his ear. "Taylor."

His side of the conversation was terse and strained. It was Jericho, she quickly figured out, going on about something. The shooting, she guessed.

But the call took long enough for her to rebutton her blouse and pinch some color back into her cheeks. She was trying to smooth the nearly-had-sex look out of her hair when Cole disconnected the call.

"He's called a meeting back at the house." He didn't elaborate on the meeting's purpose, but she could guess. "I have to go."

Tori nodded and buckled herself in. She needed the support to hold herself upright as much as she needed it for safety. "I suppose he wants retribution against whoever shot his golden boy."

"I won't let him hurt anyone. I'll convince him he can't waste his energy on anything but Daniel right now."

Tori released the brake and shifted the car into gear. "Jericho might not be the only one you have to convince. Chad got shot at too. He might not be so willing to listen to reason."

Cole leaned back against the seat and buckled in. "I don't want to talk about this right now."

She was fine with silence. She drove out of the parking lot and merged with the traffic heading south toward the eternal gloom of the Meade estate.

Tori felt him look her way, but concentrated on her driving instead of facing him. His answering sigh matched her own dark thoughts.

"For a few minutes there, I felt normal," he said. "Being with you is as real as my world's gotten for two years."

Real? Those few minutes in Cole's embrace had been

pure fantasy for her—a wonderful, guilty pleasure that shouldn't repeat itself. She shouldn't care that he hurt, she shouldn't set herself up for failing him—or her mission.

When she didn't answer, he continued. "I'm not going to apologize for kissing you."

"You shouldn't." At least she could be honest with him. "You weren't in it alone."

That small concession seemed to take the edge off his foul mood. He searched the seat for the band she'd discarded and combed his hair back into its tightly controlled style. "You'll keep my secret, I trust, Agent Westin?"

She turned onto Highway 71 and headed south. "Just like I know you'll keep mine, Detective Taylor."

"When we get back to the house, I'll turn off the cameras and let you search a few of the rooms."

That surprised her. At last, she dared a glance at his handsome face and found him watching her. She mustered a weak smile. "Thanks."

It was what she'd wanted from the start, wasn't it? As close to free rein of the estate as she could get?

But it was small consolation for turning her life and her heart upside down.

BREAKING INTO JERICHO'S office was a piece of cake the second time around. True to his word, Cole had taken her into his office, shown her the bank of television monitors and turned all of them off. Since the guard had been sent outside to patrol the grounds, there was no one around to turn them back on.

Cole had excused himself for a quick shower and fresh change of clothes, and by the time he was done, Jericho had convened the meeting in the living room, where everyone could be comfortably seated. Chad, Lana, Paulie, Aaron, Jericho and Cole were all there to discuss the shooting, and she hadn't been invited.

Tori had already gone through several of the rooms upstairs and come up empty. As long as she didn't make enough noise to activate the listening devices, she could explore to her heart's content until dinnertime.

If she should happen to stumble upon the statue itself, great. She'd wrap it up, sneak out of the house and never look back on any of these people again. But Tori wasn't holding her breath. A wiser plan was to search for Jericho's keys to the catacombs or any kind of hidden file or computer disk that might show where the missing items from Jericho's collection were stored.

Remembering Cole's warning to steer clear of the safe and Jericho's computer, she locked the door behind her and made a beeline for the bookshelves.

Though the June evening should be casting natural light through the windows, the sky overhead was heavy with rain, blotting out the sun and coating the air outside with a fine, pervasive mist. Tori relied on her penlight to dispel the shadows and illuminate the display of lacquer boxes on the shelves.

Before opening the first box, she took a deep breath and turned her head to acknowledge the portrait of Daniel and Jericho, who seemed to be looking over her shoulder like constant, silent guardians. Only, there was nothing benevolent in those unblinking, blue-eyed stares. It was as if someone was in the room with her, lurking in the shadows. Watching. Spying. Lying in wait.

Get a grip. Tori shook off the crawly sensation and chided herself. She'd thrived on fairy tales as wicked as the Grimms' and as sweet as Andersen's as a child. But since her father's death, since surviving her mother's guidance, since distancing herself from her grandfather and training with the Bureau, she'd become a very practical person. She didn't believe in ghosts, she didn't believe in fairy tales, she didn't believe in knights in shining armor.

Of course, there was one blue knight who seemed to tangle up fantasy and reality inside her head.

Tori gripped the shelf and squeezed her eyes shut as a wave of remembered longing swept through her body. She could feel Cole's pain again. She could imagine his touch against her breasts and mouth. She could sense her self-preserving distance crumbling into dust as he took her hand and insisted she be a part of his world.

Stop it. Someone was laughing at her, laughing at her fanciful notions and womanly dreams.

"You can't cut it with a man, baby," Ian had told her. *"Not with that skinny-ass body and those wide-eyed dreams."*

"Oh, sweetie. You know doctors can fix your inadequacies now." She distinctly remembered her mother thrusting out her breasts. *"They fixed mine."*

The laughter got mixed up with her pounding pulse and thundered in her ears. She snapped her eyes open and swung the light around to face the painting. Still and lifeless as always.

Tori forced herself to breathe evenly, in through the nose and out through the mouth, gathering her thoughts, sharpening her senses and firmly dismissing anything that couldn't be explained by logic or science or evil intentions.

Someone *was* laughing. A deep, rhythmic, slowly pulsing sound. A man's laugh. She frowned, turning her ear to find its source. Not voices from the hallway. No audible screen saver on the computer screen. She crossed to the window and pulled aside the drape, looking for someone outside. But the rain was falling in sheets now, making visibility for any distance impossible. Static electric lightning blinked high in the clouds and seconds later thunder rolled in the distance.

Thunder.

"Duh."

Tori's breath rushed out. She shook her head at her own foolishness and hurried back to the shelves to continue her search. Thunder. Of course. Low-pitched. Pulsing. Drawn out like a slow, lazy laugh.

What an idiot. *Specially Trained Agent Spooked by Thunder—Mistakes Storm for Someone Spying on Her.* Her supervisor and the two Bills would get a laugh out of that one if they ever found out.

But no one would ever find out her little inadequacies. She'd do her job, and do it well. All she needed were the keys to the catacombs, and she had a hunch everything else would quickly fall into place. Then she could get out of this would-be haunted house and forget about the Meades and Cole Taylor and fanciful notions for good.

Of course, she couldn't really leave Cole without a contact to the outside world. He'd be an undercover cop without any backup. A sitting duck. But there was A.J. Maybe he could be talked into helping out.

Tori shook her head. She needed to focus on the job. *Her* job.

She spent a few minutes looking through several of the boxes. Most were empty, some held folded-up notes—like an old, well-preserved love letter from Jericho's wife. She smiled at the murderer's sentimental streak and gently replaced the letter. One box was filled with pieces of broken toys—a decapitated head from a World War I iron army figure, a metal car with no wheels, beads and a string, a small wooden dagger, warped and split with age.

Keys.

Tori smiled at her success, the only outward show of charged adrenaline she'd allow herself. The keys weren't bunched together on a ring, but lay scattered throughout the box. Some were shiny, others tarnished with age. She picked out all six and stuffed them into the pocket of her black slacks. Mission accomplished.

Maybe it was a symptom of old age, she thought. Collecting things. Revisiting fond memories, preserving the past. Jericho had certainly been obsessively protective of that blue lacquer box with the silver scrollwork. Even though she'd found enough keys to unlock several doors, curiosity and a nagging instinct that there was more to find made her reach for that blue box.

Propping her penlight between her lips, she pulled the box down from its eye-level shelf. Its rectangular shape fit neatly within the span of her hand. Hearing the thunder outside like a drumroll of anticipation now, she slowly lifted the lid and peeked inside.

"Oh God!"

She dropped the box, the lid, the light, and the stiff, desiccated stump of a man's finger to the carpet and jumped back.

A split second later she realized she'd screamed out loud, clearly announcing her unauthorized presence in the room. She slapped her hand over her mouth, but it was too late.

She could hear the shuffle of furniture, doors creaking open and snapping shut, the bustle of footsteps crossing marble flooring and wood and carpet.

Tori wasted no time cursing her luck. She quickly squatted down, swallowed her revulsion and picked up the mummified appendage by the silver signet ring wedged at its base, and dropped it back into the box. She grabbed her light and the lid and replaced everything on the shelf.

As she scanned the room for the best place to hide, she heard footsteps in the hallway, raised voices and shouts. And footsteps behind her.

Behind her?

She whirled around. The wall beside the bookshelf was sliding open.

Tori bent her knees and raised her fists to defend herself.

"Get in here. Now."

Cole didn't even give her time for a startled yelp. He grabbed her fist and pulled her inside the dark, narrow passageway beside him.

"Lose the light."

Tori turned it off and poked it into her pocket while he pushed the panel door closed with a scrape of metal against wood. The panel clicked shut, plunging them into utter darkness, just as a key turned in the lock outside Jericho's door.

"Let's go," Cole whispered, his fingers butting against her shoulders and trailing down to find her hand in the dark.

But she dug in her feet when he pulled. "No. I could hear you in here. If we move, they'll—"

Cole's large hand clamped over her mouth, making the passageway as silent as it was dark. He pulled her back against the wall of his chest and wrapped a restraining arm around her waist, holding her still as the outside door opened and Jericho and company came in.

"I swear to God, it came from in here." That was Paulie, moving around the room, judging by the changing volume of his voice. "It was a woman's voice."

"Where's your artsy-fartsy friend?" Lana's condescending question came from the doorway. "She wasn't at the meeting. We should account for her."

"I'll go check her room." That was Aaron Polakis, his voice fading as he hurried to do her bidding.

Tori inhaled a startled breath, feeling the threat as if she'd already been caught. Cole's chest swelled with a deep breath behind her, reminding her she wasn't alone and she hadn't been caught.

Yet.

Lost in the blackness with nothing but touch to guide her, Tori turned in Cole's arms, seeking the anchor of his solid warmth. His arms tightened and held her close against the even rise and fall of his chest. He cradled the back of her head and tucked her snugly beneath his chin. Tori wrapped her fingers around the nubby texture of his lapels and nestled her forehead against the warmth emanating from the freshly showered skin at his neck. The clean scents of crisp cotton, wool and man replaced the dusty dampness that teased her nose.

They held each other in the dark and waited.

"Taylor left early too." Paulie again. "You don't suppose the two of them are gettin' it on somewhere, do you? Maybe that's why she screamed."

She could hear Lana's cringing sigh through the wall. "That's disgusting."

"They can go after each other like rabbits for all I care. We were talking about me and the danger I'm in." Chad had to have his say. "Taylor's not the only man I've seen her with. She comes off like money and class, but she'll go after anything in a pair of pants. You saw her with me this morning. If she's not doing Taylor right now, you'd better find out where the guards are."

Tori curled into herself at the insults, her stomach twisting in knots. Chad was calling her a tramp? If only he knew how sexless and inexperienced she was when it came to men. She should be laughing. But it hurt. It felt like a mockery, a reminder of all she could never be.

Cole's hands tightened with an almost painful convulsion around her. She felt the moist heat of his mouth at her temple, his breath stirring her hair.

"What are you talking about?" Lana seemed more concerned about Tori's social life than any threat to her engagement. "What men did Miss Westin see? When?"

"All of you, get out. Get out!" Jericho shouted, right on the other side of the wall. Tori and Cole both started, but clung to each other and kept still. A fit of chest-deep coughing seized him. Someone tried to help, but he pushed them away. "Leave me alone. I will not tolerate these games in here!"

"Jericho, here." That was Lana.

"I don't want the stupid mint!" Something tiny smacked against the wall, and Tori jumped. "Go away!"

Paulie ushered everyone out. "Let's get out of here. Give him some peace." There was a long pause before he spoke again. Chad and Lana must have left the room. "You need anything, Jer?"

Though his breathing was a labored wheeze, Jericho sounded a tad calmer. "Time alone with Daniel."

"He's dead, Jericho." There was a sharp, impatient edge to Paulie's normally jovial tone. "He isn't worth this agony. Daniel was trouble when he was alive. And he's still trouble. Let him go, and live out your days in peace."

Tori heard the *clink* of a jar and a scraping sound. An instant smell of sulfur stung her nose and she turned her face into Cole's chest to stifle the urge to sneeze. There was the creak of a chair and the beeping tone of the computer being turned on.

Tori held her breath until the standoff outside ended.

Jericho Meade, sounding like the terror he must have been in the prime of his life, uttered two words. "Get. Out."

The door closed quietly behind Paulie. Neither Cole nor Tori risked moving until the silence in the outer room ended. She heard a series of clicks. Computer keys? The fruity odor of Jericho's tobacco filtered through the cracks surrounding the passageway door.

He was in there killing himself. A man who couldn't breathe smoking himself to death. The irony of a man of Meade's reputation for violence dying such a slow, pitiful death warred with her sense of justice.

Killing him. Death. "Poison." Tori muttered the word into Cole's coat.

Jericho sucked on those mints for his cough, chewed and

smoked those cigars, and took medicine faithfully delivered several times a day by his old friend Paulie. Any of those would be an easy way to deliver a cumulative poison.

Cole must have sensed the thoughts turning in her head. Perhaps she moved or tensed, because he was suddenly massaging the back of her neck beneath her hair and humming some throaty noise deep in his throat against her ear. Mindful of the danger they still faced if discovered, she sank back into his embrace and let the whisper of his voice soothe her into quiet again.

But they both tensed when Jericho spoke again. "Talk to me, boy."

She heard a mechanical *click* and a low-pitched *buzz* from somewhere inside the passageway itself.

Cole's breath rushed out in a gasp beside her ear, as if he recognized the unfamiliar voice that had only startled her.

"Father. The time has come for you to act upon my word."

Chapter Ten

"Okay. That officially creeped me out."

"You heard the tape go on before it started?" Cole asked, typing in a command on his computer.

"I heard it. That wasn't any ghost talking."

Tori continued to pace the perimeter of his office while Cole rewound tapes from all the camera positions throughout the entire house. He'd come in here and turned them back on, just in time to realize that Tori wasn't in her room. After giving her two undocumented hours to search for her statue, he knew she was either a) in her bathroom taking a shower, or b) about to get herself into trouble somewhere in the house.

He didn't waste much time thinking about choice "a." Appealing as the idea of Tori naked and wet might be, he was counting on trouble. Sure enough, he'd detected her in Jericho's office and had taken the shortcut straight from his office to get her out before the retribution meeting broke up and she was discovered.

Now he was trying to account for everyone at the time Daniel Meade's voice was telling Jericho to name Chad as his heir and to eliminate the man who'd killed him.

Cole Taylor.

"You're sure that was Daniel's voice? Chad wouldn't shed a tear if you were out of the way. He could have dubbed it. I don't think anyone else could convince Jericho to turn against you except his own son." Tori raked her fingers through her hair and shook loose what was left of her ponytail. "Somebody's gone to a lot of effort to make Jericho believe Daniel's ghost is talking to him. I suppose that's what those cards were about—convincing Jericho that Daniel was still roaming the house, meeting up with his latest conquest in the guest room."

The same protective anger that had seized Cole inside that passageway coursed through him anew. "What Chad said about you, about sleeping around—that's bogus."

"I know. He was just making up lies to gain some sympathy. He obviously doesn't know me. Men don't..." She rubbed her hands up and down her arms, chasing away a chill. She never finished the sentence. "He doesn't know me."

Cole wanted to say something more. He wanted to do something to mend that gap in self-confidence that seemed to plague her. But Tori was in business mode now. And the thing she would appreciate most would be him sticking to business.

He went back to queuing up the tapes. "So who do you think wants to discredit me?"

It had been haunting enough to hear his own name uttered on that tape. It didn't surprise him to learn someone wanted him dead. But to know that someone thought he could replace Jericho's son, to know that Jericho valued him, loved him enough to consider naming him heir to his criminal empire—that rocked him to his bones and made his two-year journey over to the darker side of human nature complete.

"Who in this house doesn't, *golden boy?* How many times have I heard you referred to by that name?" Cole had heard it, too. "There are too many obvious suspects. We need to stick to facts to narrow it down. We need to get back inside that passageway with a light and find the electronic device. I think it was something Jericho triggered with a command on the computer.'' She stopped moving for half a second. ''He has a computer file called *Daniel*. We could go in and boot it up and see if it replays the tape.''

Cole pressed his lips together to hide his unexpected smile. He figured he was going to die a young man. If this job didn't kill him, then the tightness in his chest every time he found Tori diving up to her eyeballs into danger would.

''You're not going back inside that office a third time.''

His warning fell on deaf ears. She clutched her arms in front of her as if she was cold, and resumed her pacing. ''Do you know there's a severed finger in that blue box he worships?''

Cole stood. Understandably, she had a lot of nervous energy to work off. The threat of nearly getting caught. Being trapped in the dark. Finding dead body parts...

But he had some energy of his own that needed to find an outlet. In the short time he'd known Victoria Westin, the longest she'd been still, the longest she'd dropped her guard, had been inside that passageway. Seeking him out for comfort and safety, cuddling close as if being with him grounded her somehow.

Or maybe he was the one who'd rediscovered a sense of purpose, a reason to keep fighting and go on living each time he held on to her.

He craved her gentle, almost shy, touches. They seemed intimate—soft and honest—a stark contrast to the evil, take-what-you-want world he'd lived in for too long. He *loved* kissing her. Hell, he would have bedded her in the car if his phone hadn't interrupted them. She'd been hot to the touch, sleek and strong, and so responsive.

He was going crazy with keeping her safe and keeping up with her perceptive ideas, such as those on the poison sources she'd suggested earlier. He was going crazy with needing her, with wondering if she'd ever need him half as much for anything more than her job.

He was just going crazy.

Work, he reminded himself. He needed to concentrate on his work. He picked up the remote and flipped through the black-and-white images on the screen. "I know about the finger. It's Daniel's."

"You could have told me. It was a little disconcerting to find it."

Disconcerting was a polite understatement, judging by the cry he'd heard. No wonder she was still shivering.

"Would you have believed me if I'd told you he'd had it preserved as a souvenir?"

She paused for another few seconds, then positioned herself in front of the monitors beside him. "What are you looking for?"

"Jericho left his office about fifteen, twenty minutes ago, skipped dinner and went to bed. Told Paulie he wasn't feeling well." He pulled up the screen that showed the door to Jericho's bedroom; there was no camera inside. "It took you and me another five minutes to traverse the passage and come out here into my office. So I'm checking what was recorded a little less than half an hour ago."

"You're finding out where everybody else was when that tape was playing."

They watched together. Chad was in his office, on the phone. It wasn't a friendly call, judging by the deep frown across his forehead and his nervous pacing. Paulie had pushed his plate aside and had dealt a hand of solitaire at the dining-room table. Lana and Aaron were...

"I'll be damned," said Cole.

Lana and the butler were going at it, hot and heavy, in the upstairs hallway. His hand was on her thigh beneath her skirt and she had her tongue halfway down his throat. Cole and Tori cringed in unison.

"And Chad called me a slut," she exclaimed.

"Couldn't they at least get a room?"

"Wait a minute." Tori had him replay the scene. "Is that hair on his head?" Lana was running her fingers through Aaron's hair. Make that an off-kilter wig.

"Now that's a bad toupee."

"He actually looks better with his devil horns."

"Devil horns?" He knew there was a story with that one.

She pointed to her own forehead. "You know, receding hairline points. The description fits his personality."

Cole switched the monitors back to live-action shots. Maybe Lana wasn't as heartbroken over Daniel's death as she'd led other members of the household to believe. And her loyalty to Chad was certainly questionable. Perhaps having an affair with the hired help was her way of getting back at the men who cheated on her. It would explain the numerous passes she'd made at him over the past months.

But that picture triggered another, more troubling possibility in his mind. Brown, shaggy hair. A familiar face out of context and unidentifiable. What might Aaron's motive be for trying to kill Chad? Or him? Or Tori?

Tori had resumed her pacing. Her thoughts dragged him away from his own.

"So each of them was *occupied*," she said. "That means the tape was already cued up and ready to play at whatever command Jericho inadvertently gave. Someone's been driving that poor man into thinking his murdered son is haunting him."

"It's something that's been planned for a while." Cole speculated further. "I'd bet good money that was Daniel's voice on the recording."

"Really?"

"Really."

He grinned at the knowledge that that brief interchange was all it took to convince her.

She stopped pacing. "That means Daniel felt threatened by you, too."

"I knew a lot of his secrets."

"But how could a son do this to his father?"

"Daniel had everything he ever wanted from the moment he was born." Cole couldn't help but compare life in Meade Manor to his own poor beginnings, living over his father's butcher shop in the City Market District. But he knew whose life had been richer. "It was never about family to him. It was always about Daniel. And Daniel didn't endear himself to many people. They put up with him because of Jericho."

"Chad did tell me Daniel had ruined several business deals. He feels like he's had to clean up Daniel's mess."

A lot of people had cleaned up after Daniel's impulsive mistakes. Himself included. He could see Daniel coming up with a clever scheme to ensure a massive inheritance. Get rid of the competition. Get rid of his father. "I don't think he could pull off something like this on his own."

"Who? Daniel?"

Cole was piecing random thoughts together now. If he could talk this through with Tori, maybe he could even have it make sense.

"Daniel comes up with this wild idea to have Jericho get rid of me. At the same time, he's poisoning his father, so that once I'm out of the way and Jericho's gone, he can come back and claim his position as head of the family."

She was thinking too. "He'd need an ally to plant the tape, deliver the poison while he's hiding out."

"An ally who could run things while he was gone. Someone who'd benefit from his return."

Tori frowned. "But from what you've said, Daniel

doesn't sound like the kind of man who would cut off his own finger. You did verify that was his?''

"I ran the fingerprint. It's Daniel. And the lab said it came from a corpse."

"So his ally betrayed him. Killed him. Continued the plan for his or her own benefit? If you and Daniel are gone, who would take over for Jericho? Chad thinks he's the man. What about Lana?"

He shook his head. "Jericho would never leave the business to a woman. He's from a different generation, old-fashioned."

"Well, who's left?" Tori shrugged her confusion. "Aaron? He's the butler-slash-thug. He doesn't have the power or the business sense to manage all of Jericho's holdings."

"What if it's not about betrayal?" Cole had another possibility in mind.

She frowned. "You mean his murder's a coincidence?"

"Daniel and his ally may have had this scheme in place, with every intention of reaping the rewards. But if he's hiding out—away from the family's protection—he'd be vulnerable. Someone he cheated or owed money to may have seized the opportunity to help Daniel disappear permanently."

Tori put her hands over her face and rubbed at her eyes. "So we're back to square one. You have to find Daniel Meade's body and prove who murdered him."

Cole sank into his chair and scraped his palm over the scruff of his five o'clock shadow. "Yeah. Square one. Everyone's a suspect. Everyone has a motive."

In a resurgence of boundless energy, Tori sprang toward the door. "I need to get out of this place and go for a run."

Cole shot to his feet and followed her to the door. "You're not going back to that park alone."

"Like this house is any safer."

He braced his hand above her head, just in case she turned the knob. He had a feeling this woman could outrun him if she got a head start. She was still facing the door. Cole resisted the urge to move closer, to align that long, lithe body of hers with his, the way she'd done in the passageway.

But he didn't resist the urge to lean in and inhale that scent she called perfume but his senses called nirvana. "There's a gym you can use out back, if you don't mind getting wet or waiting until the rain lets up. You can run the treadmill there."

"I need the fresh air. It's not just the physical outlet. It clears my head. It makes me feel like I…" She shrugged.

Cole took a guess. "Like you can stay ahead of those demons if you just keep running?"

She turned and pressed her back into the door, forcing as much distance between them as possible. The stunned look on her pale face told him he'd struck a nerve. But when he reached out to touch her, to apologize, she blinked and lifted her chin away from his hand.

"I was just going to say that it's something I'm good at. Running makes me feel like I can do anything."

Cole pulled both hands back but didn't retreat. "Is there something you think you *can't* do?"

That, she wouldn't answer. "Okay. I'll go run the treadmill for half an hour. Then I'm going to bed. I intend to be down in those catacombs bright and early tomorrow morning."

Cole read the determination in those green eyes and matched it.

"Then so do I."

TORI UNWRAPPED THE TOWEL from her damp hair and blotted one last time before hanging it up and reaching for her comb. With her teeth brushed and the shorts and tank top she wore for pajamas on, she figured it was safe to go back into her bedroom and parade before the camera and whoever might be watching.

She stopped in front of the mirror on her dresser to comb her hair back from her forehead and temples. Her stomach rumbled over her decision to skip dinner and run in the gym. But even though she'd worked up an appetite after her workout, memories of all she had seen and survived today made the idea of food register somewhere between unappealing and nauseating.

A murdered young man. Cole being shot. A mummified finger. Cole kissing her. A dead man's voice. Cole holding her close. Cole.

"Ow." The comb snagged in her hair. She freed it from the tangle and massaged the tender spot on her scalp.

She'd gotten too preoccupied with her thoughts and lost track of what she was doing. With a resolute sigh, she worked loose the tangle and started combing again.

The repetitive motion was soothing to her frayed nerves. It calmed her the way Cole's hand rubbing the back of her neck did. It mesmerized her the way that incredible voice of his could lull her past her inhibitions. Low-pitched and even-cadenced, working its magic on her high-strung sensibilities the way a horse whisperer's magic tames a skittish mare. Tori's eyes drifted shut and she could almost hear that sexy voice, soothing her, exciting her. Loving her.

Her eyes popped open at the foolish thought.

"Ian Davies." She said the bastard's name out loud.

It was enough of a reminder to shock her system out of wanting what she didn't need and couldn't keep.

Tori set the comb on the dresser and headed for her bed. She paused as she went past the wardrobe. The door was held shut with nothing more than a skeleton key. What she wouldn't give for a dead bolt or her own Glock handgun tucked beneath her pillow at night.

She settled for propping the desk chair in front of the door. The knob was too high to wedge it tightly, but it would make plenty of noise should any nighttime visitors try to come in that way. She locked the door to the hallway and pulled back the covers.

Another mint rolled out from between her pillows and bounced across the floor. "I told you to keep your candy," she announced to anyone who might be listening.

Of course, there was no answer. She picked it up, but instead of heading for the trash can, she dropped the mint inside her bag. She'd call A.J. tomorrow and ask him to run it through the lab and test it for poison. She needed to get a hold of one of Jericho's cigars and a sample of his prescription meds, too.

If nothing else, she was beginning to sort out *how* the crimes against this family were being committed. It was the *who* that remained the big problem. Everyone was a potential suspect.

Except for Cole.

"Damn."

She'd almost gotten him worked out of her system.

"Ian Davies," she said again. But it seemed impossible to summon his smiling blond image to replace Cole's sterner, darker one.

No wonder her mother despaired over her ever finding a man to love her. She was just too neurotic.

Recalling some of her mother's choicest comments took the edge off her fascination with Cole, and Tori crawled beneath the covers, turned off the lamp and made herself go to sleep.

TORI'S RESTLESS SLUMBER was plagued with nightmarish laughter and images of body parts floating through her subconscious mind. Her mother chased after them, wielding a scalpel.

She got up and splashed water on her face, then filled a glass to set beside her bed in order to get past that vision. After a few sips, she lay down and tried to sleep again.

First, she was cold, with the rain outside dropping the temperature several degrees and the air conditioner still running inside the house. Then she was hot, her dreams erotic images of Cole's long, dark hair caressing her naked body as she reveled in his kiss. Then Cole himself was sliding over her naked body.

She woke herself enough to kick off the covers and hug a pillow tight in her arms, seeking a release her body wanted but her mind refused to pursue.

When the cool air chilled her long legs and bare arms again, she reached for the covers and cocooned herself beneath them once more, sinking into a deep, dreamless abyss that finally gave her peace.

Minutes, or maybe hours, later, she heard a creaking sound. She swatted at it like a fly buzzing her ear, disturbing her rest. The jangle of metal against metal had her squinting her eyes open as she tried to identify the sound and decide whether it was real or part of another nightmare.

She sat bolt upright at the smack of wood against wood.

A split second later, when the chair in front of the armoire crashed and skidded across the floor, she threw off the covers and scrambled to the side of the bed.

But a shadowy figure, blacker than the rain-drenched night around her, leaped from the armoire and charged the bed, shoving her back onto the mattress. Tori pushed up on her feet and elbows and crab-crawled to the far side of the bed. But the man was as quick as he was strong. He snatched her by the ankle and jerked her back across the mattress.

Tori raised her free leg and smashed her heel into the center of his chest. The momentum knocked him back a step, but he didn't let go. As he stumbled, he jerked her leg in its hip socket and dragged her to the floor.

Grunting at the jolt of pain, Tori swung around, trying to knock him off his feet. But suspended by the ankle, she couldn't get the leverage she needed.

When she connected with his shinbone, his muffled curse told her he was wearing a mask. That's why she couldn't see his face. Her attacker was a nameless, faceless brute in black.

He bent over her then and smacked his club-shaped fist into the side of her face. Her whole skull rang with the impact and a circle of stars swirled in the shadows. She squeezed her eyes shut to override the dizziness and block out the pain.

But her disorientation gave her attacker enough time to switch his grip to her arm. He lifted her and tossed her onto the bed. Tori landed on her stomach and tried to crawl. But he flipped her over and climbed on top of her. His hips pinned hers, rendering her kicking legs useless.

His thick, leather-gloved hand closed around her throat. He leaned his weight into her windpipe and cut off her air.

Tori pounded his arms with her fists. She clawed at his hand. She thrashed beneath him. She snatched at his mask. But he was too tall. He tipped back his head and he was beyond her reach.

No! Her throat gurgled as she struggled to make a sound. Her lungs burned as they used up the last of their oxygen.

Tori struck out for anything she could reach. She wouldn't die. She was too tough to die!

She grabbed a pillow, shoved it at his face. He batted it aside.

Her vision was fading, her world creeping toward black. The perpetual gloom of the Meade estate seemed to be rushing in, consuming every part of her. *No!*

She reached out, knocked the lamp from the bedside table. She barely heard the crash through the stuffing that filled her ears. Her lips sputtered. Her eyes closed.

She closed her fingers around a solid cylinder of glass.

Summoning the reserves of strength her training had inspired, Tori swung her arm and smashed the glass into the side of his neck.

Her attacker gave an unearthly screech that rattled the bed and echoed in her brain. He grabbed at the spot with his free hand.

Water ran down her arm along with something warmer.

His death grip loosened. Her chest heaved as it sucked in its first gasp of air. She beat against his wrist and his arm buckled.

She was free!

Free enough. She twisted her hips, rocking straight up between his legs. This time he rolled onto his side, writhing in pain and damning her with every foul name in the book.

Tori pushed his legs off her and tumbled off the side of the bed. Scrambling on her hands and knees she tried to put distance between her and her attacker until she could catch her breath, until she could see.

She was aware of other sounds now. Doors opening and closing. Footsteps running up the stairs. Voices.

"Help," she croaked, her throat raw with pain. She coughed and tried again, managing a whisper. "Help me."

But as oxygen flowed through her body once more, she gathered strength. Help wouldn't come in time. Her attacker was crawling off the side of the bed, tripping over the chair, kicking it aside, holding his neck and crotch and climbing back into the armoire.

Tori pushed to her feet and dashed after him.

"Tori!"

She ignored Cole's voice and the pounding on her door and jumped up into the armoire. She shoved her clothes aside and bolted into the dark corridor, chasing the sound of fading footsteps.

"Dammit, Victoria, you open this door or I'll knock it down!"

Tori stopped short, suddenly swallowed up by the darkness surrounding her, and the dizziness returned. She'd been running on instinct, but intellect was trying to reassert its control. Dust and grit caught beneath her curling toes. She thrust out her hands to find either wall and orient herself.

Her attacker had vanished into the bowels of the hidden corridors and she had no way of knowing whether he was thirty feet or three feet in front of her. She was unarmed, barely dressed, and a little worse for wear following that struggle.

"Go ahead, open it."

"If you're in there, stand back from the door."

She would survive the night and resume her search in the morning. It sounded like a plan.

Tori felt her way around and hurried back toward the wardrobe. "No!" she shouted, raw pain tearing at the lining of her throat. "I'm coming."

She hit the edge of the armoire, jumped down and ran for the door. "I'm coming."

She flipped the lock, and the doorknob turned in her hand. She jumped back a step as the door swung open and Cole swept in. He scooped her up off the floor with one arm around her waist and clutched her tight to his body. His free hand carried a weapon, pointed past her toward the bed.

The light from the hallway flooded in, illuminating the evidence of her fight. Cole angled her away from the center of the room and backed toward the door, carrying her away from the threat of danger. "What the hell happened in here?"

For a few needy moments she wound her arms around his neck and just held on, letting his strength sustain her.

"Tori?" He slid her feet to the floor and rubbed his hand in circles across her back. She heard an uncustomary catch in his voice. "You'd better start talking to me."

Other voices talked instead.

"Is she hurt?"

"How'd he get in?"

"I can't believe this happened in my house."

"Can we get a light in here?"

"I'll go."

Tori didn't know which alarmed her more—the notion that she was clinging to Cole's bare chest and shoulders, or the realization that she was surrounded by a circle of concerned, frightened faces—none of whom she felt comfortable turning her back on.

Latching on to modesty and common sense a little too late, she let go of Cole and stepped away to face those potential enemies. "A man broke in—" she pointed "—through the wardrobe. I fought him off. He tried to kill me."

"He?" Cole questioned.

Tugging the hem of her shirt down past the waistline of her shorts and hugging her arms to give herself at least the semblance of protection, she couldn't help letting her gaze slide to each man in the room. She saw nothing so obvious as anyone wearing a mask or even dressing in black. They'd all been awakened from their sleep and wore robes and pajamas and slippers.

Except for Aaron. She caught her breath when he appeared in the doorway, carrying a large flashlight and his gun. He still wore his black uniform with the white shirt, though the tie was missing and his clothes were wrinkled. Could he have stashed a black stocking mask and gloves somewhere? She tried to remember what else the man had been wearing. But she hadn't been able to grab hold of anything loose like a jacket. Still, she kept staring.

"Can you tell us anything about him? Did he say anything? What did he look like?"

Cole was pressing her for answers, thinking the way a good cop or chief of security would. The way *she* should be thinking.

"He wore black."

Aaron swung his light around and shone it in her face, as if he'd taken her statement as an accusation. Tori squinted and turned her face away from the high beam.

Cole swore. "Dammit, Tori, you're hurt."

Unable to see his intention, she jumped when his fingers touched her throat. Goose bumps radiated out across her skin from the brush of warm heat.

"He tried to strangle you, didn't he. I can see the marks."

Then his fingers were in her hair, gently lifting it aside to frame what must be a bruise or swelling forming on her cheek.

"Son of a bitch," he muttered.

His fingers stroked behind her ear, giving her neck a gentle massage. His touch was remarkably gentle, considering the absolute fury darkening his eyes.

"I'm okay." She wondered if her reassurance could reach him through the layers of guilt he wore like an invisible cloak. She summoned a weak smile. "I think I did more damage to him."

His gaze riveted on that smile before he released her.

"What's that on your hand?" Chad stood across the circle from her, his hands thrust deep into the pockets of his cashmere robe.

Cole seized her wrist and lifted it into Aaron's light. "It's blood."

Odd. Her head ached and her throat burned, but she

couldn't feel any pain in her hand. Pulling away, she flexed her fingers and turned her hand from side to side.

"There's blood on the bed, too." Paulie had moved on into the room to inspect the damage. The snub-nosed revolver he carried was incongruous with the paisley robe he wore over his silk pajamas.

Tori shook her head. "It's not mine."

"Should I alert the guards and have them search the grounds?" Aaron asked, his accent thick with urgency.

Cole nodded. "Do it."

"Wait." Tori caught Aaron at the door.

If she hadn't been cut, then… She grasped his chin and turned it to the side, inspecting the unblemished surface of his beard-roughened skin and receding hairline.

Tori released him and quickly circled the room, openly checking the right side of everyone's face and neck. Chad. Paulie. Jericho. She even brushed aside Lana's hair and checked her for cuts, though Tori knew her attacker had been a man. His size and weight and voice had been a man's. And when she'd racked him between the legs, the goods had been there.

She nodded to Cole to dismiss Aaron.

"You can go," he ordered. Aaron passed the flashlight over to Cole and disappeared. "What is it?" he asked her.

She even took a glimpse at Cole's face. "The blood. It has to be his."

Comprehension dawned. "None of us has injuries."

Tori crossed her arms in front of her and shivered at a very discomforting thought. Facing down an enemy she recognized was one thing. But…

Jericho, his face ashy, his eyes distant, leaned heavily on Lana's arm. "It was Daniel, wasn't it. He came back to hurt you because I haven't done what he asked."

"No, it wasn't Daniel!" She paused and took a deep breath to drain the harshness from her tone. "I'm sorry."

She tried to make him understand. "This guy was solid and real and he had a nasty right hook."

She paused to let the suspicion she felt register with everyone in the room.

"There's someone else in this house. And it's no ghost."

Chapter Eleven

The Meades weren't exactly the sort of people who called the cops when there was a crime committed on their property. But Cole had acted like true KCPD, questioning everyone before sending them back to bed, and combing Tori's room from top to bottom, inside and out, looking for anything he could use to piece together clues to the attack.

Paulie had brought her an ice pack for the swelling on her cheek and she'd curled up in her overstuffed chair to watch Cole work. She decided she had a fine appreciation for his investigative style, though she couldn't honestly say whether it was his quick, precise, miss-no-detail thoroughness—or his attire.

She'd never seen him dressed in anything but a suit and tie, which he filled to classic proportions. But there was something almost untamed about a barefoot man prowling around her bed in nothing but a pair of faded jeans with a Glock 9mm tucked into the back of the waistband.

Even his hair was loose and falling around his shoulders as he picked up a bloodstained sliver of glass and dropped it into a brown paper bag. Sexy as he was, she almost wished he'd pull those long mahogany locks back or cut them short so she could get a clear look at his chiseled features and remarkable blue eyes.

Of course, she could look all she wanted. That didn't

necessarily mean he'd be looking back. There was something about being a skinny redhead with too much attitude that kept men from seeing her as any kind of long-term option. There were bigger boobs and safer careers and less-headstrong mates out there to be had.

"That's it, then."

When Cole spun around, she dropped the ice pack into her lap, startled to think he might have caught her staring at him with some sort of wistful look in her eyes.

"You can deliver this tomorrow when you meet with A.J."

Deliver? Tori snapped out of her self-conscious haze and pressed a finger to her mouth, shushing him. She pointed to the floor. The lamp might be in pieces, but the listening device was still intact, indicating anyone could be eavesdropping at any time.

Cole tipped his head back. His reaction was half curse, half sigh. At two in the morning, a man could be expected to be a little short-tempered. But the moment passed. He dropped his chin and looked at her again.

"That settles it."

"Settles what?" Tori rose to meet him as he crossed the room.

He snatched her by her wrist and dragged her toward her bedroom door. "You're sleeping with me."

Automatically rebelling against anyone making decisions for her, she planted her feet and twisted free. "Neanderthals became extinct centuries ago."

"Don't argue with me." He took her hand again, more gently this time, and backed toward the door. "It's the safest room in the house."

Right. No cameras, no bugs. But Cole would be there, and the whole *sleeping with* idea had her rattled. She was following him out the door, but said, "I'm not sure this is a good idea."

He stopped, his expression as patient as she'd ever seen it. "Look. Do you want to stay in a room with a broken armoire door, sleeping with one eye open because that bastard might come back and finish what he started? Or do you prefer a room with no secret entrances and no way for anyone to spy on you, so you can actually close your eyes and get a few hours of sleep?"

Sleep. He really was just talking about sleep. Tori tried to hide how deflated she suddenly felt. Probably it was the chilly air against her bare arms and legs. But his argument was logical and she was beat. "I guess I am a little tired."

He led her quickly down the hall past all the other bedrooms, pushed open the door to his room and pulled her inside. He released her to lock the door and stow his gun and sack on the bedside table, giving her a few moments to note the four-poster bed and masculine navy-and-cream decor. She supposed the love seat in front of the window would be her spot to curl up in for a few hours, so she headed for it.

But she hadn't taken half a step when Cole blocked her path, backed her up against the door, wrapped his hand around the nape of her neck. "What?" she said. And kissed her.

Desperately. Thoroughly. His hips drove into hers, his hands cradled her head. His lips devoured hers, his tongue thrust in and claimed her own. The energy in her reignited by his passionate touch, she reached up to frame his jaw, comb her fingers through his hair, open herself to his demands. He worshipped, apologized. Pulled away with a forcible gasp and left her hungry for more.

He touched his forehead to hers, and her downcast eyes watched the ragged expansion and contraction of his chest as he struggled to regain control.

Tori let her hands slide down to a debatably neutral position against the mat of dark hair that curled across his pecs, and fought to regain some control herself. "I suppose you just needed to do that, too?"

"Yeah." He nodded. "I did."

He jerked his hips back first, as if just now realizing what she had—that a few thin layers of cotton and denim couldn't hide the fact that he was nearly as aroused as she.

But his hands and forehead still encircled her face. "You're not badly hurt, then?"

She lifted her gaze so he could read the reassurance there. "A couple of bruises. The aspirin helped."

"Good." He kissed her forehead and pulled away.

Her overheated body rapidly chilled as the damp, cool air swept in between them. He ran his fingers through his hair and tossed the length of it behind his back. "I promised you sleep." He crossed the room and retrieved his gun, stashing it behind his waist. "I have a couple of things to check out to secure the place. Go ahead and make yourself at home in the bed. I'll take the couch. I'll try not to wake you when I come back in."

"It's a love seat, not a couch. You're too big for it. I'll take it."

His shoulders heaved with an impatient breath. "Whatever you call it, you've got goose bumps I can see from here. Get under the covers."

He was making a quick, polite exit. She should take the hint. Tori lifted her chin and opened the door for him. "Be safe."

He paused and looked down at her, wanting to say something more. But all she got was "Lock the door."

FORTY-FIVE MINUTES LATER, Cole was pacing the carpet outside his door, wondering how the hell he was going to actually get any sleep while Tori was in there. He had no regrets about insisting she stay in his room. He'd found truck tire tracks outside the cellar door. And his computer log showed the gate alarms had been deactivated and turned back on after he'd sent everyone to their rooms.

She was right. Someone else *had* been in the house.

And the thought of that someone hitting her, the imprint of a man's hand around her throat… Cole stopped his pacing and let every muscle in his body tense as the fury worked through him.

When the anger had passed and the need to protect was all that remained, he expelled a cleansing breath. Her attacker's accomplice was someone in this house. He had to do this. He had to go in there, keep his emotions in check, his rod in his pants and hope to hell she was tucked in up to her chin and sound asleep so he could keep watch over her.

There was only so much temptation a man could take.

It just wasn't fair that he had to be a gentleman when he could see all that creamy skin exposed by the skimpy top and short shorts she was wearing. He'd sworn to keep her safe. But it'd be a lot easier if he didn't have that smart mouth or those pert little breasts to distract him.

His will resolved, Cole picked up the package he'd stolen and went inside.

"Damn."

All he could do was stare and silently curse the urges that betrayed his best intentions. She was in bed, all right. Wide-awake, sitting cross-legged on top of the covers, thumbing through a magazine. She closed it and set it aside while he locked the door.

"What's that?" she asked.

She was referring to the package, of course. He set it on the chair beside the door. "A couple of Jericho's cigars and a sample of everything I could find in his medicine cabinet."

"I'll take them to A.J. when I see him tomorrow."

At least she'd had the decency to cover up. Sort of. "I see you helped yourself to one of my shirts."

She wore it like a mini-dress, the sexiest kind possible, one that didn't do a thing to hide all ninety miles of those long, powerful legs. She had it buttoned up the front with the sleeves rolled to her wrists. Her cheeks flooded with color. It didn't take much for him to trigger a response in this woman. Or her in him.

"Sorry. I was cold. I couldn't find a robe and I didn't want to go back to my room. And I still think you're too big to sleep on the couch."

"You just like to be difficult, don't you," he challenged.

Her green eyes sparkled. "It makes logical sense. I'm tall, but you're taller. You should have the bigger bed."

Seeing her wearing something of his sparked a little possessive streak that was his undoing. Or maybe it was the argument he refused to lose. Because logic didn't have a damn thing to do with his next impulse. He strode toward the bed.

"Move over."

She rolled her eyes and swung her legs out over the side, sticking her hands up in surrender as he approached. "I'm moving."

"Not that far."

He grabbed her around the waist as she stood and pulled her down onto the bed with him, rolling over and pinning her with his body.

"Cole!"

She shoved at his chest and he let her have a little room. He pushed up on his elbows and slid to her side, keeping one leg draped over both of hers and his arm firmly cinched around her waist. "This bed's big enough for both of us," he announced.

"But—"

"No but's." He reached behind him and removed his

gun, secretly loving how her protesting hands stayed wedged against his chest as he moved across her to lay the Glock on the nightstand. "I'm done arguing with you, woman."

"I wasn't arguing."

"Sure you were. It's what you do to keep me at arm's length." He settled back in beside her, propping his head up on his hand so he could look down and read every nuance in that beautiful face. "But not tonight."

"Cole." She shoved in earnest now and twisted beneath him.

But it only took the gentle stroke of his fingers across her forehead and a few soft words to calm her. "I want you to stay with me. If I can hold you in my arms, I'll know where you are and I can keep you safe."

Her eyes darted back and forth, studying his. Her fingers started that unconscious kneading against his chest. She swallowed hard, and he watched the elegant movement of muscle down the length of her throat.

"To sleep, right?"

He reached up, caught her fingers in his and stilled them. "Maybe later."

"Cole—" She was moving again.

He tightened his grip and held her in place. "Do you honestly not *get* the chemistry between us?"

"I get it. It's just that I'm afraid of it."

He propped himself up higher, wanting to get a good look at the stark honesty in her eyes. "I never thought I'd hear you admit to being afraid of anything." He touched the tip of his finger to the tiny line between her brows and felt the tension there. He traced his finger along the auburn curves until he felt her relax. "Does this have anything to do with Ian Davies?"

Everything in her tensed again. "You were listening?"

"By the tone of your voice, I take it that chanting his name is some kind of curse?"

She pressed her head back into the pillow, breaking eye contact. She pulled her hands away from him and clutched one over her stomach. The other plopped to the bed beside her and nervously drummed against the quilt. Cole wished he could take back the question.

But he'd underestimated Tori's courage. She took a steadying breath and looked back into his eyes.

"Ian and I worked together on an undercover assignment. Posing as a couple. Somewhere along the line I blew the cardinal rule and it became real for me." Cole reached for the hand at her side and laced his fingers with hers, silently urging her on. "Ian sold us out. He was just using me. I'm not, you know, real whippy when it comes to handling men, anyway. My mother always says I scare them off."

"Because of your temper?"

She swatted at his chest and he took that playful gesture as a good sign, easing his guilt a fraction.

"Because of my money. My name. My badge. Men don't like women who can kick their ass."

He, apparently, was the exception. "Do you think your strength and smarts make you less of a woman?"

Her fingers tightened around his. "Look at me, Cole. My hair's too red, my skin's too pale. My boobs are nonexistent."

Beautiful hair, beautiful skin. And the nonexistent items perked to attention beneath his scrutiny.

Tori touched his chin and brought his gaze back to hers. "My mother's always giving me pointers on how to improve myself. Ian basically told me the same thing, that I lacked a few, you know, feminine skills. I can't do my job *and* have a relationship."

She stroked his jaw, abrading her fingertips against the stubble of his beard, petting him, soothing him until the gut-deep need to punch a certain guy passed and he could give a rational response. "Did you kick Ian's butt?"

"I set him up to be arrested, if that's what you mean. He was killed when he tried to escape the sting we'd set up."

He grinned and turned his head to press a congratulatory kiss into her palm. "That'll do."

Her hand stayed against his cheek and he savored her touch. "You really are a nice guy, Cole."

"Nice?" He groaned and let his head fall forward, sending his hair cascading down into her face.

She gathered up the long strands, tucked them behind his ears and held them in place. "You're an annoying pain in the butt because you won't let me do my job, but..." She was holding him harder now, clinging to him, demanding something of him. "I am attracted to you. And I have feelings for you. But I don't want to get the job mixed up with what's real. I don't want to get hurt again. I don't want to think there's a relationship when there's not." She shook her head and her hands slid to his shoulders. "And I don't trust that I'll know the difference."

Cole didn't know what to say to her honest confession. He wasn't the kind of man who could make guarantees. All he knew was the humbling touch of her hands and the aching coolness of her body and the peace he felt being with her like this. She didn't believe in permanence and he didn't believe in promises.

But he believed in her. He believed in this.

"Forget relationships. Just think about tonight. Think about now. Think about how crazy the world is outside that door." When she turned to look, he cupped her face and pulled it back to him, rubbing his thumb along her chin, pressing it to the fullness of her mouth. His pulse throbbed when her lips parted and her warm breath caressed his skin. "Holding you, kissing you, is the most real thing I've known in two long years. I don't know what to tell you about tomorrow.'' Her fingertips dug into his skin as she held her breath. ''I just need now. Stay with me.''

''You need me?''

Her eyes searched his and he hoped she found what she was looking for.

''Really?''

He died and went to heaven with the gift she'd just handed him. ''Really.''

Her arms slid around his neck and, with the slightest of tugs, Cole obliged and bent his head to claim her lips.

He'd intended to be gentle, but like always, the chemistry between them ignited. When her tongue found his, something inside him caught fire. With the explosive jolt of a starter's pistol, Cole angled his body over hers and joined the race to complete the sweetest seduction of his life.

Tori tangled her fingers in his hair and urged him to kiss her this way, then she begged him to kiss her like that. He obeyed every persuasive demand and made a few of his own.

''Cole.'' Her voice was a breathless whisper that danced against his skin. He skimmed his hand down to the curve of her hip and squeezed the taut muscle there. She kissed his chin, his jaw. ''Cole.'' He spread his thighs wider and dragged her firmly between them, closing his eyes against the luscious meeting of heat against heat. She nibbled on his ear, rubbed her cheek against his and gasped. She rubbed it again.

The lady liked that, huh?

''I don't know how… What do you want me to do?'' she asked breathlessly.

''Whatever feels right.'' He swept his fingers into the silk of her hair and guided her mouth back to his.

The second lap intensified and gathered speed. While he delighted in the needy exploration of her hands across his shoulders, arms, back, neck, chest, he unbuttoned the shirt that she wore and slid his hand inside.

He groaned in frustration when he encountered the second layer of her cotton knit top. "I want to feel your skin," he rasped against her neck, dipping his lips to taste the creamy smoothness there.

What felt right to Tori felt very, very right for him when she moved into the lead. With a little coaxing and a little athletic strength, she pushed him off her and sat up. He rolled onto his back and reached for her hips as she followed him over and straddled him.

He eagerly helped her lose the shirt and tagged along with her hands as she pulled the tank top up and off over her head. Her back arched as she shook her hair loose, and Cole nearly lost it right there.

But he caught only a glimpse of those perfect porcelain mounds and their pale straining tips before she crossed her arms in front of her and her gaze dropped to a self-conscious point near his chin.

"I don't know," she whispered, her voice itself a heady stroke against his senses. "Maybe I shouldn't have done that."

Cole sat up and dropped her into his lap. He looked straight into those darkening green eyes and thanked her. "You absolutely should have."

He kissed her then, deeply, fully, telling her with everything in him how much he desired her. Her back was an endless expanse of velvet skin and sleek muscle, and he touched every part of it he could reach.

When she finally relaxed and wound her arms around his neck, he let her pull herself as close as she wanted. They were skin to skin, muscle to muscle. He skimmed her ribs and flicked his thumbs into the tight space between them, catching the tips of her breasts. Tori gasped. Her fingers dug into his shoulders and he teased her again. She buried her mouth against his neck and called his name again and again—and it wasn't any curse.

"Let me," he urged. Needing something more, needing to give her more. "Trust me."

She nodded, leaned back against his hand and let him pull a taut bud into his mouth. The perfume of her skin went straight to his head. Her husky moan cut straight to his groin. He wasn't going to last much longer. But he wanted her in the homestretch with him. He laved the other breast, and she was squirming in his lap, squeezing her thighs around his hips, clutching at his hair and holding his mouth against her.

"Oh God, Cole. Cole?"

He lifted his mouth to hers and answered every greedy demand of her kiss. He dipped his fingers beneath the waist of her shorts and cupped her bottom, lifting her against his bulging, burning heat.

"Tori…" He bit back *baby* so he wouldn't spoil the moment. "I don't think I can wait."

"Neither can I."

Her fingers clawed at the snap of his jeans. She rose up to her knees, and he worked her shorts off her legs. The zipper came next. She peeled the denim from his hips and he sprang free.

"Cole! There's nothing—"

She blushed, and he kissed her for it.

"You think I sleep in a suit and tie?"

She laughed and grasped at his bottom as he rolled her onto her back and settled between her legs.

"I want this, Victoria Westin. I want you."

She nodded. "Now."

He found her wet, slick heat and eased inside.

Her fingers skimmed right up his spine and she pulled him down on top of her. "I said now."

Yeah, he had his work cut out for him, keeping up with

this lady. "Bossy britches." He grinned and gathered her into his arms.

She closed those long legs around his hips and Cole plunged into her, again and again. Then, in one blazing moment, her back arched, he thrust, and the world exploded deep inside him, all around him, as their amazing chemistry consumed them both.

Catching his breath sometime later, Cole pulled up the covers and spooned himself against Tori's back. He buried his nose in the perfumed silk of her hair and smiled. He'd finally discovered a way to slow her down.

Her fingers laced through his where they rested against her stomach. She made a valiant effort to speak, but it wasn't much more than a drowsy slur into the pillow. "I'm not bossy."

He grinned. "Yes, you are."

"No, I'm not." She yawned.

He pulled her hair aside and kissed her neck. "Go to sleep."

"Okay, I'll do what you say. See?" She squeezed his hand and in a few minutes she was snoring softly against her pillow.

Cole lay awake in the darkness and absently stroked her hair, memorizing every touch, every scent, every imprint of her body. He recalled her shy words and bold actions. He noted how such a strong woman could feel so vulnerable curled inside his arms.

Holding Tori, he felt a peace and contentment that had eluded him for too long.

He stayed awake and memorized what this felt like.

Because he knew it wouldn't last.

HOMICIDE DETECTIVE GINNY Rafferty-Taylor looked across the seat at her younger partner, Merle Banning. Of course, a few scars and some hard experiences on the job had stripped him of his youthful edge. Nobody thought of him as the precinct's rookie computer geek anymore. But then, it had been a long time since she'd thought of him as anything but one of her best friends.

"Are you thinking this was a wild-goose chase too?"

"It crossed my mind." He pointed through the windshield. "The sun's coming up. Even the hookers have gone to bed for the night. I'm guessing our informant isn't going to show."

Her frustrated sigh stirred the wisps of silver-blond hair that framed her face. "I hope it's just cold feet and not the alternative."

Nine prostitutes had been murdered in downtown Kansas City over the past eleven years. Seven of those unsolved deaths had already been transferred over to the cold-case-file section. Two of the most recent killings shared enough of the same M.O. that Ginny was thinking she had some kind of serial killer on their hands.

But there were no leads. No fingerprints. The victims had nothing in common except their profession.

Until that call she took yesterday afternoon at the Fourth Precinct offices. A frightened woman, claiming to be a prostitute, said she had information on the last hooker's murder. She said there was a client—a man who had threatened her life—who'd been bragging about how he was cleaning up the streets of K.C. when the cops couldn't. He claimed he was a killer who could never be caught.

Ginny's gut had responded to that woman's fear. Her keen intellect had responded to the details about the last murder she'd shared. This prostitute, calling herself Daisy, had promised to meet with Ginny on the street where she worked.

But the neon lights had been turned off an hour ago. Even the streetlights were starting to fade.

"I gave up my weekly cooking lesson with my mother-in-law and an evening at home with Brett to do this stake-out.'' Her cooking skills were showing improvement, though her husband never once complained about burned dinners or take-out food.

"How's that going?" Merle asked, scanning his side of the abandoned street while she studied hers.

"The cooking or the marriage?"

He laughed. "Both, I guess."

"I haven't killed anyone yet, and amazing. Brett and I are talking about starting a family, but we both seem to work all the time. We're trying to change priorities and get our schedules—'' A flicker of movement in the doorway of one of the black-painted brick buildings caught her eye. "Half a block down. Check that out."

"I see it."

A woman dashed out of the tenement building, clutching a shiny silver coat around her neck, obscuring her face. Her garish blond hair bobbed back and forth as she turned her head from side to side. The woman either wore too much makeup or sported two black eyes. She took a couple of steps toward Ginny and Merle's car, darted a glance behind her shoulder, then spun around and took off as fast as her silver spiked heels could carry her.

"Do you suppose that's Daisy?" Ginny asked.

Merle shot to attention behind the wheel. "That'd be my guess."

A man, dressed in black from his stocking cap to his toes, slammed the door behind him as he ran out of the building, cursing and shaking his fist. He spotted the woman in silver and took off after her.

Ginny had her door open first. "Call it in as an assault and get backup. If it's anything more, we'll take it from there."

"Ginny, wait!"

But she was already charging up the sidewalk, her petite

legs pumping as fast as they would go. She unsnapped her holster and pulled her gun from her waist. Daisy turned the corner and disappeared into an alley.

"Police!" Ginny yelled. "Freeze!"

But the man ignored her warning and darted into the alley.

She heard a scream, the bang and crash of garbage cans against brick and steel. The man threatened to kill Daisy.

Ginny slowed her pace as she reached the alley. Before she turned the corner into unknown territory, she pressed her back against the wall, gripped her gun between both hands and steadied her grip.

"Ginny, wait up!" Merle was running to join her, drawing his weapon.

Daisy screamed, and Ginny heard another crash.

With the threat to life imminent, Ginny took a deep breath and rounded the corner, temporarily blinded by the alley's impenetrable shadows. She held her gun in sure, steady hands. "Police. On the ground, now."

Through a trick of the light, she thought she saw Daisy standing on one side of the alley, and the man in black on the other, tossing garbage cans against the wall.

"What the hell?"

Daisy wasn't the woman in trouble.

"All you Taylors are gung ho hero types, aren't you."

The flicker of movement on the fire escape above her registered a split second too late. Ginny raised her gun. But the second man in black fired first. An explosion of pain ripped through her chest and knocked her to the ground.

Her head bounced off the pavement and her gun flew from her hand. She was vaguely aware of Merle calling her name, firing his weapon. One man in black collapsed in the pile of garbage cans. She saw sparks fly as the other man ran up the fire escape stairs.

Merle grabbed her by the shoulder of her jacket and dragged her back to the sidewalk.

She never did see where Daisy went. But the other woman's voice, damning the Taylors for ruining everything, echoed in her ears until darkness claimed her.

Chapter Twelve

Cole paced the hospital waiting room while the rest of the family huddled around Brett.

Cole's oldest brother—big, bad Brett Taylor—sat on the couch, crying and praying and talking tough while he waited for any word from surgery. His mother, Martha, sat on his left, hugging him close. His sister, Jessie, sat on his right, holding his hand.

Brett was the one who always handled things. He'd taken charge when their father had been hospitalized. He'd worked an extra job through school to help support a family of six siblings. He was the one who shook some sense into his younger brothers when they did something stupid, then stood beside them when they needed a friend.

But indomitable Brett had been leveled when he learned his wife had been shot. That the bullet had pierced a lung, broken two ribs and nicked her heart. That it would take four hours of surgery or longer to maybe—hopefully—save her life.

Cole stopped in his tracks, some distance away. Was that what love did to a man? Was that the same fierce emotion that had nearly crippled him when he heard the struggle in Tori's bedroom so soon after she'd been shot at? Love?

Did Cole Taylor even have it in him to love anymore?

Or had guilt and cynicism and too much death destroyed his heart?

He seemed to find enough of it last night in Tori's arms. It wasn't just the sex, though that had been a mind-blowing ride. It was the talking and the cuddling and the sharing.

It was the regret he felt when he took that call from Mitch about Ginny and tried to argue Tori out of investigating the catacombs by herself. It was her game-faced acceptance that it was back to work as usual, that their night together had been a wonderful fling but she didn't expect him to commit to anything.

His heart had been reborn with the possibility of loving Victoria Westin. It had been crushed with the idea that he'd already lost her.

Suddenly, Brett surged to his feet, snapping Cole from his gloomy thoughts. The surgeon, drying his hands on a towel, came out of the OR. The rest of the family gathered around, and Cole drifted closer, as anxious as his brother to hear the doctor's report.

Critical but stable, with the expectation that Ginny would be upgraded to guarded condition once she was moved from the surgical ICU. Brett picked up the surgeon and hugged him and there were *thank you*'s and *thank God*'s all round.

"Penny for your thoughts, son."

Cole stood a little straighter as his father broke off from the group and walked over to him. He stuffed his hands into his pockets and summoned a smile. "That's great news about Ginny."

"Yes, it is." Sid's brown eyes warmed with a smile. "The doctor says it'll take her a few months to recover, but that's all right. I can't imagine she'll have a more attentive nursemaid than your brother. And, of course, the rest of us will be there to help out."

The rest of us. "Yeah." Cole's shoulders sagged as his

smile faded. "I don't suppose Brett will be wanting my help."

Sid frowned. "He doesn't blame you."

"He should. Mitch said Merle Banning reported specific threats against the Taylors. That it was a setup." He shook his head, knowing the Meades had to hate him an awful lot to be so cruel and vindictive to his family. "It's my fault."

"How do you figure that?"

"I'm responsible for you guys getting hurt—"

"*You're* not hurting us—"

"Dad—"

Sid grabbed him by the arm and led him farther down the hall, well beyond earshot of the others. He turned Cole to face him before releasing him. "Do you remember a few years back, when I went into the hospital for my heart and had bypass surgery?"

He remembered it all too well. "Yeah. We almost lost you. I couldn't get there soon enough, then I couldn't stay, and Brett chewed my butt. Kind of like today."

"But you were there. You came to see me in my room. Do you remember what you said to me that day?"

Cole shook his head. "I just recall being scared and feeling useless."

Sid dropped his voice to a whisper. "You said to me, 'I'm working undercover, Dad. Something long-term, something dangerous.'"

His dad remembered that five-minute conversation? "I didn't know how sick you were. I wanted you to know that I was still trying to do the right thing. Just in case..."

Neither one finished the sentence. Sid Taylor hadn't died that day.

"I kept your secret. Didn't even tell your ma. Though she'd have been relieved to have proof that you were still working on the right side of the law. I didn't tell her because you said your life would depend on keeping your assignment secret.''

But someone knew his secret. Someone who'd resort to violence against his family to punish him. To break his will.

"I guess I forgot that." A strange sort of feeling—something humbling, something proud—took root inside Cole. "I know it's hard keeping things from Ma."

Sid waved aside that comment. "She's probably guessed it on her own. She believes all her boys are good guys."

"Some days, I can't tell if I am anymore." Sid gave him one of those 'Dad' looks, putting Cole on guard. "What?"

"You told me you were out to get some very, very bad men. That you wanted Kansas City and your family to be safe from users and killers like them." His father placed his hand on Cole's shoulder and didn't let go. "Don't you think for one moment that you're not protecting us, Cole. My brother was gunned down in the line of duty. All my boys give to their community. They make it better. They keep it safe." That tiny root listened and began to lift up his soul as it grew. "Men like Jericho Meade take advantage of people when they're down. They take what they want without any concern for what someone else needs. They create fear. They smell it. They feed on it. They don't raise themselves up to be better men. They put others down so they feel superior, powerful.

"You, son, and a few others like you, are the only thing that stands between the people I love and men like Meade. You might not be there to hold your sister's hand when she's going through something awful—" Sid squeezed Cole's shoulder, and shook him a bit to make his point "—but she can walk the streets of her town, run her own business, marry the man she loves because you've made her world safe. Now, go to work, son. Ginny's going to be fine. We'll be fine. You take care of Mr. Meade and his business. So we can continue to be fine."

Cole couldn't help himself. He reached out and gave his father a hug. He crushed him tight and held back his tears and thanked God for this man in his life.

When he pulled back, he knew what he had to do. "I gotta go, Dad."

"I know. I'll give your mother your love."

"Do that."

There was no confusion in Cole's mind as he walked out of the hospital and climbed into his car. Jericho Meade might have a paternal influence on Cole's current life, but he didn't own Cole's loyalty.

Sid Taylor was a rare breed. A good man who'd raised a family of good men. A strong man who did the right thing, provided enough, talked the tough talk and backed it up, loved—and was there for—his children.

His father set a mighty high standard to live up to—but he was damn determined not to disappoint him.

TORI'S MEETING with A. J. Rodriguez went a hundred percent more smoothly than it had the day before, considering Cole hadn't spied on her and no one had gotten killed.

A.J. promised to take the items she'd brought straight to the lab and test them for the synthetic poison, and try to ID her attacker through his DNA. Then he'd pay a visit to the Kramer clinic as well to collect any data related to Jericho's treatment.

She'd listened intently to his information about the waiter who was killed. The young man was an immigrant from an Eastern European nation that had once been part of Yugoslavia. Martín Lukasiewicz was from the same country. As were the chauffeur and hit man killed at the Kramer clinic.

"What do you think they have against the Meades?"

A.J. didn't like to speculate, but his thoughts echoed her own. "Lukasiewicz has traveled to Europe more times than I've eaten at the corner deli. He imports and exports rare works of art. I'm guessing Daniel Meade reneged on a deal. Maybe he acquired something they'd already paid for, but conveniently forgot to deliver.''

"Like *The Divine Horseman.*"

"You said Daniel was in New Orleans when the statue was stolen.''

"He takes a bundle of money from them, then keeps their national treasure for himself." Players and motives were falling into place. "So Chad didn't set up Lukasiewicz yesterday. It was the other way around. The waiter got caught in the cross fire."

"Cole said he recognized the shooter, though. How does that tie in?"

And so the conversation turned back to Cole.

She resisted the urge to ask A.J. about Cole's personal life. If he even had one, what kind of women he dated, if she had any chance of measuring up. But pride and common sense prevailed. She'd told Cole that it had to be strictly business between them. She'd thrown out a tired excuse about attention to duty and responsibilities that couldn't be compromised, but inside, she'd simply been a coward. She already loved Cole, maybe she had from that first encounter in Jericho's office. She'd been afraid then, too. And the only reason was that she didn't want to hurt the way she had hurt with Ian.

She didn't want her last memory of Cole to be the one where he broke her heart.

So she'd met with A.J., had put in a call to Bill Brady to arrange their meeting and had driven back to the overcast gloom of the Meade estate to finally explore the catacombs.

The house seemed oddly deserted, with only Aaron lurking in the hallways and Jericho resting in his room. That meant Paulie was upstairs too. Cole was still at the hospital with the family emergency that had transformed him from caring lover to cold-hearted cop. With Chad and Lana gone for meetings, she practically had the run of the house.

Her elation wasn't anywhere near where it would have been twenty-four hours ago. Still, Tori changed into her running shoes, grabbed her flashlight and opened the door that led down into the pit called the catacombs.

There were some lights available as she crept down the stairs. A serpentine wire had been draped along the stone walls, powering a dim light bulb about every twenty feet or so. But she relied on the flashlight to find her way through the maze.

The temperature dropped a degree or two with every few steps she descended. The dank, musty air reminded her of the cold chill that swept through the secret passageway into her room. She should have worn a jacket over her blouse, but she was too close to finding the truth to want to go back for one. She trailed her hand along the walls. ''Yuck.'' Then she snatched her hand away and wiped the dusty slime that clung to her fingers on her pant leg.

Several feet down the first stone corridor, she stopped to get her bearings. To the left was the wine cellar, stacked high with vintage bottles and locked behind an iron gate. Straight ahead she found the vault where Jericho stored the records and collectibles Chad had mentioned.

No paintings or artifacts yet.

She turned at the next right and discovered the corridor doubled back on itself. She followed the twists and turns and tried her keys in every locked door she passed. An empty room, abandoned to decades of stone crumbling into dust, bit by bit. Next, she found a vault, sealed with a re-frigerator-like door instead of a wooden one.

Her heart beat faster as she stepped inside and found a treasure trove of paintings, wrapped and stacked and well-preserved. She searched through each shelf and opened any crate large enough to hide the statue. Her breath puffed out on a cloud in the chilly air.

"Nothing."

Disappointed but undaunted, she closed the vault. She had to shine her light on the floor to find her footprints, to see which direction she'd come from and where she should go. Choosing the less-traveled path, she turned another corner and followed the long corridor to the end of the line. The Meade family vault.

Blaming the sudden eruption of goose bumps across her skin on the cold air, she unlocked the iron gate and stepped inside to view the names and dates carved into the stones on the wall. Jericho's wife. His parents. An uncle. His brother, Chad's father. Four blank stones, each the size of a small television, completed the set.

She shone her light at the ceiling and down into the corners, hoping there might be yet another exit, another hidden passage to check. But there was nothing but dust and slime.

She'd been so certain she'd find the *Horseman* down here. So sure that Chad's bookkeeping and Daniel's lies and Jericho's hidden keys would lead her to the catacombs. Her disappointment was as palpable as the air she was breathing.

Backing out through the gate, she was reaching to close it when… She hit the bottom right stone with her light again. "It couldn't be."

Dust had collected in every other crevice, but the groove surrounding that stone was relatively clean. She tried not to raise her hopes. "I've come this far, I might as well try it."

Tori kneeled down. She laid her flashlight on the floor, ignoring the giant, distorted shadows it cast up on the wall. She ran her fingertips around the edge of the stone block. It was loose. Rocking it back and forth, she moved it out an inch from the wall. Then she could get her hands beneath it, lift it and pull. She breathed out as her arms took the weight and her muscles clenched to keep from crushing her fingers underneath.

The block fell to the floor and she shoved it aside. She grabbed her flashlight and pointed it into the opening. But the glint of something bright and shiny reflected into her eyes and she had to look away.

Her heart thumped in her chest as she closed her eyes and reached inside. Her fingers closed around something cold and bumpy. The adrenaline rush was singing in her ears now. She pulled. Heavy. "Oh, mister, this better be you."

She dropped the light to reach in with both hands and pull out the object. She dragged it a few inches until it caught on something. Shifting her position, she braced her feet against the wall for leverage and used the strength of her legs to pull as well. It fought her efforts until sheer willpower freed it from its snag and out tumbled a golden knight astride his noble steed, with rubies for armor and a history more valuable than any jewel carried inside his heart. It clunked to the floor between her legs and Tori whooped for joy.

"Yeah! We're going home."

She still hadn't failed a mission. She'd nearly botched this one as badly as the debacle with Ian Davies by getting involved with Cole, but she hadn't failed. Her personal life might still be a shambles, but she had this.

She gave a bone-deep sigh, stirring the dust and making herself sneeze. Funny. This victory didn't seem so sweet, after all.

Returning to her senses, she scrambled to her feet and reached down to pick up the statue. It would be heavy to lift, but not impossible to carry. "Oh my God."

Tori froze bent over like that, her hands on the statue. Looking behind it now, she could see what it had snagged on inside the vault. A man's hand.

Or, more accurately, the flesh-eaten skeletal remains of a man's hand, with "one, two, three, four" fingers.

Inside her head she was screaming. *Daniel Meade*. Cole needed to see this. Daniel had been buried along with the statue he'd stolen.

She shut down her squeamish reaction as the federal agent in her took over. With a little more maneuvering, she pulled out enough of the corpse to get a look at the remnants of his tailored suit and the bloodstain and bullet hole over the left side of his chest. "One in the heart." She checked the skull and let the body rest. "And one in the head."

A professional hit.

"Lancelot?" No. He'd have taken the statue with him.

Who else benefited from Daniel's death?

Tori cut short her speculation. There might be bullets to run ballistics tests on, trace elements to check. The sooner she could get this dead body to Cole and the cops, the sooner they could ID his killer.

She didn't bother to lock the gate. She hoisted the statue onto her hip and anchored it with her left arm. Using her light to retrace her footsteps, she hurried down the corridor. She couldn't run, and she had to stop once at the base of the stairs to catch her breath. But minutes later she emerged into the kitchen.

The cameras. Oh, damn, where were the cameras?

She stopped for a towel to wrap around the statue, then walked sedately out into the main part of the house. She was going to grab her purse and walk straight out to her car. She'd call Cole from there. She'd drive away from this nightmare house and find him and tell him his debt to Jericho was paid.

She headed for the front door, brushing the dust off her clothes and shaking the cobwebs out of her hair. A shower could wait too. She paused at the foyer table near the base of the staircase and shifted the *Horseman* to her other hip so she could dig her keys out of her purse and sling it over her shoulder.

"I'll take that."

Tori turned her head to the woman's voice at the top of the stairs. She wasn't going to just walk out of here, after all. "Good afternoon, Lana."

"Don't be smart with me."

She wasn't surprised to see the gun Lana carried as she came down the steps. Nor was she surprised to see loverboy Aaron entering from the dining room with his gun drawn as well. Tori nibbled on her bottom lip so she wouldn't laugh at the irony of her brain finally putting two and two together. He worked for Lancelot.

"You wouldn't know Martín Lukasiewicz by any chance, would you, Aaron?"

"Martín is a patriot for my homeland. Hand it over." He jerked the statue from her grip, but it was too heavy to control and he dropped it.

Tori cringed when it hit. But only the floor was dented. The *Horseman* stayed true. "Careful. You don't want to break that before you get it home or collect your money. Which is it? Are you a patriot or an entrepreneur? I like you better without the wig, by the way."

"Shut up." Aaron wasn't the brightest guy on the block, but judging by yesterday's shooting, he knew how to use that gun.

"I promised I'd get it back for you, didn't I, darling?" Lana had reached the main floor now. "So you finally found out where Daniel had hidden it. That jackass wasn't any good to me when he was alive, and he was even more trouble dead."

Where Daniel had hidden it. Not hidden *with* Daniel. Lana didn't know her ex-fiancé was buried in the basement. Aaron didn't, either, or he'd already have the statue.

Oh God, where was Cole? He needed to know everything. Even if she didn't get out of this, he needed to know the truth so he could free himself of the Meades. She needed the intervention of a divine hero now more than ever. But those guns weren't part of any fairy tale, and the only one she could depend on right now was herself.

Tori forced herself to breathe evenly, in and out. She'd taken out an armed assailant before. Two of them would be tricky.

Her heart sank.

Three would be damn near impossible.

A man in a black stocking cap and gloves opened the front door and invited himself in. Tori curled her toes inside her shoes, antsy with the need to take action, but sensing the odds weren't in her favor yet. He pulled off his gloves. Black skin. He peeled back his mask and hope surged within her.

"Bill."

But hope died. The bandage on his ear was proof enough that he was the man who'd attacked her in her room last night. She swung around to Lana and Aaron. That meant...

"That's right, Agent Westin. We've known who you are all along." Lana was practically cooing with the thoroughness of her plan. "Agent Brady works for me. I paid him a lot of money to recruit whoever was most qualified to find that statue for us."

"And to do a few odd jobs, too."

At Bill's interruption Lana snapped, "Yes, and if you were any better at them, Backer wouldn't be dead. The police will tie him to Miss Westin, and that will bring them straight to us."

"That's why we're getting rid of her, right?" Aaron was practically slathering at the prospect.

"Backer's dead?" The situation was spinning beyond Tori's grasp. "Then why did you try to kill me last night if you needed me to find the statue?"

"Because you became a liability." Lana crept closer.

Tori could see she carried something in her other hand. A syringe. Instinctively, she backed away, but her hip butted the table. She had nowhere to go.

"You were helping him," Lana continued. "Running errands. I could control him until you came along."

Tori planted her feet and stood her ground against the other woman. Her hands curled into fists. "Cole."

"Yes. Cole Taylor. Like a second son to Jericho." Something ugly and hateful leaped through the beauty of Lana's face. "*I* run this business. Not that sick old man, not his selfish son or incompetent nephew. *I* deserve to take over. But I can't. I have to run it through a man. But Daniel disappeared and Cole wouldn't have me."

"So you hooked your talons into Chad and tried to discredit Cole."

Lana threw out her hands. "Distract him, discredit him. Bill and I arranged for another family tragedy to keep him occupied today. Once Jericho changes his will to inherit Chad, I'll arrange for a much more personal tragedy."

"You greedy bitch."

Before Tori could guess her intent, Lana lunged. Tori automatically dodged to the side and brought her fist down hard on Lana's wrist. The other woman cursed, but the gun sailed through the air. She jerked Lana in front of her to use as a shield against Bill and Aaron. Too late, she realized she'd made a huge tactical mistake.

Lana swung around, jabbed the needle into her shoulder and emptied the syringe. Pain spread down Tori's arm and up into her chest. She clasped at the wound and stumbled as the walls around her suddenly began to spin. Lana grabbed her beneath the chin and shoved her up against the table. She spat her words in Tori's face.

"Cole's not here to charge to your rescue this time. I guess you'll just have to die."

"What did you give me?"

"The same thing I've been feeding Jericho for weeks, only I gave you a much larger dose. It's an experimental chemical from Aaron's homeland. You can be our second test subject." She winked, and Tori almost gagged. "I think your death will come a lot faster than his."

When released, Tori's knees buckled and she slid to the floor. The three of them were converging now, but Tori couldn't make any sense of their words. A heavy weight was gathering in her chest, pushing her down. Like a woman drowning, she opened her mouth and gulped air. But there was no relief. She couldn't breathe. She was still so dizzy.

A faint sound pierced the damp air and every head swiveled toward the open door. A siren. A glimmer of hope sparked in Tori's heart and cleared her head for a moment.

"Dammit, woman, you waste too much time with all your drama!" Aaron's words were almost unintelligible in his anger. "We go now!"

Lana turned on him. "Don't you dare lecture me."

"We have to return this to Lancelot before he makes good on his word and destroys us all." Ah, yes, wasn't love grand between two murdering thieves?

"Honey, you've got bigger problems to worry about than—"

"Boys, girls, we need to stay focused here." Bill foolishly tried to intervene.

Aaron whirled around and pointed his gun, shouting something damning in his native tongue. Tori closed her eyes, conserving what energy she could. A giant fist wrapped around her lungs and continued to squeeze. She could hear several sirens now.

The bickering trio had dismissed her. They seemed to shout and run in circles. Tori tried to scoot her way along the wall, working her way toward the door, fighting the chaos inside her head.

"Get her!" Rough hands picked her up on either side and she was vaguely aware of being half carried, half dragged along the polished wood floor toward the back of the house.

"KCPD! Drop your guns!" She knew that voice.

Tori crashed to the floor and the air exploded all around her. She curled up into a ball, desperate to breathe, desperate to see, desperate to know what was real and what was hallucination.

She lurched as a man fell beside her. She saw a shiny golden light and reached for it. Her fingers closed around it, cold and lifeless. She snatched them away. Another body fell. And then another.

The world went silent, and Tori raised her heavy eyelids. She wasn't dead yet. She didn't want to die.

Something warm brushed across her forehead. "Tori? Victoria? Stay with me."

A shadowy face tried to swim into focus. She reached up to touch it. It was warm and full of life. Strong arms picked her up and carried her into the light. She let her eyes drift shut and snuggled against the heat.

Her divine horseman had come to save her.

Chapter Thirteen

One week. Seven days too long to wait through this hell. Seven days wasted in a lifetime that would never be long enough to make up for all the mistakes he'd made.

Cole's eyes burned from his bedside vigil. Yeah, he'd grabbed a few hours of sleep here and there. He'd made sure someone was always in the room, just in case. He'd done everything the DA's office had asked of him, and when the investigation was officially declared closed, he'd gone to the barber and cut his hair—trimming away everything that represented his life with the Meades and reclaiming the man he used to be.

He'd spent the rest of his time here. Holding Tori's unresponsive hand. Listening to doctors. Watching monitors. Praying.

His family had come and gone, and would return. Now he just needed Tori to wake up. She'd been pumped full of enough synthetic toxin to shut down her lungs and stop her heart. That night in the E.R. had been the worst night of his life. But the doctors had stabilized her. Frank Westin had been called in as Tori's closest next-of-kin, and he authorized Dr. Kramer to use the trial antidote he'd created on his granddaughter. She'd been asleep ever since.

He studied her beautiful face, framed by a halo of that coppery hair, and rose to kiss the fading bruise on her cheek. "I love you," he whispered. "You fight this thing like you fight everything else, and you come back to me."

Then he sat back down in his chair, clinging to the most real thing he'd ever known. He laid his head on the bed and let fatigue claim him.

COLE HEARD THE DRUMMING sound in his ears. Then he felt the repetitive strokes across the back of his hand and snapped his eyes open. Joy surged through him and he sat up, turning his hand to capture Tori's drumming fingers within his own.

Those pretty green eyes were smiling at him and there was a healthy blush of color on her cheeks. "It's about time you woke up."

"Speak for yourself." He rose to his feet and moved to her pillow to brush a wayward strand of hair from her eyes.

Was she too fragile to crush in his arms? Could he kiss her? Would she want him to? The relief that had propelled him to his feet vanished and uncertainty turned his legs to jelly. He plopped back onto his seat.

"When? How?"

"The doctor left about twenty minutes ago. I told him not to wake you. He said my body just needed time to recover from the shock to my system. If I wasn't in top physical condition like I was, I wouldn't have survived." Her chest heaved with a cleansing sigh, the first deep, normal breath he'd seen her take since finding her collapsed on the floor in Jericho's house. "You look different. I like it."

"You look beautiful."

Her gaze dropped to the clasp of their hands atop the sheet and a silence that lasted an aeon ensued. Their last conversation had been an argument. All business, she'd said. She couldn't mix a job and a relationship. She'd never trust it to last.

He trusted what he felt would last forever.

If that was what she wanted.

Not knowing whether she'd take that risk left him tongue-tied too.

Suddenly, her body thrummed with energy and she lifted her gaze. "Daniel's in the basement."

She was choosing business.

Cole sighed, but didn't surrender. He'd let her run the first part of this conversation, then he'd pick his time to argue his case.

"Good to see you, too. We found the keys in your pocket, put two and two together and found the body downstairs."

"We?"

"KCPD, FBI, the DA's office. We've been pretty busy while you've been sleeping on the job." She huffed up at the implication. Cole made no apologies. "You put me through seven days of hell, Tori Westin. It's about time you came back to me."

"I guess I did need rescuing, after all." Her fingers clenched around his. "You carried me out of the house. I thought you were the divine horseman."

"That's a compliment I'll take. The little guy, by the way, is in a vault at the Nelson-Atkins Museum of Art. Since he seems to have changed hands illegally several times in the past few years, we're holding on to him until all the details are sorted out."

She pushed against her pillows and sat up straight in bed. "What else did I miss? Were there bullets?"

Her excitement pulsed through the room like a bolt of pure energy, and he knew for certain the woman he loved was back and ready for action. "Two slugs. We ran ballistics and got a match." He grinned. He'd never specified what kind of action he wanted her to try. "I'll give you a kiss if you can tell me whose gun they belong to."

Her eyes sparkled at the challenge. "Let's see. I can eliminate Lana, Aaron, Lukasiewicz, the two Bills—they wouldn't have been searching for the statue, otherwise. Daniel wasn't killed because of the statue. He was killed so he wouldn't cause his father any more trouble." She was talking with her hands now, back in perpetual motion. "So who would go that far to protect Jericho?" She paused. He waited. She knew. "Paulie. He figured out what Daniel had done, keeping the statue from Lukasiewicz and bringing the wrath of an entire nation down on the Meades. Did you arrest him?"

"Yeah. Chad and Jericho, too. Though Jericho's in the hospital ward. Your hunch was right. Lana poisoned his cigars. Lukasiewicz is being extradited to his homeland. Everybody else is dead. Brilliant as usual, Agent Westin." Cole cupped the side of her face and bent down, pausing just before he touched her lips. "But I would have kissed you anyway."

Some time later, after the nurse had checked her, her mother had visited and Tori had met several of his brothers, Cole snuggled down in the hospital bed with Tori in his arms. That same peace he'd felt that night at Meade Manor swept through him again.

Tori's voice was a husky whisper in the dimly lit room. "You don't have to stay with me, you know. I'm going to be all right. I know your family's worried about you getting enough sleep. And you have a job to do." She reached over and patted his belt, touching the KCPD badge he could once more wear with pride.

He heard the hesitation in her voice, the longing, the hope. "I'm not going anywhere tonight," he whispered against her ear in the low voice that seemed to soothe her fears. "Or any other night, as long as you'll have me."

She slid her fingers up over his ribs and splayed them

across his chest above his heart. "You sound like you're talking long term."

"I am talking long term."

Her fingers stroked him, petted him, touched his soul and made him crazy with desire.

"With me?"

He laid his hand over hers and held her close to the heart she had healed. "I'm not in love with anybody else."

"Really?"

"Really."

Her cheeks flushed with color. She smiled. She believed him. "Cole?"

"Yeah?"

"I need you to kiss me now."

He did.

Epilogue

"Do you know how hard it is to get all you people together in one place at one time?"

"Just bake a pie, Ma. We'll all show up." That was Josh, carrying his daughter, Anne Marie, as he bent down and kissed Martha Taylor's cheek before hustling over to his position beside his wife, Rachel.

Cole laughed along with the rest of the Taylor clan. That's all it took to defuse her temper. Show a little love. Heck, with this tight-knit bunch it was impossible not to show a lot of love.

"Mitch, you and Casey sit down front." Mitchell III toddled along beside them, his tiny hand latched on to one of his father's fingers.

Martha was directing traffic again, clearly in her element, as she ruffled her grandson Alex's hair and instructed him to gather his three adopted brothers and sit on the pile of leaves on the ground in front of the grouping of chairs.

This was all she had wanted for her sixty-fourth birthday, a new family picture to replace the one the two Bills had stolen from her that day in the parking lot so many months ago.

Cole bristled inside and took a cleansing breath. It still worked him up to think his job had brought harm to his family. But his mother saw the mugging as an opportunity for a bigger, better photograph. His father had repaired his shop and gotten city approval to designate it as an historic landmark since it was one of the original buildings in the City Market District. Now he was looking at full-time retirement, tinkering around his workshop and taking his grandkids to ball games.

Even Ginny had taken the tragedy of being shot and turned it into something beautiful. She and Brett had had three months of recuperating time together at home. Now she was pregnant with their first child.

"We'd better get this picture taken fast, Martha." That was Sid, urging her to come sit beside him on the two center seats.

Meghan pulled the black Kansas City Fire Department cap off her husband Gideon's head, ruffled his hair and then sat in his lap at the end of the row.

His sister, Jessie, still beaming as beautifully as the bride she'd been just last month, reached for her husband Sam's hand and cuddled up beside him in the back row.

Mac and his wife, Jules—the best damn second baseman Cole had ever had the honor of playing with—took their position to Martha's right.

"They're waiting for us, Cole."

Any remaining tension in him eased as Tori snuck up beside him and wrapped her arm around his waist. He gladly dropped his arm around her shoulders and kissed her. The crisp air had whipped a rosy color into her porcelain cheeks, and the bright, copper-red color of the trees had nothing on her gorgeous hair.

"I suppose you just needed to do that?" she smiled.

"I will always need to kiss my wife."

There were no *babe*'s, no *sweetheart*'s, no *honey*'s that he used with her. She'd rather talk shop than talk sweet. But when they took their place behind his father, Cole leaned over and whispered the words he knew would make her blush, make her crazy, make him one lucky man later that night.

"I love you, bossy britches."

Her smile matched his as the camera flashed.

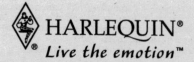

If you enjoyed what you just read,
then we've got an offer you can't resist!

Take 2 bestselling love stories FREE!

Plus get a FREE surprise gift!

Clip this page and mail it to Harlequin Reader Service

IN U.S.A.	IN CANADA
3010 Walden Ave.	P.O. Box 609
P.O. Box 1867	Fort Erie, Ontario
Buffalo, N.Y. 14240-1867	L2A 5X3

YES! Please send me 2 free Harlequin Intrigue® novels and my free surprise gift. After receiving them, if I don't wish to receive anymore, I can return the shipping statement marked cancel. If I don't cancel, I will receive 6 brand-new novels each month, before they're available in stores! In the U.S.A., bill me at the bargain price of $3.99 plus 25¢ shipping and handling per book and applicable sales tax, if any*. In Canada, bill me at the bargain price of $4.74 plus 25¢ shipping and handling per book and applicable taxes**. That's the complete price and a savings of at least 10% off the cover prices—what a great deal! I understand that accepting the 2 free books and gift places me under no obligation ever to buy any books. I can always return a shipment and cancel at any time. Even if I never buy another book from Harlequin, the 2 free books and gift are mine to keep forever.

182 HDN DU9K
382 HDN DU9L

Name _____ (PLEASE PRINT)

Address _____ Apt.# _____

City _____ State/Prov. _____ Zip/Postal Code _____

* Terms and prices subject to change without notice. Sales tax applicable in N.Y.
** Canadian residents will be charged applicable provincial taxes and GST.
   All orders subject to approval. Offer limited to one per household and not valid to
   current Harlequin Intrigue® subscribers.
   ® are registered trademarks of Harlequin Enterprises Limited.

INT03

BETTY WEBB

DESERT WIVES

Arizona private investigator
Lena Jones is hired by a frantic
mother desperate to rescue her
thirteen-year-old daughter from a
polygamist sect. But when the
compound's sixty-eight-year-old
leader is found murdered, Lena's
client is charged with his murder.

To find the real killer, Lena goes
undercover and infiltrates the dark
reality of Purity—where misogynistic
men and frightened women share a
deadly code of silence.

"...this book could do
for polygamy what
Uncle Tom's Cabin
did for slavery."
—*Publishers Weekly*

*Available July 2004
at your favorite retail outlet.*

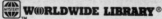 **W⊕RLDWIDE LIBRARY** ®

WBW497

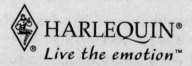

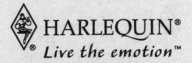

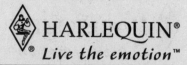